To Norm

Blessings

Judy Gerlach

Ransom My Heart

Cheapside Trilogy Book One

Judy Gerlach

Wicket Gate Publishing

Ransom My Heart

Published by Wicket Gate Publishing
Lexington, Kentucky

Printed in the United States of America

ISBN-10: 1986182045
ISBN-13: 978-1986182041

Cover design by Judy and Greg Gerlach.

Scripture quotations are from the King James Version of the Holy Bible.

ACKNOWLEDGMENTS

With heartfelt thanks to:

Monica Mynk for "teaching me the ropes" of fiction writing and getting my manuscript off to a strong start with your editing expertise.

My daughter Lindy for being the second pair of eyes on the text. I can't thank you enough for your help with proofing the manuscript.

Jan Kasten, my dear sister in Christ and prayer partner, for your faithfulness and friendship over the years. Your support and encouragement are such a blessing.

And a special thank you to my husband Greg for seeing the potential of this story and encouraging me to never give up. Your amazing creativity with the book cover and help with this project have been invaluable. I couldn't have done it without you!

ABOUT CHEAPSIDE AUCTION BLOCK

In the heart of downtown Lexington, Kentucky, is a thriving marketplace known as Cheapside Park. It's the site of concerts, celebrations and other civic events where people gather for a good time. But the name Cheapside was originally associated with an auction block and a sinister business known as the slave trade.

Until the Civil War put an end to slavery in the United States, Lexington was a major hub for the thriving slave trade, which had reached its peak by 1860. The Cheapside slave auction block was located on the west side of the Fayette County courthouse lawn. On Court Day each month, people came from far and near to bid on such items as farm equipment, cows, mules, horses—and slaves.

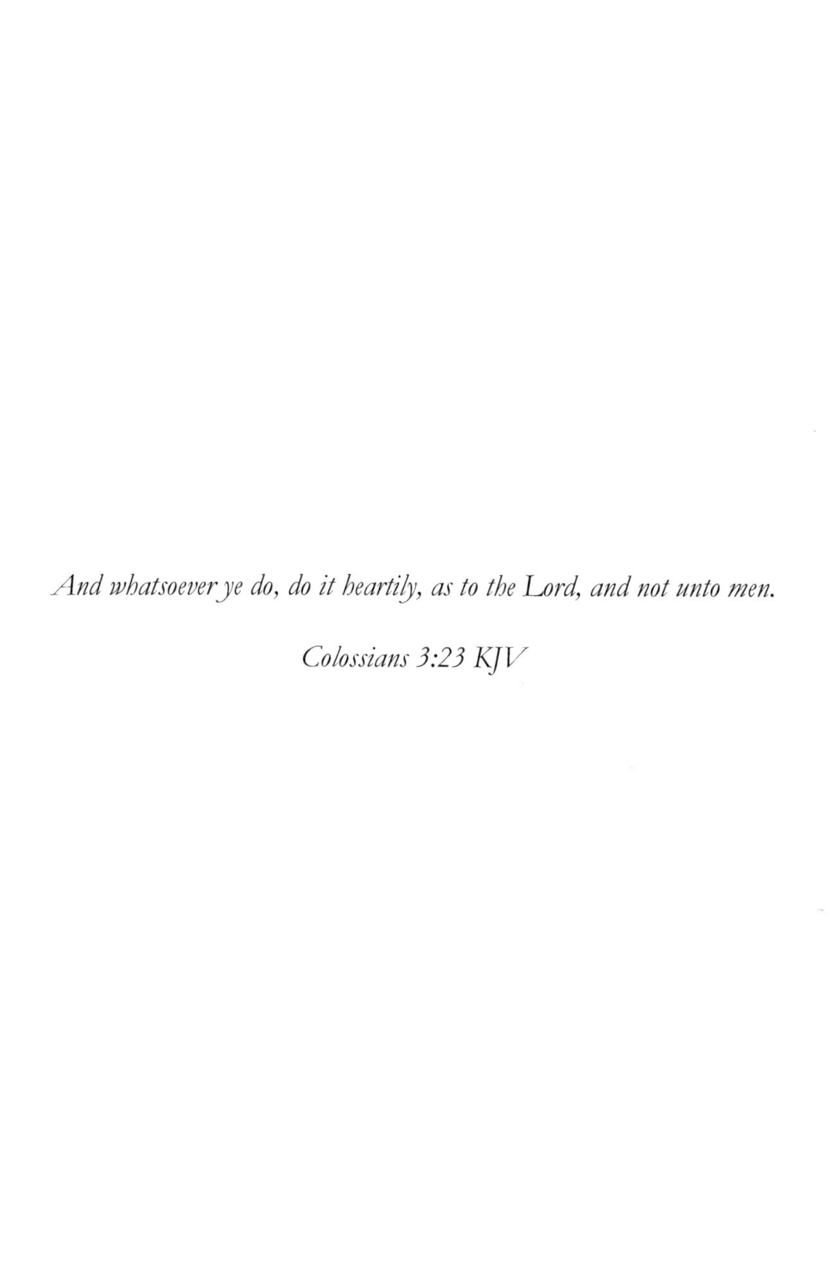

And whatsoever ye do, do it heartily, as to the Lord, and not unto men.

Colossians 3:23 KJV

CHAPTER ONE

Monday, March 14, 1859
Cheapside Auction Block, Lexington, Kentucky

A queasy feeling, heavy as lead, settled in the pit of Timothy Locker's stomach. The twenty-five-year-old itinerant preacher fixed his eyes on the auction block ahead.

Cheapside. The mere thought of it triggered a rush of anger through his veins.

Narrowing his gaze over the sea of top hats before him, Timothy caught a glimpse of the sign posted to the platform's wooden beam. He could only make out the larger words at the top, yet the injustice of Cheapside screamed at him from the first line alone: Auction and Negro Sales.

His jaw clenched.

A quick glance at the clock tower reminded him he was half an hour early. No sense in standing around doing nothing. The two men he was supposed to meet were nowhere to be seen.

The young preacher's swift strides carried him to the corner of Short Street where he crossed over to the other side. Taking a right, he made his way along the boardwalk—past the bank, an attorney's office, and a men's clothier.

Not more than a few doors away, two nurses in gray

uniforms caught his eye as they exited a doctor's office. He watched them wave to a middle-aged, red-haired gentleman riding down the street.

Just as the red-haired man stopped and dismounted, the two men Timothy had been looking for earlier approached the man from the opposite direction.

"C'mon, Frank. We really need your support today." Reverend Leonard Thompson's tone gave away his desperation as he addressed the red-haired man. "Just once, stop thinking about your own selfish agenda and help us out."

The man named Frank ignored Leonard while he tied his horse to the hitching post. Flicking his gaze to the two nurses, he exhaled a huge breath, his lips flapping from the force. A good yank on the rope followed by a forceful boot strike to the dirt, and he was soon waggling his finger in Leonard's face. With a voice loud enough to draw attention from several passersby, Frank lit into Leonard. "What I do here is none of your business, so leave me alone! Do I make myself clear?"

"Crystal!" The veins in Leonard's neck throbbed. That was never a good thing.

One of the nurses—the shorter one with blonde tresses—dipped her head as she peered out from under her bonnet. The embarrassed look on her face suggested she'd rather not be a witness to this shouting match. Her eyes met Timothy's, but she quickly averted her gaze to the other nurse, who seemed a bit frightened by the outburst.

Timothy tensed and held his breath while his other preacher friend, Micah, stood a few feet behind Leonard and remained silent. Which way was this altercation going to go?

Leonard thrust his pointer finger right back at the red-haired man. "Just once, Frank … just once … why can't you work *with* us instead of *against* us?"

Frank snapped his head away from Leonard, kicked the hitching post then excused himself and waved good-bye to the nurses. He took off in a huff across the street.

Leonard brushed by Timothy. "I'm ready to go," he rasped before he stormed off toward Cheapside, Micah trailing after him.

Timothy's chest heaved. Leonard must really have something stuck in his craw today.

Nodding politely to the nurses, Timothy doffed his hat. Without giving it a second thought, he'd locked eyes with the pretty blonde nurse. Heat crept up his cheeks. "My apologies, ladies, for my friend's lack of manners. Don't know what got into him."

"No worries." The tall brunette flashed a smirk. "We really need to get our lunch now or we'll be late to work." She cupped the blonde's elbow, prodding her toward the corner café.

The blonde wrenched her arm free, casting a shy smile to Timothy. "If you'll excuse us, sir."

"Certainly." Timothy doffed his hat a second time. "Enjoy your lunch, ladies. Good day."

Giggling, the nurses disappeared into the café.

Yes, enjoy your lunch, ladies. Go about your business like everything's right with the world.

But everything wasn't right. Didn't anyone besides himself and his preacher friends care that human beings were about to be auctioned off?

Dipping his head against the stinging March wind, Timothy pressed forward across the street. He joined his companions near the edge of the courthouse lawn.

Chilly as it was, Leonard shrugged out of his frock coat and tossed it over his arm. Perspiration dampened his white shirt below his armpits, spilling onto his black waistcoat. His jaw twitched with every throb of the veins in his neck.

Timothy balked. Best not to ask about that argument now.

The clock tower tolled twelve times. Noon. Time for the bidding to begin.

Inside the pocket of his frock, a well-worn Bible slipped through his fingers.

As the first lot of goods emerged from the pen, he ran a

finger along the inside of his high stiff collar and stretched his neck. How many times had he witnessed scenes such as this? There was no getting used to it.

Upon the block stood a young black girl named Lottie. Today, though, she was simply "Chattel No. 1."

The girl's faint whimpers, barely audible above the raucous din of voices, fell on Timothy's ears. His stomach lurched, and he swallowed it back. If only he could shake that gnawing feeling deep in his soul. "This is utter madness."

Leonard gave him a grim nod. Digging deep into his pocket, he scooped out a bulging purse. "Pray we have enough money to buy the girl. If we'd known sooner—if we'd been given more time—we could pay whatever it costs and set her free."

Timothy faced Micah, who was himself a slave and the preacher of the slaves' church. "I wish I could have contributed more, my friend." He glanced at the girl on the block, feeling guilty for not getting back in town soon enough to help raise money. God help them … they had to be able to ransom the girl.

Micah leveled his eyes at Timothy. "Lottie had papers sayin' she free. Did you know that? She a free girl until they grab her away. Ain't no law gonna help Lottie."

"That's what I don't understand. If Lottie was free, how did this happen?" Timothy searched Micah's eyes. Such deep pain.

Micah pounded his fist into his hand. "They trick her, then they kidnap her."

"Kidnapped?" Timothy quirked his brow at Leonard.

"Yes," Leonard said. "We had less than a week's notice. Micah informed me of Lottie's plight the very moment he found out from her mother." He jammed the thick purse back into the pocket of his frock. "Ruth told Micah right away, but it was hardly enough time for the congregation to collect the money we'd need. Everyone did the best they could."

The buyers put out their cigars and threw them down,

grinding the butts into the dirt with their boots. Catalogues and pencils in hand and purses padded to the full, they ceased their chatter.

Timothy secured his low-crowned hat over his tousled brown hair then shifted his focus back to the auction block. "Gentlemen, this is it."

As the sale launched into full swing on the lawn of the Fayette County Courthouse, a gravelly voice from the front of the crowd echoed off the side of the building. "Four hundred!"

"Five hundred!" Leonard waved his hand high.

One bid, then another—randomly back and forth they flew. As the bids increased to a feverish pitch, the auctioneer stopped abruptly, cut off by a sudden interruption.

"Halt the bidding!" Leonard's deafening shout rang across the lawn.

Timothy jolted. Leonard must have run out of money.

"It over." Micah's shoulders slumped.

With a sudden spring forward, Leonard pushed his way to the front. "Allow me a moment! It's important." He jumped onto the auction block.

Timothy shot Micah a questioning look, but Micah only shrugged.

The wide-eyed auctioneer laid down his hammer, stepped aside and adjusted his spectacles.

Leonard raised his arms, palms to the audience. "Please! Cease the bidding now! This girl has been fraudulently brought here for sale. She is a free black, I tell you!" His fist thudded against the auction stand. "Lottie Preston is the daughter of a recently deceased free man who purchased her freedom just before he died. Her widowed mother was tricked into handing over her daughter's manumission papers!"

Timothy's heart drummed against his ribs. Should he try to coax Leonard away?

"On with the bidding, I say!" Standing in front of Timothy, a gray-haired man with a mutton chop beard charged forward. "This ain't no time for yer dern abolition speeches. Save your hellfire sermons for Sunday morning, preacher!"

"Why that …" Timothy lunged at the mocker.

"Stop." Micah's firm hand pulled him back. "You'd only make it worse for Leonard."

A deputy rushed at Leonard from the side, jangling a pair of handcuffs.

Leonard stumbled and nearly fell. "You won't need those, sir." He straightened up and elbowed his way back to Timothy and Micah as the bidding resumed.

Here they stood—three men of God. Silent. Defeated. Dejected.

"Fifteen hundred dollars once! Fifteen hundred twice!" The auctioneer's hammer came down hard. "Sold!"

Timothy flinched. Another sale. Another life.

Micah wiped his eyes with the sleeve of his coat. "Lottie's father, he dead, and now she got no written proof of her freedom."

"I'm sorry, Micah." Timothy averted his gaze, quelling the urge to retch.

Leonard put a hand to Micah's back. "We did everything we could."

"I know." Micah shook his head. "Now how I gonna tell Ruth her daughter been sold?"

"You shouldn't go alone, Micah." Leonard buttoned up the pocket where he kept the money pouch. "I'll give you a ride out to the Trumbeaux Estate."

"I'd like to go, too, if you don't mind." Shifting his weight from one leg to the other, Timothy unfolded a paper he'd stuffed between the pages of his Bible and showed it to Micah. "I already have these flyers posted for my camp meetings so I'm free for the afternoon."

"I'd like that." Micah scanned the flyer. "Looks good, my friend."

As the three preachers made their way across the lawn, a well-dressed little black girl zipped toward them and crashed headlong into Timothy's side. Her arms flew around him, and tear-drenched cheeks nestled into his frock. "Poor Lottie! Oh, Lord o' mercy, Bro'er Tim, she done be sold!"

"We know, Brillie." Timothy's heart ached for the girl who'd been like a little sister to him ever since his host family in Lexington had rescued her from Cheapside. What if Brillie hadn't been rescued? Where would she be? Could the same thing happen to her that just happened to Lottie? "I'm so sorry you had to see your cousin get sold."

The skirt of Brillie's green pinstripe dress swirled about as she shuffled her boot on the sparse lawn. "Aunt Ruth say y'all gonna buy Lottie. What happened?"

"We tried, Brillie. We just ran out of money." Timothy gave a tug on one of Brillie's long braids. "How about you ride with us to the Trumbeaux Estate to see Aunt Ruth? I'm sure Melia won't mind if you go."

"All right, Bro'er Tim." Brillie pointed across the street. "She right over there."

With an arm across Brillie's shoulders, Timothy nudged her forward. "Let's go tell Melia you'll be with me."

As they crossed the street, meandering through the crowd, the auctioneer's hammer struck the wooden stand for the next round of bidding. Brillie gasped and jumped.

Timothy pulled her closer. What must it be like for her and Aunt Ruth?

A downtown café

Nurse Haven Haywood carefully lifted a spoonful of hot potato soup, blowing softly on it twice before letting it pass through her lips. She glanced across the table at her coworker, Nurse Sarah Goolsby. "Mmm … Millie's Café has the best soup anywhere." Plucking the blue and white checkered napkin from her lap, she patted the corner of her mouth.

Sarah slurped soup off her spoon. "Mmm … it's delicious."

A thirty-something black waitress in a coffee-stained calico dress, scuttled up to the nurses' table, balancing a wooden tray in her hands. "Be needin' some apple pie when you done with that soup?" She lowered the tray laden with several tempting slices of Millie's pie of the day, sliding it until the edge rested on their table.

Haven leaned in, relishing the plump juicy apple slivers dripping with sugary cinnamon sauce. "Oh my … looks delectable. We're short on time today, though. Could you wrap up a couple slices for us to take back to work?"

"Yessam. I can do that."

As the waitress moved on to the next table, Sarah plunked her elbow down by her soup bowl, sinking her chin into her palm. "Haven, tell me, why was your pa arguing with that preacher a while ago?"

"I don't know, Sarah. Pa argues with a lot of people." Sipping her coffee, Haven stared past Sarah to the painted letters on the glass window that read *Millie's Café* backwards. "I think it was about the auction."

"I thought so." Sarah's lips formed a playful grin. "I saw you smiling at that other preacher. You know—the younger one."

"So, what's wrong with that? Aren't I allowed to smile at someone?"

"Yes, but it's the way you smiled, and the way he looked at you." Sarah's elbow slipped off the table. She quickly straightened herself up. "I know you too well."

Haven squirmed in her chair, bumping her shoe against the table leg. "You just think you do."

"Well, I thought he was handsome. I know he had his eye on you." Sarah pointed her index finger, almost touching Haven's nose. "I saw him blush."

"Stop it, Sarah." She swatted Sarah's finger away. "You're imagining things."

Sarah pursed her lips. "I never imagine anything."

"Maybe. Maybe not." Pushing her bowl aside, Haven cleared a spot for her reticule.

"You know he was cute, Haven." Sarah lifted her coffee cup, peering over the rim.

"I've got no room for a man in my life." She had to agree with Sarah, though. He sure was cute. No … handsome. Both, actually. What did it matter, anyway? She wasn't interested.

"When the time is right, we'll know. Right?" Sarah fished around in her reticule and scooped out some loose change. Lifting her gaze, she flashed a smile to the waitress, who'd just brought them their slices of pie.

"Funny, that's what Ma always …"

The town clock tolled once. Haven pushed away from the table. "Heavens to Betsy, Sarah. How can it be one o'clock already?"

"That's what you get for flirting." Sarah slapped some coins on the table.

"Sarah, stop it. I mean it." Haven flung her mantle over her shoulders. "I wasn't flirting with anyone." Was she?

"Yes, you were."

Adjusting her cap, Haven dashed out the door, Sarah close on her heels. She made a sharp left onto the boardwalk—just in time to catch sight of the preacher Sarah thought was so cute. But her jutting elbow slammed into the red, white and blue striped pole in front of the barber shop next door. "Ow!"

Mr. *Cute* looked her way and smiled before he climbed into a carriage.

How could one handsome face possibly be so distracting?

CHAPTER TWO

The Trumbeaux Estate

Leonard turned his modest carriage into the lane of a massive estate. "Welcome to Monsieur Maurice Trumbeaux's humble abode."

Timothy chuckled as he scanned the endless acres of land. Reaching back to the little girl snuggled under Micah's protective arm, Timothy tapped on her knee. "Brillie, you've not said a word the whole way here."

Brillie frowned. "Ain't got nothin' to say, Bro'er Tim. Too angry."

Timothy skewed his lips. This was harder than he thought it would be. "Brillie, can you tell me about your aunt? What does Ruth do here?"

"Sure, I tell you about Aunt Ruth." The girl's face brightened. "She a maidservant to Miz Jeannette—that Massa Trumbeaux's wife. She real nice."

"Aunt Ruth sounds very special." Timothy smiled at Brillie then looked at Leonard. "You mentioned Lottie was kidnapped. Didn't Trumbeaux try to get Lottie back?"

"He was out of the country when it happened." Leonard kept his gaze on the lane. "The whole family went to France to visit his parents. I don't think they're home yet, so he doesn't even know."

"No wonder Brillie's upset." Timothy leaned forward. "She was counting on us."

A white mansion with six thick columns came into view as they rounded a bend. Timothy gaped. "Is that their house?"

Leonard grinned. "Indeed, it is. Greek Revival at its finest."

A plump woman in a white-trimmed black dress, bouncing her way toward the house, goaded a young boy along in front of her. He held a canning jar in each hand, whining every time she poked him.

"Ain't never knowed a boy could take so long to fetch some apple butter!" The woman scolded the boy in between pokes.

Timothy glanced back at Brillie.

"That be Cora." Brillie perked up. "She Aunt Ruth's friend."

As Leonard slowed down in the circular drive, Cora stopped by the steps and stared at them. Her hands flew to her cheeks, and she spun on her heels, facing the mansion.

"Ruth! Ruth!" Cora scuttled up the portico steps. "Brother Leonard here with Micah! Praise the Lord—they done bring Lottie back! Come on out here, Ruth!"

"Uh-oh." Timothy's heart stopped. "Did you hear that?"

"Yes … she thinks we have Lottie." Leonard shook his head. "She must have seen Brillie's bonnet and thought she was Lottie."

Micah squeezed Brillie's shoulder. "Lord, help us."

Seconds later, a petite woman wearing a dress like Cora's, appeared at the door. "Lottie!" She brushed past Cora and almost knocked her over as she raced down the steps, waving her arms high. "Thank you, Jesus! You done save my Lottie."

When the carriage came to a stop, Brillie wiped her tears, sprang from the back seat and sprinted over to Ruth. Ruth looked past Brillie and craned her neck, standing on her tiptoes.

Micah approached her slowly. "I'm so sorry, Ruth."

Timothy's stomach churned. What could be more painful than a mother's joy shattered into a million pieces?

Ruth dropped to her knees. "No, no!" Her cries rent the air from the lane to the mansion. Rocking back and forth, she lifted her face toward heaven. "God of mercy, it ain't so! Not my Lottie. She all I got left, Lord. No-o-o!"

"It a wicked thing, Ruth." Micah helped her to her feet. "Lottie draw such a high price, we just not have the money. Brother Leonard, he try powerful hard."

Leonard's gaze fell. "It weighs on me heavily."

Timothy hopped down and stood next to Micah. He tipped his hat to Ruth. "Hello, ma'am. I'm Micah's friend, Timothy Locker. I'm sorry to meet you under these circumstances. But Micah is right—Brother Leonard tried his very best."

A harsh wind whooshed in. Ruth leaned into Micah's arms. "It not supposed to happen this way." She shivered, hugging her shoulders.

Micah took off his cloak and wrapped it around her. "Let's get you inside." He flattened his hand against the small of her back, guiding her toward the portico. "When Trumbeaux coming back?"

"Massa and Missus, they be gone another week or two." Ruth rubbed her sleeves across her wet cheeks. "Oh, Micah, if only Massa Trumbeaux come home now, he fix everything. The overseer, Massa Hughes, he say this all my own doing."

Timothy walked alongside them. "It's not your fault, Ruth."

As they neared the steps of the mansion, the overseer rode up to the front where the workers had congregated. "Back to work or I'll have your hide!" Hughes lashed a whip in the air.

Suddenly, dogs in the distance barked and horses' hooves pounded louder and louder.

"Sounds like riders coming our way—and fast." Timothy lifted Brillie into the carriage. "Stay here with Brother Leonard and don't get out. You understand?"

Brillie twisted clusters of her pinafore in her trembling

fingers. "I won't, Bro'er Tim."

Three men on horseback and two hounds turned into the circular lane by the front portico. Great puffs of dust and dirt billowed up in their trail. One of the men held his gun high as his horse slowed to a walk.

"Blast those catchers, anyway!" Hughes jerked the reins to the right forcing his horse to face the intruders.

The three horsemen stopped in front of Hughes. The man waving the gun spoke first. "Hughes, where's Trumbeaux?"

"Away on holiday in France. I'm in charge now." Hughes flashed a scowl. "What do you want, Cal?"

"We been deputized by Sheriff Hines to search for two runaways, both of 'em boys. One's nineteen and the other's thirteen. Names are Pete and Shadow. Been missing since late morning, right around auction time." The gunman named Cal did a quick scan of all the workers.

Micah squeezed Ruth's jittery hands, and Timothy kept an eye on both of them. Hadn't Ruth been through enough already?

Beady little slits sharpened Cal's sneer as he rode down the line of slaves and back. Snapping up a brown leather pouch hanging from a lanyard around his neck, he thrust his pointer finger and thumb inside. A few thick, shredded leaves of chewing tobacco escaped from the pinched wad as he crammed the rest into his mouth and began chomping away. "We're gonna have us a look around the place and let these here hounds do some sniffing. You know the routine."

"Yeah, I know your routine." Plunging forward in the saddle as his mount sidestepped and reared, Hughes grabbed a fistful of mane and patted the horse's neck. "Whoa, boy! Easy now." Turning to the tobacco-chewing man, he rasped, "Get on with it!"

Cal spat, then flashed a snarky grin. "Everyone stay right where you are until we're done. Tolbert, you take the north grounds; Artie, you take the south."

Timothy glanced over at Brillie as Tolbert and Artie galloped off in opposite directions. Good—she hadn't budged.

Thirty minutes later, they all convened near the bottom of the portico steps, empty-handed.

Walking up to the carriage, Cal pointed at Brillie. "You was at that auction today, weren't you?"

Timothy eased closer to the carriage, a prayer on his lips for Brillie. Terror marked her face. If that man so much as laid a hand on Brillie …

"Look at me, girl!" Chewed tobacco sprayed from Cal's mouth. "Answer me!"

Timothy mustered all the fruit of the Spirit he could—especially the self-control part. He could sure use an extra dose of that. "Go ahead, Brillie. Answer the man."

"Yessuh." Brillie's lower lip protruded.

Cal swiped his stained sleeve over his wet beard. "What do you know about Pete and Shadow running off?"

"Nothin'!" Brillie's voice took on a higher pitch. "No ways."

"Don't lie to me, you little—"

"The young lady said she doesn't know anything about it, Cal!" Leonard sprang to his feet. "She's been with me every moment since the auction!"

"Don't take that tone with me, preacherman. If there's anything I can't stand, it's a loud-shoutin' preacher." Cal plopped one arm on the side of Leonard's carriage and leaned in. "And why are you out here, anyway?"

"Reverend Locker and I brought this little gal and Brother Micah here to inform Ruth that her daughter was sold. That's all." Leonard's scowl deepened. "Now, if you don't mind, I must get Brother Micah back to his master before he gets reported as missing or runaway."

Cal walked over to Micah. "Let me see your pass."

Micah reached in his pocket, but all three gunmen cocked their pistols quicker than a duel at high noon. Micah froze.

With a flick of his wrist, Cal waved his partners closer. "Tolbert, Artie, check him for weapons."

After a brief frisking, Micah again reached into his pocket

and pulled out his pass. He handed it to Cal who looked at it and handed it back.

"All right, you can go." Cal unhitched his horse and mounted, the dogs following him. "Blast those dogs! Couldn't track a scent if you spread it out on a platter in front of 'em."

Hughes rode up to Cal. "Are you about done?"

"Done for now! 'Spect we'll be back afore long, though." Cal spit a wad and rode off with his partners.

Micah walked with Ruth up the steps where Cora stood waiting then returned to the carriage. Cupping his mouth, he shouted, "Take good care of Ruth, Cora!"

Timothy puffed his cheeks and blew it out before landing a hearty slap on Micah's shoulder. "Ruth must be pretty special." No mistaking the longing look on his friend's face.

Haven Hill Farm

Haven Haywood tucked her youngest brother in bed and tousled his hair—a habit she knew greatly annoyed him. "Have a good nap, Hank."

"I'm way too old for naps." The ten-year-old boy rolled over and punched his pillow.

"Ma makes me take naps sometimes, too."

Frowning intensely, Hank straightened his hair where she'd mussed it up. "And don't do that again."

Haven stuck her tongue out at him and closed the door then walked down the hall to her parents' room. Finding the door slightly ajar, she poked her head inside. "Ma? May I come in?"

"Of course, dear." Ma lowered the book she'd been reading. "You're home early today."

Sitting on the edge of the bed, she kissed Ma's cheek. "Dr. Wright sent us home because of the storm threat. But he asked us to come early in the morning to organize supplies before patients start trickling in. I have to leave before breakfast."

"All right, dear."

Haven tapped the cover of Ma's book. "I thought you already read *Jane Eyre*, Ma."

"It's still good the second time around."

Haven stayed seated on the bed.

Ma tucked a bookmark between two pages, clapping the book closed. "All right, sweetheart. Something's eating at you. What is it?"

"Ma, I was wondering … does it bother you that I chose a career over courting?"

"Don't be silly, Haven. Your pa and I are very proud of you."

"I needed to hear you say that." Haven rose to her feet. "Sarah's been flirting with every man that looks at her cross-eyed, and she teases me relentlessly about getting a beau."

Like that preacher I met today.

"You'll know when it's time, dear." Ma cozied down into the mattress and grinned.

"That's what I told Sarah you'd say!"

The Roberts farm

Fast-moving charcoal clouds threatened the darkening sky during the short jaunt to the Roberts farm—an unassuming place Micah called home as a slave. Timothy angled his face upward to the thick pockets of water overhead. "Doesn't look good, Leonard. Hope it holds off until we get back into town."

"Me, too." Leonard turned the open carriage into the lane of the small hemp farm. "Wouldn't that be the perfect way to end this day?"

"No, thanks." Timothy looked back over his shoulder at Micah. "How's Brillie?"

"Still asleep." Micah glanced down at the child nestled under his arm.

Timothy drew in the crisp farm air. "I think it's been a year since I was here."

Micah nodded. "I believe that's right. You brought Brillie out to my church social. Not sure if we'll have a social this year. Massa been havin' some health issues off and on."

"Sorry to hear that." Leonard drew the carriage to a stop by the slave quarters—three modest, one-room cottages.

A dog yelped, and Brillie bolted upright in her seat. "Who's that?"

Micah reached over the side and scooped the puppy up in his arms. "Lazarus, my boy, you came to greet me." He placed Lazarus on Brillie's lap. "What you think, Brillie?"

Brillie's face brightened as the puppy bathed her with wet puppy kisses. "He so cute."

Timothy reached back to stroke the pup. "Nothing like a cute puppy to cure what ails ya. Right, Brillie?"

Brillie giggled as she burrowed her fingers into a pile of fur. "This here puppy sure do like me. Wish I could take him home." She lifted the puppy and kissed him on the nose. "Why you call him Lazarus, Bro'er Micah?"

"Well, Brillie, when that pup come out, his little body be limp as a wet rag." Micah tickled the puppy behind its ears. "Thought he was dead, but after I stroked him, he come alive—just like Lazarus in the Bible."

Brillie squeezed Lazarus, pressing her cheek against his snout. "This here's a special pup."

A slave woman named Martha skittered over to the carriage and looked up at Micah. "If it weren't for this here pup, I might be done with my chores by now." She gathered the puppy from Brillie's arms.

Micah climbed down and stood next to the carriage. "Brillie, you come visit soon. You can play with Lazarus."

"I will, Bro'er Micah." A huge grin stretched across Brillie's face as she wiggled in her seat.

Picking dog hairs off his cloak, Micah faced Martha.

"How Massa Roberts today?"

Martha's smile faded into a frown. "Massa done took sick again. Been in bed all afternoon, givin' Miz Cilla fits." She cuddled the squirming puppy closer. "Bear, he try and help Miz Cilla, but she be a frettin' all day."

Timothy furrowed his brow. "I'm sorry to hear that, Martha. Tell Bear I said hello."

"You should go check on Roberts, Micah." Leonard gathered up the reins. "I'd best be getting Brillie and Timothy back to Melia's house before that storm hits." He looked up at the bulging clouds.

"You're right. I best be seein' what I can do to help. Keep my mind off ..." Micah rubbed the back of his neck as he turned away and faced his small log cottage.

"Off what, Micah?" Martha sported a mischievous grin as she stroked the pup's fur. "Or who?"

Micah shook his head. "Martha, Martha, you need to be a mindin' your own business."

A snicker escaped Timothy's mouth before he could stop it. At least he knew he wasn't the only one who suspected Micah had a woman on his mind. *That widow I just met at the Trumbeaux Estate? Fancy that ... Micah's in love.*

Martha planted her free hand on her hip. "You need a good wife, that what you need. I just a tellin' Bear last night how our friend Micah need a good woman." She pivoted and walked toward her cottage.

Micah trailed after her. "And what Bear say?"

Martha glanced over her shoulder. "He say, 'Martha, you need to be a mindin' your own business.' That what Bear say."

CHAPTER THREE

The Delaney home

Timothy strode across Melia's foyer to the hall tree, Brillie stringing along with him. "I'll hang up your coat and bonnet. Run on upstairs and let Melia know we're home."

The moment Brillie's shoe hit the first step, Melia's voice floated down from the upstairs hallway. "Avery? Is that you?"

"No, Miz Meely, it's me—Brillie." Her plaited hair dangled down her back as she tilted her head upward. "And Bro'er Tim."

Melia appeared at the top landing. "Thank goodness you're home. Come up here and freshen up while I talk to Timothy. Avery and his sister are due in today." She made her way down the staircase as Brillie skipped the rest of the way up.

"Sorry we're late, Melia." Timothy hung his coat next to Brillie's.

Melia set her needlework on the bench by the stairwell. "How did Brillie's aunt take the news about her daughter?"

Timothy leaned against the balustrade. "Not well, I'm afraid."

"Oh, Timothy, I can't imagine such pain." Melia stared at the front door sidelights, adjusting a hairpin in her dark blonde tresses.

"Me neither. How can people be so cruel?"

"Very sad. Come … let's have a cup of tea in the parlor while you tell me everything that happened." Melia picked up her needlework. "Take this, please. Set it on the table by my chair. I'll have Mrs. Perky prepare a tray. Be right back."

Timothy warmed his hands by the hearth while he waited. The house seemed so quiet—except for the occasional clanging of a pot or pan in the kitchen.

A few minutes later, Melia returned to the parlor and set a tray with teacups and a plate of gingersnap cookies on the pedestal table. "I know you must be hungry, young man." She took a seat in one of the two wing chairs by the table.

Timothy plopped into the other chair. "Come to think of it, I am."

Melia lifted her teacup, balancing the saucer in her other hand. "Did you get your flyers posted for your camp meeting?"

"Yes, ma'am." Timothy snagged a cookie.

"Good." Melia rested her cup and saucer on her lap. "Now tell me what happened at Cheapside."

Timothy finished off the cookie then relayed the chilling events of the auction.

Melia's eyes widened. "Heavens be … I might have fainted!"

With a heave of his shoulders, Timothy nodded. "I came close."

"If only Avery had been home." Melia patted her lips with a napkin. "He had to pick up his sister in New York. Alifair's coming to live with us, you know. Her husband recently passed away. A bad bout of cholera took him."

"I'm sorry to hear that."

"Did I mention she's pregnant? She didn't find out about the baby until after William died." Melia ran her finger around the rim of her teacup. "Avery insisted she come here. She doesn't have any other family."

"How kind of you and Avery to open your home to her."

He brushed some crumbs off his shirt then fixed his gaze on the crackling flames of the hearth.

Melia reached across the table and patted his arm. "You're still thinking about the girl at the auction, aren't you?"

"Sorry." Timothy set his cup and saucer next to Melia's.

"Oh, don't be. But what's done is done."

"I'm certain Trumbeaux won't let this matter rest when he returns from France." Timothy slapped the chair arm.

Someone knocked on the front door, and Melia shot to her feet.

Timothy hurried past her. "I'll see who it is."

"Telegram for Melia Delaney." A teenage boy waved an envelope.

"I'll be right there!" Melia vaulted into the foyer, her fingers stuffed into a reticule jingling with loose change. She tipped the messenger and snatched the telegram.

Timothy closed the front door. "What's it say?"

"Good gracious, Timothy!" Melia's jaw dropped. "Avery and Alifair are due to arrive by stage at five o'clock. Would you mind picking them up? If you leave now you can make it."

"Don't mind at all." Timothy snatched his coat and hat from the hall tree as a flash of lightning triggered a window-rattling rumble of thunder.

"Better take an umbrella." Melia opened the front door and looked up at the sky. "And take the large carriage, too. Alifair is sure to have quite a bit of baggage with her."

"I'll take care of it, ma'am." Timothy buttoned up his frock and headed to the back door.

As he passed through the kitchen, Mrs. Perky stopped stirring the custard for the pudding. "Will you be joining the family for supper, Reverend Locker?"

"Mmm, mmm … yes, Mrs. Perky. Whatever that is you're cooking, it sure smells good!"

The plump housemaid blushed. "Thank you, sir." A few whimsical curls bounced beneath her white maid's cap.

An hour later, Timothy lumbered through the kitchen, escorting a very travel-weary Alifair. "We're back, Melia!" He supported the pregnant woman with one arm around her waist and his other hand under her elbow.

Melia rushed to meet them. "Oh no! What's wrong with Alifair?"

"She needs to lie down … quickly. Says she's having contractions."

"Let's get her to the parlor. She can lie on the chaise." Melia draped Alifair's other arm across her shoulders.

Rapid flashes of lightning lit up the room as Timothy eased Alifair onto the chaise.

Melia spread an afghan over her. "Where's Avery?"

Timothy backed away from the chaise, his eyes fixated on the lovely creature lying there.

"Timothy?" Melia poked his arm.

"Oh … he's in the carriage house tending to the horses. He'll be in shortly."

Brillie sauntered into the room and over to Melia.

Crack!

"Gracious me!" Melia jumped, pulling Brillie with her.

"I'm skeerd of lightning, Miz Meely."

A fierce hammering at the front door followed by the maid's ear-splitting scream sent Melia airborne again. "What in merciful heavens?"

Timothy dashed toward the foyer, and Melia darted after him, leaving Brillie with Alifair. Her hands flew to her cheeks, and Timothy pulled her back as they faced the intruders.

The maid cowered by the staircase landing, wringing her apron and trembling like a cornered mouse.

"Who are you?" Melia's shrill voice just about split Timothy's eardrums.

"I know who they are." Timothy glared at the trespassers. "They were out at the Trumbeaux Estate this afternoon looking for some runaways."

Cal kicked the front door shut and faced Melia, brandishing a gun while the others restrained their hounds.

"Sorry to frighten you, ma'am. The name's Cal." Tobacco juice dribbled down his beard. "You wouldn't happen to know where I might find those runaway boys, would you, Mrs. Delaney?"

"I don't have any idea what—"

Crack! Crack! Lightning flashed in broken spurts.

Cal moved closer to Melia, his beady eyes narrowing even more. "Now see here, Mrs. Delaney, we got reason to believe you do."

"I do not!"

Timothy dived at Cal. "This is ridiculous!"

"Get back and shut up, preacher." Cal took aim at Timothy's chest.

"Miz Meely?" Brillie's tiny voice trembled from the parlor. "Who's out there? I skeerd."

"Hmm … who might that be?" Cal shifted his beady eyes to the parlor. "Reckon I'll have to have myself a little look around."

"No!" Melia pushed past Cal and blocked the parlor entrance. "This is my house! I don't give you permission to go traipsing through it—you and your disgusting bounty hunters!"

"Don't need your permission, ma'am." Cal sported an evil grin.

Timothy eased closer to Melia, but Cal grabbed Melia by the arm and shoved her aside.

"Blast you, Cal!" Avery Delaney had entered the foyer from the back of the house. "Don't you ever lay a hand on my wife again!"

"You know him?" Tears glistened in Melia's eyes.

"Unfortunately."

"Look here, Delaney, I don't mean to cause no harm, but I gots a job to do here, see." Cal backed away from Melia. "Just calm down."

She ran to Avery's side. "Oh, Avery, these dreadful men burst into our house like they own it."

"Silence!" Cal glowered at them.

Avery drew Melia closer. "All right, then, why *are* you here, Cal?"

Cal lowered his gun. "Lookin' for a couple of runaways, Delaney."

Melia's knuckles whitened as she tightened her grip on Avery's arm. She nodded toward Mrs. Perky, who hadn't budged from her spot by the landing. "I'd appreciate it if you'd allow the maid to go in the parlor, too."

Cal waved the maid over. "Go on. Get in there."

Avery glared at the slave catchers. "My sister is with child and needs immediate medical attention. I'll thank you to leave my house now!"

"Not until we search the place, Delaney." Cal got right up in Avery's face. "Now move aside."

"Back off, Cal." Utter repugnance contorted Avery's features. "Man, you stink. Just take your hounds and hurry it up!"

Timothy stood by the parlor entrance as Mrs. Perky sat wringing her apron in silence.

Cal stayed near the front door. Snatching the empty, floral-painted tole tray—the one Melia used for the family's missives—from the small foyer table, he spat out the foul-smelling wad of tobacco and slammed the tray back on the table.

Avery's face twisted into a sneer. "Nice to see you've refined your manners, Cal."

The clock in the parlor chimed seven times. Raindrops pattered against the windows before hammering down like a cloudburst. A few minutes later, Cal's men returned to the foyer.

"Satisfied?" Avery's face radiated an angry crimson. "Now, I'll thank you to remove yourselves from these premises!"

Cal tipped his hat to the family. "Thanks for your hospitality. Much obliged."

As soon as Cal's boots hit the porch, Avery slammed the front door. He turned the key in the deadbolt and checked it twice.

Melia pulled Timothy aside. "I hate to send you out in the rain but I need you to fetch Dr. Wright from his house. His office is closed now." She scrambled through the pigeonholes of the maple secretary for a scrap of paper then wrote down the address. "It's only four blocks."

"I'm on my way." Timothy took off in Avery's small covered buggy and returned with the doctor in less than thirty minutes.

Melia's face lit when Dr. Wright entered the parlor. "Oh good! I'm glad Timothy found you. Alifair's right over here."

"If you'll excuse me, I'll wait in the foyer." Avery turned, tapped Timothy's shoulder and nodded toward the parlor entrance. "Come, Timothy. Fill me in on what happened today."

Timothy took a seat on the foyer bench next to Avery, leaned over and rested his elbows on his lap. Time to relive the ordeal. Again …

"What a day, Timothy." Avery straightened his back and leaned against the wall. His eyes hardened. "Listen … about those boys, I have to tell you …" He cleared his throat. "I think I saw them as the stage was nearing Lexington."

Timothy sat up straight. "I'm all ears."

"I'd been staring out the window of the coach, half asleep. Just northeast of Lexington a sudden movement at the edge of the woods caught my attention." Avery stretched out his short legs, crossing his ankles. "At first, I thought I'd seen a couple of animals, but it soon became clear the figures were human. Looked young to me."

Timothy raked his fingers through his hair. "You know I must go check it out."

"Now?" Avery quirked his brow. "In the dark?"

"No, but I must leave before dawn. Sounds to me like they're lost." Timothy angled his head and put a hand to Avery's shoulder. "Pray that my connection in Ripley will be available. The conductor there can give them passage across the Ohio on a little skiff."

"My prayers always go with you, son." Avery fingered the watch fob on his waistcoat and glanced at the time. "It's half past eight already."

Dr. Wright walked into the foyer. "Your sister's going to be fine. The contractions have stopped. I'm certain it was the long, bumpy ride in the coach."

Avery pushed himself up from the bench. "That's what I suspected."

Timothy crossed the foyer with the doctor. "Finally, some good news."

Dr. Wright faced Avery. "Keep her on bed rest a few days." He grabbed his coat and hat from the hall tree. "Looks like the rain has stopped. I'll just walk home."

The aroma of cinnamon chicken wafted past Timothy's nostrils. His stomach growled. He could eat the whole chicken.

The family gathered in the parlor, and he took his regular place at the dining table, surprised to see Alifair seated directly across from him. She smiled, and his breath caught. A strange lump lodged in his throat. Wasn't she supposed to be on bed rest?

Those eyes of hers … a rare pale green … like the sun-kissed surf of the sea. Fascinating. Except she's a widow. A pregnant widow.

For the second time in one day, he found himself captivated by a pretty face. First the nurse downtown and now Avery's sister.

This nonsense had to stop.

Making every effort to divert his attention to anything but Alifair, he rushed through his meal and pushed away from the table. "If you'll excuse me, I think I'll retire to my apartment."

"Goodnight, Timothy." The whole family spoke at once, but for some reason, his eyes locked with Alifair's.

"Goodni—" His voice cracked. He cleared his throat. "Goodnight."

How embarrassing.

CHAPTER FOUR

Haven Hill Farm

"Stick 'em up or I'll shoot!"

Haven dropped a comb, and Ma sprang from her vanity stool.

The two Haywood women turned to find themselves face to face with the business end of a small gun. Ma shook a gilded hand mirror at the bandit. "Henry Colton Haywood, you put that thing down right now or I'll tan your hide!"

"Ah, Ma." Hank thrust his lower lip out and stuffed the makeshift toy gun into its holster.

Grinning at her little brother, Haven stooped to pick up the comb. She'd been helping Ma pin up her long brown hair.

The boy hooked his thumb in the holster. The pistol had been fashioned for him from a broken and unusable gun by their uncle, Brady Haywood—a real life cowboy complete with jeans, suede vest, bandana, boots with silver spurs, and a wide-rimmed, felt hat made out of beaver hair.

Ma sported her "this is your last warning" frown. "You know I think the world of Uncle Brady, but I don't like the way you behave whenever he's about to visit."

Haven tugged on Ma's hair and put the last pin in place. "Hank, how many times has Ma told you it's an outdoor toy?"

"Sorry. Guess I forgot." Hank's head drooped. He peered up at Ma through his uncombed brown locks. A pair of large brown eyes begged for mercy beneath the rim of his kid-sized western hat.

Ma took his hand and walked him over to the door of her bedroom. "Oh, Hank. Where's Ella this morning anyway?" She poked her head out into the hall. "Ella!"

Hank's mammy skipped up the stairs. "I right here, Miz Becky! Where that boy go? He slippery as a baby pig in the mud!"

"Ella, see to it that Hank refrains from playing with that toy in the house." Ma fingered a tuft of Hank's messy hair. "And please see that he is cleaned up and ready on time for his tutor when she arrives this morning."

"Yes, Miz Becky." Ella reached for the toy gun. "Hand it over, boy." She palmed his back and pushed him out the door.

Ma returned to the vanity, muttering complaints under her breath as she patted her cheeks. "Why, if that Brady Haywood wasn't your pa's brother, I'd … I'd—"

"You'd what, dear?" Pa sneaked up behind Ma.

"Frank! You startled me." Ma puckered her brows at Pa's reflection in the vanity mirror.

"What is it about Brady that's got your dander up this morning?" Pa bent over and kissed Ma on the temple.

"Oh, it's nothing, Frank." Ma stood up and smoothed her skirts.

"Good morning, Pa." Haven gave him a hug. "Hank pretended he was a robber and scared us out of our wits with that gun Uncle Brady made for him."

Pa looked Ma in the eye. "Now, Becky, the gun doesn't work, you know. It's useless." He dipped his head to the vanity mirror and combed his fingers through his curly red hair. His blue eyes held a glint of mischief.

"Well, it looks real, and I don't like him playing with it in the house." Ma stood in profile in front of the mirror, adjusting her bodice.

"Brady's a good man, Becky. Got a heart as big as all outdoors. And as for Hank, he's just at that age to begin shooting lessons. He's gonna turn out fine." Pa shrugged. "Besides, we've got enough to worry about with one prodigal son out there somewhere. God only knows where we went wrong with Harley."

"How long's Harley been gone this time, Ma? A month? Two?" Haven shook her head at the thought of her third oldest brother—the one closest in age to her and her twin sister, Harmony. "And no word of him from anyone?"

"I know, dear. That's why I worry so much about Hank." Ma arranged her hand mirror and the matching brush and comb in a neat row on the vanity shelf. "I know he's only ten, but if he turns out anything like Harley, I don't think I could handle it."

Pa scratched his chin through his bushy red beard. "I've said it before, Becky—I think God gave us Hank to see if we learned anything from raising Harley."

"Frank, you're impossible." Ma poked her finger into his chest.

Pa wrapped an arm around Haven's shoulders. "What about this beauty here? She makes me proud."

Haven smiled. "Aww, Pa … thank you."

Ma patted the side of Pa's face. "You're right, dear." She faced Haven. "See, dear … didn't I tell you how proud your pa and I are of you?"

A huge grin split his beard. "Well, of course we are, sweetheart. Why wouldn't we be?"

"Oh, it's nothing, Pa. I thought maybe you and Ma might be worried because I'm twenty years old and never been interested in having a beau." *Until that cute preacher I saw today.*

"Nonsense." He extended one elbow to Ma and the other to Haven. "Let's go to breakfast. Shall we?"

"Sorry, Pa … didn't Ma tell you? I can't join the family for breakfast. I have to go in to work early. Big Joe's waiting for me outside." She waved and ran on ahead. "See you this afternoon!"

&

The woods in the country

"Well, Danny Boy, dawn has broken." Timothy put the bulls-eye lantern aside and picked up the reins. "Time to get to work if we're gonna find those boys."

The horse snorted and pawed the dirt.

Driving along at a snail's pace, Timothy stopped every now and then to remove fallen twigs and branches that had blown onto the road during Monday's high winds. What if the boys had wandered farther away or deeper into the woods before he could even begin his search? "Sure hope they don't get caught by the pattyrollers, Danny Boy."

A mile or so into the sunrise, he passed one rider on horseback headed toward town. Other than that, nothing seemed unusual.

Finding the perfect spot to pull off the road, he waited and watched. The birds of early spring flitted about in the trees, singing their chorus. With the sun rising higher, the morning frost that dusted their woodland home began to thaw. Had the boys kept warm overnight?

As an occasional gust of wind whistled through the pines, he hugged his chest and shivered. Too hard to sit still.

A grayish-brown squirrel paused on the branch of an old elm, eyed him for a second and scurried down the trunk. It scampered to a neighboring tree, darted up the trunk and hid in the branches.

Timothy slipped his pocket watch from his waistcoat and noted the time. Almost seven. A crumpled piece of paper fell from the pocket and drifted to the floor. He picked it up and smoothed it out, perusing its content for about the fourth time. A reward notice for the two runaways. He'd snatched it from a post on his way out of Lexington. Some of the ink had smeared, but he could still read the message:

> *Two hundred dollars Reward, From the subscriber, on the 14th of March, two Negro bucks of the following description, to wit: Pete, 19 years, dark complexion, 5 feet 7 inches high, lean, quick spoken. Had on, when he absconded from Cheapside auction, brown wool overcoat, black linsey pantaloons, and pegged shoes. Also Pete's brother Jim, nickname Shadow, 13 years, very black, about 5 feet, very lean, scar on left leg, easily excitable. Attired similar to Pete. The above Reward will be paid for the return of both or one hundred dollars if only one is returned. Asa Short, Fayette County.*

His fist clenched, crumpling the notice again. He jammed it into his pocket as his eyes scanned the length of the road. Being an expert woodsman, he looked for any unique markings on either side to help him identify his location.

"Danny Boy, I think this might be the best place to start." With a canteen strapped over his shoulder and his rifle secured, he led the horse off the road.

Whispering soothing words to Danny Boy as he walked, Timothy took the horse and rig far enough into the woods where they wouldn't be visible from the road. Finding a suitable hitching spot, he stroked the horse's withers. "There now, Danny Boy, I don't think you'll attract the attention of any travelers back here."

For the next fifteen minutes, he wandered from one clearing to the next. With the trees still bare from winter, the morning light filtered through to the ground. Good visibility. He glanced at his pocket watch. Past seven-thirty.

Doubt started to plague him. He prayed short, silent prayers. If the boys were still in the woods, they couldn't have gone far.

As familiar woodland creatures went about their activities, his eyes searched every detail. But one sound stopped him cold in his tracks.

Something swift. Footsteps?

Whatever it was came to an abrupt halt, and something else followed. He crept toward the sound just as the running picked up again. The snapping and cracking of fallen twigs trailed the creatures through the thick brush.

Then he heard voices. Human voices. Young. Frightened.

The clatter of hooves and the creaking of wheels on the main road started to pick up. He had to get this taken care of soon.

"Aaah! Aaah!" The sudden screams began at a low pitch, increasing to a high-pitched squeal.

Timothy ran like the wind toward the source, but the screams stopped. Two frantic voices bantered nearby. He slowed his pace then froze before ducking behind the large trunk of an old elm. Pete and Shadow. Good … they hadn't noticed him yet. He watched for a minute or so. He had to be careful.

The older boy lay writhing on the damp soil, which was strewn with clusters of rotting leaves. "Go on, Shadow."

"Pete … no, Pete." Shadow knelt, rocking his body beside his brother.

"Forget about me, Shad." Pete shoved Shadow's chest, knocking him back on his rear. "Go on without me." Pete's pleading grew weaker. "Hide somewhere till dark. And remember—follow the North Star."

"No, Pete, I skeerd." Shadow wiggled closer to his brother.

Pete rolled to his side, his features contorted. "Run, Shad. Run … before the pattyrollers come … and beat us with they whips … till the blood runs."

In a flash, Timothy pounced on Shadow, wrestling the kicking and punching boy flat on his back. Without so much as a scratch to Shadow, he'd managed to straddle the boy. Eye to eye.

Shadow spat in Timothy face, spraying his chin.

Timothy caught his breath and lowered his chin to his sleeve, wiping away the spittle. He'd had worse greetings than that. "Listen to me, boy. I don't want to hurt you. I want to help you. Do you understand? I want to help you."

Shadow stopped struggling long enough to glance at Pete. Then he switched his gaze back to Timothy.

"Listen here … it appears your brother's done got himself caught up in a claw trap. Looks like he could use some help real fast." Timothy kept his eyes locked on Shadow. "Now, are you able to help him by yourself?"

Shadow's whining faded. "No, suh."

"That's what I thought." Timothy smiled. "Your name is Shadow, isn't it?"

The boy nodded.

"I'd like to help Pete. Would you let me do that?"

Shadow's lips quivered. "You gonna take us back to Massa Short?"

"No." Timothy relaxed his grip. "You have my word on that."

The boy's eyes stayed locked on his.

"I'm a preacher." Timothy wondered if that even meant anything to Shadow. "You might know a good friend of mine. His name is Micah. Do you know Brother Micah?"

Shadow's demeanor brightened. "He your friend?"

"Yes, he is—a really good friend." Finally. He was getting somewhere. "Now what do you say? Will you let me help your brother, or are we just gonna let him lay there and bleed to death?"

"Help him."

"All right … that's better. I'm going to let go of your arms, and I'm going to get up. If you decide to run, I'm not going to chase you. I'll stay right here with Pete." Timothy glanced at Pete's bloody leg. "Now, I could sure use your help getting that claw open. How about it, boy? Can you help?"

Shadow squirmed and wriggled his arms free. "Yessuh."

Timothy got up cautiously and pulled Shadow to his feet. Taking off his coat, he walked over to Pete and got down on his knees. "Listen to me, Shadow. As soon as I open this trap,

I want you to ease your brother's leg out. He may scream. Do it anyway."

"Yessuh." Shadow lifted his brother's leg as the claws opened. "Don't scream, Pete."

"Good job, Shadow." Timothy patted his back. "Now, I'm going to pour a little water from my flask over the wound. I don't think it will sting too bad. But just in case, hold his hand."

Pete flinched.

Shadow clasped his brother's hand tighter. "You all right, Pete?"

"Pete's doing great. Next, we're gonna make a tourniquet." Timothy ripped the sleeve off his own shirt. "Do you know what a tourniquet is?"

Shadow shook his head. "No, suh."

"Just watch. I'll show you." Timothy tied the sleeve around Pete's leg. "This will keep him from losing too much blood."

Clearly, he couldn't take Pete to Ohio like he'd planned. "Shadow, I think we need to get Pete to Shaker Village. It's about thirty miles southwest of here. The Believers there have helped me out many times. They can fix up Pete's leg, and they have excellent places to hide fugitives. They'll let you both stay there until Pete is well enough to travel. Then I'll come back to get you. Sound all right to you?"

Shadow nodded. "Yessuh."

"Good." Timothy smiled, but a loud neigh from Danny Boy suddenly echoed through the woods.

Shadow shot to his feet.

"That's just my horse." Timothy got up and drew Shadow close. "Something must've spooked him. You stay here while I . . ."

A swishing noise in the nearby patch of trees hissed into the clearing. "Shhh! Quiet." He held his palm up to the boys. "Don't move."

Footsteps followed, and Shadow scurried behind a large tree.

Swish, swish.

Cocking his rifle, Timothy waited. Probably just a deer, but one could never be too sure.

Another footstep. Someone emerged from the copse and appeared where some early morning sunrays sliced through the bare trees, creating a blinding aura. An apparition?

His heart about to leap from his chest, Timothy jerked his rifle up and took aim.

The visitor froze. "Please … don't shoot!"

CHAPTER FIVE

Timothy lowered his rifle to his side. His pulse slowed, but words failed him. There before him stood what at first appeared to be a beautiful angel.

"I heard a scream a while ago as my carriage passed by. Sounded like someone got hurt." The young woman didn't move. "I told my driver to wait while I checked it out. Since I'm a nurse maybe I can help."

He narrowed his gaze. "I saw you downtown yesterday, didn't I?"

"Yes, that was me." The woman's familiar warm smile calmed his jittery nerves. "I'm on my way into town to the office where I work."

Words stuck to Timothy's tongue as he assessed his predicament. A face like hers could tempt a fellow to feign a malady. But could he trust her?

"Well? Is your boy hurt?" She planted her hands on her hips. "Do you want me to help or not?"

"What can you do for him? He's lost quite a bit of blood."

"I have some yarrow in my medicine bag. It's in the carriage." The nurse pointed toward the road. "I have tea tree oil to cleanse his wounds and clean wraps, too. What happened to him?"

"Claw trap." Timothy nodded toward the contraption. "It's off now."

"Shall I get my bag?" Her voice sounded genuine enough.

"I'll go with you." Timothy inched closer to her, still a little skeptical. He paused to glance back at Pete. "I'll be right back."

"Is that your horse tied up over there?" Her gray skirt swayed with a distinctive feminine flair as she shifted her body.

"Yes, I need to check on him. You go ahead." Timothy waved her on. "I'll catch up with you."

He watched her walk away until she was no longer in his view. Then he rounded the tree where Shadow had hidden and found the boy all curled up, shaking.

Timothy squatted next to Shadow, his hand braced against the tree. "I think the Lord sent her here. What do you think?"

The boy shrugged.

Timothy placed his other hand on Shadow's shoulder. "We're just gonna have to trust God on this one, Shadow. You can stay here and hide if you like until she's gone. It's up to you. I'll be right back. All right?"

Shadow nodded.

Timothy ran straight to Danny Boy, said a few soothing words to the horse then caught up with the nurse.

A tall, muscular black man, well over six feet, stood waiting by the nurse's carriage. Though finely dressed in a handsome driver's uniform, he was none-the-less a menacing figure with his large stature and stern face.

"Don't let Big Joe's looks fool you." The nurse kept her voice low as they approached the driver. "He's harmless as a kitten."

"Good, because I need to ask him to pull the carriage off the road into the woods. Do you think he'll mind?" Timothy shot a quick glance at the towering driver.

"No, of course not." She angled her face to Timothy. "But why?"

"I don't want to attract attention from anyone on the road." Timothy caught her inquisitive gaze.

"I see." She retrieved her medical bag from the carriage and faced Timothy. "The boy's not yours, is he?"

"No, ma'am." Why had he accepted her help? Now what? He watched her as she spoke to Big Joe.

The driver nodded and led the carriage and horse off the road into the woods.

So far, so good.

By the time Timothy and the nurse got to Pete, they found him nearly unconscious, but Shadow never came out of hiding.

Timothy exhaled a ton of nerves when the nurse went to work on Pete's leg. So caring. Gentle. Kind. Her soothing manner, her medical knowledge—very professional.

"I see why you're missing your shirt sleeve." She slipped her finger beneath the tourniquet then faced him. "Perfect. I'm impressed."

That smile … *mercy!* Timothy's chest swelled as he handed the first aid items to her one at a time. "Thank you for helping him."

"You're welcome. I'm glad I could help." The nurse started putting things away in her medical bag. "I think he's going to be fine, but he'll need further treatment to prevent infection."

"I know. I'll see that he gets it." Timothy pushed himself up and extended his hand, pulling the nurse to her feet.

She picked up her bag and turned to leave.

"Wait." He raised his hand.

She met his gaze. "Yes?"

He bent down and whisked his frock from the ground, draping it over his bare arm. "Do I have your word that you'll say nothing of what took place here?"

"You have my word." Raising her palm like she was taking a vow, she shifted her weight. A twig snapped under her shoe.

"To absolutely no one—ever?"

"Absolutely no one—ever." Her arm fell to her side.

Timothy inched closer to her. "What about your driver?"

"Trust me. He won't tell anyone."

"How can you be so sure?"

"Big Joe can't talk."

Timothy furrowed his brow. "Why can't he talk?"

The nurse switched her bag to her other hand. "When he was a boy, his first master cut out his tongue for saying something he shouldn't."

Timothy grimaced. "I'm so sorry."

"Well, I've got to get to work. I was supposed to go in early." She left the clearing, fading into the shadow of the trees.

Timothy cupped his mouth. "Thanks for helping! I hope we didn't make you late."

The nurse kept walking as she looked over her shoulder and smiled then disappeared from his view. But that smile … it stuck with him.

Timothy coaxed Shadow out of hiding and carried Pete to the rig. He sat Pete on the rig's side step as Shadow scrambled up next to him.

"I bet you boys are hungry. I brought some rolls with me." Timothy uncovered a basket and held it in front of them. "Help yourself. And here's a flask of water. Share it."

While they ate, he told them about the rig's false bottom. "A Quaker Friend of mine in Ohio built this rig especially for me. It can hide up to three people. You boys will be just fine."

Ten minutes later, with the boys well hidden, they headed out. A quarter mile down the road, Timothy's thoughts returned to the pretty nurse. He hadn't even gotten her name.

He could have kicked himself.

~

Shaker Village

A little before noon, Timothy approached Shaker Village with the boys in tow. When he reached the main building, he left them hidden in the rig and rapped on the door. A middle-aged man with salt and pepper hair and a long black beard greeted him.

Timothy stepped inside. "Thank you, Brother Robert. I've got two young'ns this time. They're brothers. Pete, the oldest, has an injured leg. The younger one is Shadow."

"Follow me." Brother Robert led Timothy out the back door to a stable. A younger man brought Timothy's horse and rig to the stable where they unloaded the boys.

Timothy and Brother Robert carried Pete on a wooden stretcher, and Shadow stayed close to his brother's side for the short walk to the men's dorm. When Shadow entered the small room with two quilt-covered beds, his cheeks stretched into the biggest grin.

Timothy's heart melted. "You like this place, don't you, Shadow?"

"Yessuh!" Shadow flumped onto the edge of one of the beds.

Timothy helped Brother Robert transfer Pete to the other bed. "How long do you think it'll be before Pete can endure a lengthy trip?"

"At least two weeks, I'd say."

"That'll work out fine. I'll be back to pick them up in two weeks." Timothy sat down next to Shadow. "That boy's leg really had me worried."

❧

Friday, April 1, 1859
A downtown Lexington tavern

"To all the fools of the world!" A tavern patron—a young man with long, stringy dishwater hair—lifted a pewter stein from the bar in his shaky hand, beer splashing onto the floor. He clinked his stein against the tankard of the young man sitting next to him.

Gales of coarse laughter bellowed from the bar.

At a table on the opposite side of the room where a more civilized group of gentlemen sat, Timothy shook his head at the rabble-rousers. *Misguided young men. A few too many drinks for their own good.* He tossed a glance to Avery Delaney.

"April Fools' Day." Avery regarded the unruly men with a scowl. "Wouldn't you know?"

Timothy scoffed. "Perfect day for the likes of them. Are the patrons always that rowdy?"

"Not always." Avery picked up a newspaper, opened it and gave it a good shake. "Couple of ne'er-do-wells."

Timothy leaned into the thick wooden slats on his chair. "They don't bother me."

The tavern, a favorite gathering spot on Friday nights, provided the men with a chance to catch up on the week's news. Too bad it had to be next door to a popular inn for out-of-towners.

Leonard Thompson walked in and pulled up a chair next to Timothy. "Hey, my friend. Good to have you back in town. When did you get in?"

"Leonard!" Timothy proffered his hand. "Earlier today. I'm leaving again tomorrow for a short trip, but I'll still have ample time when I get back to set up the tents and get everything ready before the camp meetings begin."

Avery put a hand to Timothy's back and tossed a look to Leonard. "Oh, to be young again and do all that traveling. Right, Leonard?"

"I'm too old to even think about it." Leonard chuckled. "Say, has anyone heard if Trumbeaux got back from his trip to France?" Leonard's gaze landed hard and heavy on a red-haired man who'd just walked in and seated himself at their table.

The red-haired man shifted his weight and cleared his throat. "Listen, Leonard, I know you hold the sale of that former slave girl against me, but I'm afraid I have to disagree." He glared at Leonard. "I admit the details of her case are cruel—being kidnapped and all—but she was Trumbeaux's problem, not mine."

"That's typical of you, Frank." Leonard splayed his fingers against the tabletop. "Always thinking of yourself first."

"That's not true!" Flame red hues spread around the man's eyes, matching his beard.

Timothy sat up straight. Their quarreling triggered a flashback. Was that the man Leonard argued with before the auction? He folded his arms and settled back into his chair. *This should be interesting.*

"You may run a big, fancy horse business, Frank, but you're a minister, too."

That man's a minister?

Leonard's chest heaved. "Your Christian calling should be reason enough for you to step up when asked to help a poor soul in need."

"Everyone here knows I treat my slaves with dignity and respect and give them everything they need and more." Frank looked around at everyone and back to Leonard.

Across the table, Pastor Watson leaned in and fixed his eyes on Frank. "Yes, but Frank, that still doesn't make it right to own another human being."

"What about Delaney over there?" Frank pointed a finger at Avery. "You're all the time calling slavery an evil institution, yet you yourself own a slave girl!"

Timothy's jaw clenched. Surely Frank didn't mean little Brillie. That was uncalled for.

Avery slammed his fist down on the table. "Brillie's not a slave!"

Leonard stood up and leaned over, bracing his arm on the table. He eyeballed Frank. "You know better than that." Rubbing his throbbing neck veins, he sat back down.

Frank crossed his arms. "Then tell me—what is she?"

Avery plucked his spectacles off and waggled them at Frank. "We rescued her, and we treat her the same way we treat our own daughter."

"If you say so." Frank shook his head and looked away.

Leonard faced the man to his right. "Luke, you're a lawyer. Tell me … wasn't it just recently that the U.S. Supreme Court upheld the Fugitive Slave Act in a Wisconsin case?"

"Yes, the Court did indeed do that." Luke Staton took a sip of his soda water. "The state of Wisconsin tried to declare the Act unconstitutional and released that fellow Sherman Booth for helping a fugitive. Then the U.S. Marshall stepped in and contested the judgment, appealing it to the U.S. Supreme Court. The Fugitive Slave Act still stands, strong as ever."

"The Fugitive Slave Act has certainly made my missions more dangerous." Timothy folded a newspaper he'd been skimming through and handed it to Leonard. "There's an article right here in the paper dealing with that ruling."

"I wholeheartedly disagree with it." Leonard glanced around the table. "The free states should not be held to the acts of the South! If a person up north wants to provide shelter and food to a poor soul as the Lord has commanded us to do, then he should have the right to do so!"

A sudden rush of horse's hooves outside the tavern brought the discussion to an abrupt halt. The door flew open, and a frantic young man, his face dusted with ash, pushed his way through the gathering of patrons. He reeked of burnt wood smoke.

"Pa!"

Frank bolted to his feet. "Harrison? What's wrong, son?"

"Pa …" Breathing heavily, Harrison hugged his sides. "One of the stables burned down!"

The company of men with Timothy all stood up at once.

Frank locked eyes with his son. "How did it happen? Was anyone hurt?"

"No one was hurt, Pa. One of the stable boys was close by and rang the emergency bell." Harrison's breathing slowed. "We got all the horses to come out. They're fine."

"Thank the Good Lord for that."

“The fire was Harley’s doing. He finally came home tonight—drunk as ever. Ma wouldn’t let him come in the house, so he started throwing a fit and cursing.” Harrison’s voice calmed as everyone at the nearby tables stopped talking and stared at him. “He knocked over a kerosene lamp.”

“Harley doesn’t have a lick of sense.” Frank kicked his chair against the table with his boot. “How’s your ma? And Haven?”

“Haven’s fine, but Ma’s in a bad way. She won’t let anyone help her.”

Frank slung his coat over his shoulder. “Where’s Harley now?”

“We got him bedded down in another barn.” Harrison raked his fingers over the back of his neck. “He’ll be passed out for a while.”

“Frank?” Leonard put a hand to Frank’s back. “Would you like us to come out and help?”

Avery stepped closer to Frank. “Timothy and I would be glad to help, too.”

Timothy nodded. “Absolutely.”

“I appreciate the offer, fellows, but I think we have enough help.” Frank swatted Harrison’s arm, and they meandered their way around tables to the door.

Timothy walked with Leonard back to their table. “Thank God no one got hurt.”

“That man has to be the most complex person I’ve ever met.” Leonard flopped into his chair. “I really do feel for his family.”

CHAPTER SIX

Haven Hill Farm

Haven leaned against the doorjamb of her parents' bedroom, watching Pa try to console Ma. Was Ma ever going to stop crying? How could Harley do this to her?

Haven's brother, Howard—second in line of her older brothers—stood beside her at the door, his arms crossed. He sported an intense frown. "Sometimes I hate Harley." He removed his spectacles and rubbed smoke from the fire out of his eyes.

"I know." Haven kept her voice low. No need to get Ma any more worked up.

"Is Ma gonna be all right, Pa?" Howard repositioned his spectacles and blinked.

Pa smoothed Ma's hair, tucking a few tresses behind her ear. "She'll be fine, son."

Haven straightened up and stepped inside the room. "Pa, if you don't need me, I'm going to head out to the barn to make sure Harley has enough blankets to keep warm for the night."

Pa nodded. "You go ahead, sweetheart."

"I'll go with you, sis." Howard mumbled under his breath as they turned to leave. "But I really don't care if Harley stays warm tonight."

Haven pulled on the door, leaving it open a crack. The two of them listened to Pa's voice for a moment from the hallway …

"Ah, Becky, don't cry. No one was hurt, and all the horses are fine. We can be thankful for that."

Ma replied through her sobbing …

"Why, Frank? Why is that boy such an incorrigible reprobate? God knows I love Harley, but sometimes he just pushes me past my limits."

Silence. Then Ma spoke again …

"Honestly, Frank, I don't know how much more of this I can take."

Haven tugged on Howard's arm, and they tip-toed down the stairs.

Early Saturday morning, Haven sat yawning atop her horse while she waited for Harrison to ride out to the barn with her. Dressed in riding breeches, she gazed over the rolling hills of bluegrass at the pink hues of the Kentucky sunrise.

She yawned again for about the hundredth time. Thoughts of the handsome preacher had been keeping her awake every night even though she really had no intention of ever giving him the time of day.

"Ready, sis?" Harrison rode past her.

She caught up to him as their horses cantered over the hills. A warm spring zephyr breezed through her long blonde tresses.

They passed the springhouse and one of the stables before rounding Lake Harmony. Gentle ripples on the water caught the first rays of sun as they glinted and scattered light across the surface.

Haven slowed to take in the beauty of the spring floral burst—the crowning touch of slave Elias Parker's artistic landscaping and the handiwork of God. She marveled at the mix of pink angel wing begonias, violet crocuses and the delicate pale yellow of the Polly's Pearl jonquils.

Her smile faded as she caught up to Harrison. "It amazes me that one person in our family can cause so much trouble."

"I know, sis. Harley only cares about Harley."

As they approached the barn, Haven took a deep breath and exchanged glances with Harrison. She dismounted and walked over to the door while Harrison tied the horses.

Her eyes scanned the interior of the barn. "He's not here. You don't suppose ..."

Harrison joined her and went inside. "His horse is gone. Unbelievable! He's taken off again without telling anyone."

"Look over there where we fixed his bedding. The place is a mess. Looks like he threw a tantrum." She stooped to pick something up off the straw-covered dirt. "A scrap of fabric. He must have torn his clothes."

"Let's not worry about Harley right now. I'm just glad he didn't burn down this barn." Harrison headed to the door. "We'd better tell Pa before they go to breakfast. I'll send Elias to clean things up later."

Haven dropped the torn piece of cloth and followed Harrison out. "I hate what this is doing to Ma."

As they rode past a small brick cottage about a hundred yards away from the barn, Haven fixed her gaze in that direction. A maiden's blush shrub covered one side of the cottage, and white verbena lined the front.

Slave Elias lived in the cottage with his wife, Anna, and their four children—Sapphire, Ruby, Pearl, and Andy. The whole family worked together to beautify the grounds around the lake. Over the years, Haven had forged a friendship with them.

She noticed Elias standing by his front door and waved. But Anna opened the door, grabbed his arm and yanked him inside.

Harrison quirked a brow. "Was that Elias?"

"Yes." Haven glanced back over her shoulder. "Wonder what that was about."

"Don't know, sis." Harrison gave his horse a light kick in the flanks. "C'mon. We'd better hurry home for breakfast."

~

The Trumbeaux Estate

After picking up Micah at the Roberts farm, Timothy drove his rig around the circular drive of Trumbeaux's mansion and parked off to the side. Time to check on Ruth.

Micah's incessant fidgeting, annoying as it was, made him laugh. "You did ask Ruth if you could see her today, didn't you?"

Micah tossed him a confused look. "No. Was I supposed to?"

"It might have been a good idea. Pfft … too late now." He hopped down. "She works in the big house, right?"

"Yessuh."

"All right. You wait here while I go up to the door. We should find out if we're even welcome today."

A few minutes later, he came back to the rig. "The Trumbeaux family is supposed to return from France today, but the house servant named Jim said you could visit with Ruth on the portico." He waited a few seconds while Micah stared at him. "Well, are you coming or not?"

Micah snapped out of his stupor and jumped down.

Timothy pulled on his arm. "Now remember, we can only stay a couple of hours. You have to get back to your master, and I have to make a run to the river tonight. You know … the two boys I left at Shaker Village."

"I remember." Micah led the way to the portico where Ruth waited at the top of the steps. He tipped his hat. "Hope you don't mind my dropping by like this, Ruth."

"I don't mind, Micah. I happy you come to see me." She gestured toward a white wicker table and chairs. "We can sit here. I have my work done for now."

At the first lull in the small talk, Ruth's eyes welled. "I dread having to tell Massa Trumbeaux about Lottie." She dipped her head and sniffled.

Micah placed his hand on her shoulder. "It be all right, Ruth. Don't worry yourself."

A rapidly approaching horse veered off the lane, bringing its rider straight toward the portico. As Cora peeked her head out the door, the field worker came to a halt by the steps. "Massa Trumbeaux just turn in the lane!"

Cora gasped and quickly disappeared into the house. Her muted voice trailed behind her as she hollered to the other house servants. "Massa Trumbeaux here!"

The house servants paraded onto the portico where they formed a greeting line. Ruth sighed and rose to her feet, joining them in the line.

Timothy and Micah walked down to the lawn to wait.

A large carriage came to a stop in the circular drive, and Monsieur Maurice Trumbeaux climbed down, smiling and waving to his waiting crew. With an upward swing, he hoisted his young son, Master Eric, high into the air before setting his feet on the ground. In a more reserved manner, he helped his wife, Madame Jeannette, and his daughter, Mademoiselle Marie.

While Micah kept his eyes on Ruth, Timothy took in all the pageantry—especially Madame Jeannette, who radiated the height of Paris fashion in her leaf-green silk dress and matching hat with golden feather plumes.

The children ran on ahead as Maurice escorted his wife to the portico. He almost walked right past Timothy and Micah but stopped to face them.

"Well … what a nice surprise." Maurice removed his hat. "I didn't expect visitors."

Timothy proffered his hand. "Welcome back, Maurice."

"Welcome home, Massa Trumbeaux." Micah bowed.

"Won't you come inside?" With a wave of his arm, he gestured toward the portico steps. "Please … be my guests."

Timothy and Micah followed Maurice up the steps and stood a few feet away from the greeting line. As each house servant bowed or curtsied, Maurice and Jeannette greeted each one by name. Jim held the door while everyone filed into the house.

"It looks as though everything is in tip-top shape." Maurice paced up and down the line while Jeannette appeared to be focused on Ruth. He ended his speech and slipped his arm around his wife's waist. "Madame Jeannette and I are very happy to be home."

After he dismissed the servants, Jeannette walked over to Ruth. "Ruth, dear, you look so forlorn." She put her hand on Ruth's shoulder. "Whatever is the matter?"

Ruth's eyes glistened.

Timothy's jaw tightened. *Here we go.*

"Ruth?" Jeannette lifted Ruth's quivering chin with her finger. "Talk to me."

A sudden hush fell over the house servants. Two of them, who were carrying the trunks up the stairs, exchanged glances before continuing to the top.

Timothy noted the puzzled look on Maurice's face at the inexplicable silence throughout the house.

Maurice eyed the servants as they poked their heads into the foyer. "All right. What does everyone here know that my wife and I do not?"

No one answered. Instead, they all scurried off to work.

Maurice faced Micah. "What's going on?"

Micah locked eyes with Ruth. "It all right, Ruth. Tell Massa Trumbeaux and Miz Jeannette what happened."

Jeannette took Ruth's hand. "Yes, Ruth … do tell me. I know when something is not right with you."

"Oh, missus, I done a most foolish thing." Ruth withdrew her hand, clutched a corner of her apron, and used it to wipe her tears.

Jeannette glanced at Maurice then back to Ruth. "What, Ruth? What have you done?"

"I-I let my Lottie fall into … the hands … of some wicked traders!" Ruth buried her face in her apron.

Maurice cupped Jeannette's elbow. "Maybe we should take this to the drawing room." He gestured to Timothy, Micah and Ruth to follow him. "Shall we? Right this way."

Jeannette and Ruth sat at a round, mahogany tea table in the fanciest armless chairs Timothy had ever seen. His eyes scanned everything. So this was a drawing room? Maurice nodded to Timothy and Micah, indicating a plush, plum-colored settee that faced the women. Awestruck, he hesitated before he sat down.

Maurice remained standing. He offered Ruth a sympathetic look. "Ruth, I want you to tell us everything from the beginning." He draped his arm over the back of Jeannette's chair. "Just take a deep breath and begin when you're ready."

Ruth's chin quivered. "It happened the week before auction. George, he take Lottie and me to town to buy flour and meat. He wait in the carriage while we walk down to the butcher's. Then two men, all dressed up fine and dandy, comes up to us and calls us by name like they knows us. They say they's good friends of you, Massa Trumbeaux."

Maurice rapped his fingers on the top of the chair. "Hmph!"

"They say they gonna open a new restaurant, and they offer Lottie a good paying job, cooking and cleaning and such. Three dollars a week to start, and if business be good, they raise it to four. Me and Lottie, we look at each other—can't believe it true. They say you be right proud of Lottie for getting herself paying work, now she free and all." Ruth paused to catch her breath.

"Oh, Ruth." Maurice puffed air through his nostrils. "What happened next?"

"The men tell Lottie if she want that job, she to show up at eight o'clock next mornin' and bring her freedom papers." Ruth's fingers worked the edge of her apron. "They point to the building where they starting the new restaurant and say if she not there, they gonna hire someone else."

Timothy had heard Ruth's story from Micah, but hearing her tell it in her own words wrenched his heart. *So naive.*

"So we thank 'em and tell 'em we think on it." Ruth let go of her apron and laced her fingers together on her lap.

"When we get back to the carriage, we tell George. He say, 'What good fortune that gal has.' So Lottie take the job."

"I see." Maurice massaged his temples and paced a full circle. "All right, Ruth … finish your story."

"George drive Lottie to town next mornin' and drop her off at eight o'clock, just like they say. He watch Lottie till she go inside before he drive off. He not get too far and notice Lottie's lunch still in the seat. So he drive around the block and park then take her lunch to her.

"When he get close to the back door, he hear the men laughing and Lottie trying to say something, but it all muffled like she got a gag on. George say Lottie try to scream, but he hear one of them slap her and say, 'Shut up, you stupid wench!' And they laugh again." A stream of tears washed down Ruth's face.

Jeannette reached across the table and cradled Ruth's hands in her own. "Ruth, I can't imagine."

"And that not all." Ruth sniffled. "George peek through the keyhole to see what they's doing. Lottie gots fetters on her hands and feet. They ain't no restaurant in there at all. George saw one man hold up Lottie's manumission papers and the other man strike a match and set the papers on fire." Ruth broke into sobs. "Oh, Massa Trumbeaux, my poor Lottie watch her freedom go up in flames right before her eyes!"

Timothy managed to quell the anger coursing through his veins as he gripped the front of the settee's thick cushion.

Maurice leaned against Jeannette's chair. "Ruth, you didn't do anything wrong."

Ruth wiped her eyes. "George hurry to tell Micah. Then Micah go and tell Brother Leonard. By the time they get back to the warehouse, ain't nobody there!"

Ruth's gaze swung from Timothy to Maurice. "Brother Leonard find which trading firm they sell her to. But that evil trader say he paid good money, and he not gonna let her go without no proof. Her name weren't Lottie no more, but he knew which gal Brother Leonard lookin' for. They take her to

Cheapside." Ruth let out a wail. "She gone."

Micah pushed himself up from the settee and faced Maurice. "Brother Leonard try to buy Lottie, but the price go up too high, and he run out of money."

Maurice leaned over the table in front of Ruth. "Do you remember the name of the firm?"

"Baxter and Drake." Ruth sniffled.

"I can't make any promises." Maurice gave the table a good thwack. "But I'll do my best to track her down—starting Monday morning with a visit to Baxter and Drake."

Timothy pulled Maurice aside. "I'll go with you."

As much as it disappointed him that Maurice owned slaves, he thanked God for Maurice's compassionate heart.

CHAPTER SEVEN

Shaker Village

"How are my boys, Brother Robert?" Timothy stepped inside the front door of the Shaker Village men's dorm for the first time since he'd dropped Pete and Shadow off.

"Pete has healed well." Brother Robert led Timothy across the room, the thud of their boots on the wood floor echoing off the walls. "He's ready for travel."

"That's what I hoped to hear." Timothy unbuttoned his frock and slid his arms out.

Brother Robert paused by a row of slatback chairs, and a big grin broke across his face. "Shadow likes it here so much, he's asking to stay!" The elderly Shaker belly-laughed and gestured with his hand for Timothy to sit down.

Timothy pulled up a chair. "I figured he would."

Brother Robert sat in the chair next to him. "Pete's ready to go to Canada. He's a fine young man and very resourceful. He'll find work."

Pursing his lips, Timothy considered the possibilities. "They have a long road ahead of them. Are they ready to leave now?"

"I believe they are, sir. How far do you plan to take them tonight?"

"If I leave now, I hope to make it to the river before dawn." Timothy crossed one leg over the other. "I've arranged for a conductor in Maysville to get the boys across the Ohio to another station—to some Quaker Friends."

"And where will you be headed from the river?"

Timothy met his gaze. "Back to Lexington. I have camp meetings coming up."

"Perfect. Since you're heading back this way, I have a traveling companion for you." Brother Robert tapped Timothy's arm. "Brother Thomas is prepared to leave with you right away. It will be safer all around."

Timothy quirked his brow. "Thank you. How very generous."

A black-bearded, muscularly built man of about forty, dressed in the Shaker fashion, entered the room. "I'm ready whenever you are."

Brother Robert stood up. "Brother Thomas, this is Timothy Locker."

Timothy stood to shake the man's hand.

"Brother Thomas will drive you in one of our wagons." Brother Robert flicked his gaze to the window then back to Timothy. "We have a load of Shaker supplies to be delivered at a small market close to Maysville. This will provide a good cover for the trip. You'll use two of our horses and give your horse a rest."

"Follow me, Timothy." Brother Thomas gestured with a wave. "I'll take you to the boys. You'll need to change into Shaker clothing so no one will suspect anything in case we're stopped."

Shadow's eyes lit up when Timothy walked into their room. "Are we leaving today?"

"Today's the day, boys. You fellows look like you've gained ten pounds each!" Timothy sat down between the boys on the bed. "How's that leg, Pete?"

"Much better, Brother Tim. I'm ready to go to Canada."

Shadow scooted closer to his side. "How far is Canada?"

Timothy put his hand on Shadow's shoulder. "Farther

than you think, Shadow."

"I'm sorry to interrupt the camaraderie." Brother Thomas stood framed in the doorway. "We must leave soon."

Baxter and Drake Slave Traders
Downtown Lexington

Fists balled, Timothy rubbed sleep from his eyes as he and Maurice waited for Drake in the lobby of the slave trader's building. Monday mornings after a weekend of traveling and very little rest always called for extra coffee. Unfortunately, he'd turned down Melia's offer for a second cup. Big mistake. At least the trip to the river with Brother Thomas and the boys had been successful.

The secretary, a tall, skinny young man with slick hair parted in the middle, walked over to them. "Mr. Drake should be arriving any moment."

"Thank you. We'll wait." Maurice removed his immaculate, silk stovepipe hat, flipping it right-side-up.

"All right, sir. When Mr. Drake arrives, I'll let him know you're here." The secretary straightened his plaid bowtie and headed toward the hallway.

Timothy started to hang his modest hat on a brass hook by the front entrance.

Maurice grabbed his arm. "Better hold on to that."

"Good idea."

The front door swung open, and a short, stout, fifty-something man in brown trousers, wrinkled white shirt and no waistcoat strode in like he was in a big hurry. He brushed past them, meeting the secretary at the opening to the hallway.

Maurice leaned close to Timothy's ear. "That's Ephraim Drake. He knows who I am. Probably not happy to see me here."

The secretary pointed to Timothy and Maurice, and Mr.

Drake nodded before waving them over.

"Mr. Trumbeaux and Mr. … I don't believe I know you, sir." He proffered his hand to Timothy.

"Locker." Timothy accepted Drake's hand with a weak grasp, preferring not to shake hands with the man at all.

"All right, Mr. Locker … Trumbeaux, my office is down the hall." An old, worn hardwood floor creaked noisily under the heavy gait of the slave trader as he led Timothy and Maurice to his office.

The man's secretary held the door as they walked in.

"What's this, Percy? What are those papers on my desk?" Mr. Drake seemed to be in quite a surly mood. He sat down rather forcibly on his wooden desk chair and began riffling through the papers.

The secretary leaned over Drake's desk and pointed to a place on the first paper. "If you'll sign these documents, Mr. Drake, I'll get them mailed this morning."

"Where's Baxter, anyway? Hasn't he come in yet?" The balding man twirled the tips of his dark brown mustache.

"Yes, sir. He's in his office." The skinny secretary palmed the door knob. "Shall I bring him in, sir?"

"Not now." Drake's voice foamed with agitation as he gave Maurice the evil eye. "I'll handle this myself."

"Yes, sir." Percy slipped quietly out of the office and closed the door.

"Well, are you two going to pull up some chairs and tell me what I can do for you this beautiful, sunshiny spring day?" Drake's words reeked sarcasm. He pointed to the chairs along the wall.

"I'll stand, thank you." Maurice placed his hat on a chair and folded his arms.

Timothy scooted a chair up to face Drake's desk. "I'll sit. I'm a little tired this morning." He raised one foot and rested his ankle on his knee.

"All right, somebody get to the point. I haven't got all day." Drake lit up a cheroot and began to puff.

Maurice marched right up to the front of Drake's desk.

"It has come to my attention, Mr. Drake, that you purchased a young girl who once belonged to me before her father purchased her freedom."

"Oh?" Drake pushed some papers aside and rested his elbows on the desk. "And what has that to do with you if she was no longer your property at the time of purchase?"

"I have always treated my slaves well, Drake. The girl was living on my estate, and I resent that she was abused and falsely claimed by some no-good wolves in my absence."

"Get to the point, Trumbeaux."

Maurice stared at Drake in silence for a few seconds. "And her mother, who is still my property, is left to bear the burden of her grief at having fallen prey to their lies."

"It seems to me, Trumbeaux, that you're barking up the wrong tree. I've done nothing wrong. My purchases are perfectly legal."

Timothy's boot hit the floor hard. "How can you sit there and say you've done nothing wrong?"

"How dare you come into my office and accuse me otherwise!"

Timothy started to get up. "Because we—"

"Let me tell him." Maurice pressed down on Timothy's shoulder.

Drake leaned forward. "Do you have the girl's manumission papers and proof of her identity?"

"No. That's the kink in this whole thing." Maurice shifted his weight from one foot to the other. "The liars, whoever they are, took the papers and destroyed them before they sold the girl to your firm."

"You don't say." Drake skewed his face. "And how did these papers come into their possession in the first place?"

Timothy shook his head. Of course … Drake had to ask about the papers.

Maurice rubbed the back of his neck. "Well, the girl's mother believed their lies and, thinking they were making a legitimate offer, handed the papers over to them."

Drake broke into an almost diabolical fit of laughter. He

laughed so hard he had to hold his sides.

Anger flared like fire through every fiber of Timothy's being.

Maurice's face turned crimson. "I demand to know who these men are! And I want you to tell me who purchased her and where she was taken from here!"

The fat man plopped against the back of his chair, panting to catch his breath until his laughter died down. "Trumbeaux, I'm afraid if what you say is true, chances are these wolves, as you call them, didn't give their real names. I will tell you this, though—they were good ol' Georgia boys. You know the new law in Georgia—free blacks can be sold back into slavery."

Timothy shot to his feet. "Yes, we know about that law. But that doesn't give them the right to come here!" He wanted to spit in the man's face.

Maurice stomped his boot against the wood plank floor. "I want names, Drake! Give me some names."

"Percy! Come here please!" Drake took another puff on his cheroot.

Percy stepped inside Drake's office immediately. He must have been listening right outside the door. "Sir?"

"Mr. Trumbeaux would like the names of a couple of traders who sold us a young wench … when did you say it was?"

"She went to Cheapside on March 14. It was sometime the week before that. I don't know exactly what day."

"Pull all the files for that week, Percy. Look for a deal on a wench named …" He looked at Maurice. "What's her name?"

Maurice faced Percy. "Lottie. Lottie Preston."

"Yes, sir. Right away." Percy closed the door.

"Now if you don't mind, Trumbeaux, I've got a lot of work to do here. Would you gentlemen please wait in the lobby?" Drake drummed his fingers on his desk. "You're costing me time and money with this wasteful attempt to amend something that's out of my hands."

"I'm not leaving this room until you tell me what I want to know." Maurice took a seat on a scratched up wooden chair in the corner. "I'll wait right here until your secretary comes back."

Timothy scooted his chair away from the desk. "I'm staying, too."

"As you wish." Drake scowled, took a puff of his cheroot and began signing the papers Percy had given him.

A few minutes later, Percy returned and stood before Drake's desk holding a stack of files. "There's no record of a slave girl named Lottie. I've been through them twice, sir." Percy separated three files from the top of the stack and handed them to Drake. "These files are purchases from the Georgia traders."

"Just as I thought. Thank you, Percy." He picked up the documents he'd finished signing. "Here, you can take these and get them ready to mail."

"Yes, sir."

Maurice stood facing Drake. "Well, what are the names?"

Drake began twisting the ends of his mustache again. "Like Percy said … there's no record of this Lottie Preston that you say my firm purchased."

"I know that you know who these men are! Tell me their names!"

"I can only guess, sir! And I don't appreciate your tone of voice. It's been nearly a month ago that you speak of, you know." Drake flipped one of the files open. "The one who signed these documents was named Bill Spencer. Obviously, if he sold us your wench, he called her by a different name."

"What names do you have there?"

"Let me see." Drake read the first name aloud. "Sam." He laid it aside. "No." He opened the second one. "Margaret."

"How old is Margaret?" Maurice dug a notepad out of his pocket and swiped a pencil from Drake's desk.

"It just says she's in her teens."

"Any more?" Maurice scribbled the name Margaret on the notepad.

"One more … hmm." Drake ran his finger over the document. "Another teen named Betsy."

"Is that all?" Maurice pressed the pencil to the notepad and wrote "Betsy."

"That's all. They were sold to a firm out of Louisville—Clarke Brothers." Drake straightened up the three files into a neat stack. "You're grasping at straws here, Trumbeaux. If I were you, I'd let it go."

"Of course, you would! How do you people sleep at night?" His neck veins throbbing, Maurice slammed the pencil down on Drake's desk. "Have you no shame? You're snakes! All of you!"

"Such scathing words, Trumbeaux. How dare you call me a snake when you burst into my office shaking your rattler!" He picked up his cheroot and took several deep puffs.

"Why, I have half a notion to …" Maurice raised his fist, but Timothy clamped his arm in a firm grip.

Drake shot to his feet. "Percy!"

In a flash, Percy popped in. "Yes, sir?"

"Please show Mr. Trumbeaux and Mr. Locker the way out."

Maurice glared at Drake. "We can show ourselves out!" He nudged Timothy out the door ahead of him and left Percy inside. As he slammed the door behind him, something made a loud crash in Drake's office. Timothy and Maurice stood there staring at each other as they listened to the conversation coming from the other side of the door …

"Look at that, Percy. Trumbeaux's gone and done it now. What a pity. That was my favorite framed picture."

"I'll get a broom and dustpan, sir."

"Oh dear, look at this, Percy." The wicked timbre of Drake's voice made the hairs on Timothy's neck stand on end. "Trumbeaux's little door banging tantrum has dislodged the doorknob, too. See if the locksmith can come today and install a new knob."

"Yes, sir, Mr. Drake."

"But first clean up this broken glass and order a new

frame for this picture. And Percy?"

"Yes, sir?"

"Send the bill for both of these items to Monsieur Maurice Trumbeaux."

Maurice spun on his heel, grabbed Timothy by the arm and spoke in a low throaty voice. "Let's get out of here before I do something else I'll regret."

The two hurried through the lobby and out the front door.

"I appreciate you coming with me. Helps a lot." Maurice donned his top hat and flicked lint off his dark gray cape. "Can I give you a ride to Mr. Delaney's house?"

Timothy slapped his slightly tattered hat down on his head. "Thank you, but I'll walk. It'll give me a chance to calm down."

Maurice drew a big breath and exhaled. "That makes two of us." He turned to leave. "I'll keep you posted."

Timothy headed in the opposite direction, slowing down as he passed by the doctor's office where the pretty nurse worked. Hmm … he *did* feel rather ill from the conversation with Mr. Drake. No … he'd need a better excuse than that. But she sure had been helpful with Pete's injury, and he'd never forget it. That was two weeks ago. Would he ever run into her again?

CHAPTER EIGHT

Haven Hill Farm

A thrill tingled through Haven as a carriage pulled up the drive in front of the Haywood mansion. Her whole family had been anticipating Brady Haywood's arrival for days, and she'd asked for Monday morning off from Dr. Wright's office so she could be home when he arrived.

Uncle Brady jumped down from the carriage, grinning from ear to ear. His red bandana flapped against his reddish brown beard.

"Brady!" Pa locked his denim-clad brother in a huge, Texas-style embrace. "Good to see you!"

"Good to see you, too, Frank! The place looks wonderful. I always forget how beautiful Kentucky is." The fringe on Uncle Brady's buckskin jacket swayed with his arm movements.

Haven curtsied. "So good to see you, Uncle Brady!"

Brady took her hand. "Howdy, darlin'! Look at you … beautiful as a Texas sunrise."

"Uncle Brady, you're making me blush." Haven withdrew her hand.

Brady lifted his gaze to the house. "Speaking of beauty …"

Ma, looking as radiant as if she'd just dropped out of heaven in her light blue spring taffeta dress, had just walked out onto the second floor balcony and waved.

Uncle Brady waved back. "Yee doggies! If she ain't purtier than maple syrup drippin' down a stack of hotcakes!"

Uncle Brady stepped aside to make way for his traveling companion, who'd just hopped out of the carriage. "Frank, I'd like you to meet my business partner, Larkin Smith. He's in the market for a couple of fine quarter horses, and like I tell everyone, Frank's the man to see."

Pa greeted the business partner with a handshake. "Welcome to Haven Hill, Mr. Smith."

Mr. Smith looked much younger than her uncle—closer to the age of her older brothers.

"Lookin' forward to seeing your stock, Mr. Haywood." Mr. Smith sported a black western hat and vest and a white shirt with a black corded bolo tie.

Haven sharpened her gaze to an emblem on the tie's brass clip. Was that a longhorn?

Pa flashed a proud grin. "Frank. Please call me Frank."

"Yes, of course … Frank." Mr. Smith smoothed the wrinkles on his vest. "Brady tells me I won't find a finer horse than those born and bred in Kentucky."

"He's right about that! Just got two new quarter horses last week." Pa never missed a chance to brag about his horses. "Glad to have you as our guest here at Haven Hill."

"Larkin, allow me to introduce you to my lovely niece. This is Haven." Uncle Brady wore that silly grin like he always did when he was up to mischief.

Mr. Smith removed his hat and bowed like a gentleman. He smiled but didn't say anything. Haven forced an awkward smile in return. What a strange man. Why didn't he speak to her?

Uncle Brady turned to Pa. "Where's your other lovely daughter, Frank?"

"Harmony's been in England this past year studying equestrian arts." Pa glanced at Mr. Smith then back to Uncle

Brady. "Chances are she'll be home before you head back to Texas."

"That'd be dandy." Uncle Brady slapped Mr. Smith on the back and winked.

"Let's go inside. Becky's waiting for us." As Pa started to lead his guests to the steps of the veranda, two very young "Indians"—one white and one black and both crowned gloriously with homemade feather headdresses—ambushed them from the side of the house.

A medium-sized, speckled gray mutt scampered about, wagging his tail and barking. Red stripes streaked across the dog's fur, matching the boys' cheeks. Haven covered her mouth. Poor dog had no idea how ridiculous he looked.

Uncle Brady laughed. "Whoa, boys! All that whoopin' and hollerin' is loud enough to frighten a totem pole."

"Uncle Brady!" The white-skinned Indian chief rammed into Brady's leg like a wild bull from a bullpen.

"Whoa, pardna!" Uncle Brady swooped Hank up into his arms. "Good to see ya, boy!"

Slave Noah quieted the black-skinned Indian chief—Elias's son, Andy.

Pa leaned over to pet the dog. "What'd these boys do to ya, Scratch?" He traced the red stripes with his finger.

"That's war paint, Pa." Hank broke into a spasmodic trot, going round and round, and Andy joined him in the war dance.

"Of course, I should've known." Pa grinned, rubbing his chin through his beard.

In her usual graceful manner, Ma descended the veranda steps. "Welcome to Haven Hill, Brady."

Uncle Brady removed his western hat and lifted Ma's hand for a kiss. "Glad to be here, Becky." He turned to Mr. Smith. "This is my sister-in-law, Rebekah. We call her Becky."

Larkin removed his hat and placed it over his chest. "Pleased to meet you, ma'am." As he returned his hat to his head, he fixed his eyes on Haven but said nothing. What a strange habit.

Haven couldn't care less if Uncle Brady had plans to hook her up with Mr. Smith. She felt very uncomfortable around that man. And if he didn't stop staring at her, she might … she'd have to … fiddlesticks, she didn't know what she'd do. Mr. Smith didn't hold a candle to her handsome hero from the woods.

The Delaney House

By the time Timothy got back to Avery's house on Monday evening, all he wanted to do was grab something to eat real quick, go to his apartment and collapse in his bed.

Mrs. Perky had just finished up in the kitchen when Timothy walked in through the back door. She hung a towel up to dry. "Well, look what the cat dragged in!"

"Good evening, Mrs. Perky." He removed his hat and rubbed his eyes.

"You look exhausted, sir."

"I am." Timothy yawned. "I've been meeting with people all afternoon about the camp meetings. It took a little longer than I expected."

"I bet you could use a bite to eat." Mrs. Perky started unwrapping leftovers before he could respond. "Go on to the parlor and relax. I'll bring you a tray. The family has gone for an evening stroll with that new puppy Mr. Delaney brought home."

"They have a new puppy?"

"Yes. They call him Lazarus."

"Oh, I've met Lazarus. Brillie's been wanting that dog." In spite of his sore feet, he laughed as he shuffled to the parlor. "So Avery went and got the girls a puppy."

Timothy plopped himself down on a chair, stretched out his long legs and kicked off his boots.

Whump! Then w*hump* again.

"Gracious me!" A copy of Dickens' *Hard Times* slid off

Alifair's rounded belly and tumbled to the floor next to the chaise.

Timothy flew out of his chair, his energy restored in one grand surge. "I'm so sorry! Please forgive me, ma'am. I mean, I didn't see you there." How had he not noticed her?

He sat back down and grabbed his boots, bumbling about as he attempted to put them on. "I had no idea." He got one boot on, but it was the wrong foot. Heat crept up his neck to his cheeks. Was Alifair watching him? Eventually, both boots made it on the correct feet.

He raised his head and stole a glance at Alifair, who'd covered her mouth. At least she wasn't laughing at him … yet. "I was so tired I guess I couldn't see straight. I didn't mean to disturb your nap."

"It's quite all right, Timothy. I shouldn't be sleeping so much anyway." She yawned and patted her lips. Such perfect lips. "I guess I dozed off while I was reading."

"Mrs. Perky said the family went for a stroll, so I just assumed that … well, you know." What was it about Alifair that made him act like a dimwit?

"Don't worry yourself so. I didn't feel up to a stroll this evening so I stayed home." Alifair removed a hairpin, allowing her auburn locks to drape over her shoulders. "Mrs. Perky probably didn't know I was in here."

Mrs. Perky entered the parlor carrying a tray of leftovers from supper. She set the tray on the dining table and turned to Alifair. "Can I get you anything before I leave?"

"No, thank you, Mrs. Perky. I'm fine." Alifair recovered her book from the floor.

Timothy stood and faced Mrs. Perky. "You're leaving? I mean, do you have to go now?"

"Yes, my husband is waiting out front." Mrs. Perky walked over to the window. "Is there something you need?"

"No." How could he say it without being too obvious? "When will Avery and Melia be back?"

Mrs. Perky pulled the lace sheers back for a clearer view. "Hmm, I think I see them now."

Timothy heaved, blowing air through his lips, then took a seat at the dining table by the tray of food.

Mrs. Perky sniggered at him and held the door for the family to come in before she left.

"Timothy, you're home!" Melia sprinted over to him as Brillie and Sylvia headed upstairs with the puppy. "I worried like a mother hen all day that you might have left again without telling us." She tapped the edge of the dinner tray. "Oh, good. I see that Mrs. Perky has taken care of serving your meal."

"Yes, she did."

"Well, you go on and enjoy your supper. Don't mind us." Melia walked over to the settee and sat next to Alifair.

He lifted a plate off the tray. His stomach grumbled as Avery pulled up a chair next to him.

"Glad you're home!" Avery put a hand to his shoulder. "Missed you at dinner and supper."

"It's been a long day."

"Well … while you were gone our family grew by one."

"I heard. So the girls twisted your arm, did they?"

"Yes, and Melia, too." If the grin on Avery's face was any indication of how he felt about the puppy, Timothy guessed it didn't take much arm twisting.

As the grandfather clock chimed seven times, Timothy silently gave thanks for his meal.

"Seven already." Avery locked his fingers together over his belly. "So, tell me, did you get much accomplished today for the camp meeting?"

"Quite a bit, actually. I've been in meetings all afternoon." Timothy took a hearty bite out of a turkey sandwich and washed it down with several gulps of water.

"Do you have a location picked out?"

"I think so. We're going out there tomorrow to check it out." A large mound of cole slaw made its way into his mouth. As he lifted a glass of water to his lips, he caught Alifair staring at him. Was she flirting with him, giving him sultry looks like that?

"This sandwich is delicious." Timothy kept his eyes on his plate. "I was starved." As he chewed, Alifair got up from the chaise. He chewed faster.

"I think I'm going to turn in now." Alifair crossed the room and stopped right next to him. "It was so nice to see you again, Timothy."

His eyes met her sea green gaze, and he nearly choked on that last mouthful of turkey. "Pleasure's all mine, ma'am." Gulping down more water, he listened to the graceful rustling of her silk dress when she walked out of the parlor.

Time to hide from the world in his little backyard apartment. If he hadn't been so famished, this was one meal he could just as well have done without.

~

The slaves' church

Timothy had spent the entire week working on plans for the camp meeting. When Sunday came around, he decided to visit the church where Micah preached instead of going with the Delaney family to Leonard's church.

Rain drizzled outside the windows then faded into mist. Whiffs from a cool breeze murmured in through an open window. He tilted his head back. The fragrance after the rain smelled so sweet. Rays of sunlight slashed through the window like glowing blades and warmed the room.

Glancing around the small sanctuary, he waited for Micah to come out of his study to begin the service. The building had been given to the slaves by the previous congregation after they'd moved into a newly built structure next door. Micah's master, John Roberts, had given him permission to be their preacher—a rare privilege. That made Timothy happy.

As church bells chimed all across Lexington, he savored the glorious sound. The houses of God were open, but Cheapside was abandoned for the day. Yes … this was the

Lord's Day.

Right before the service, Micah stepped up to the pulpit, and Elder Jack took his seat on the stage beside him. The room grew quiet. After greeting the congregation in the name of the Lord, Micah read aloud the scripture for his sermon, Lamentations 3:17 and following: "'Thou hast removed my soul far off from peace: I forgat prosperity. And I said, My strength and my hope is perished from the Lord: Remembering mine affliction and my misery, the wormwood and the gall.'"

Several worshippers shouted all at once. "We be afflicted *all* the time!"

Micah glanced toward the back of the sanctuary where Deputy Grant Powell kept watch by the entrance doors.

Deputy Powell had the job of checking every slave's pass. If they didn't have a pass, the deputy would have to take them to the jail to await pickup by their owner. In order to avoid a possible whipping at the whipping post down by Cheapside, they'd best be carrying a pass. Timothy was glad he'd never witnessed anything like that—yet.

Micah raised his hand high. "You want hope? Jesus gives us hope! Are you listening?"

"The Lord! He our hope!" An old, gray-haired man pounded his walking stick on the floor in rhythm to a chorus of *amens* and *hallelujahs.*

Timothy leaned back on the pew, crossing his arms. Oh, how he loved watching them worship.

Micah wrapped up his sermon and shared an update on his master's health. "Remember the social I told you about before Massa got sick? Well, he be feeling fine now, and he say I can host it on the farm Friday night. So, make sure you get your passes and come on out!"

After the service, Ruth made a beeline to Micah. She took a deep breath and grabbed both his hands. "Did Brother Tim tell you about Massa Trumbeaux's visit to Baxter and Drake?"

Timothy walked up and put his hand on her shoulder. "I

was just getting ready to tell him, Ruth. You beat me to it."

Micah kept one of Ruth's hands in his and faced Timothy. "How did it go?"

"Maurice got a couple of leads, and he plans to follow up on them." Timothy stepped aside to make way for Cora and Martha, who bounced up to Ruth in grand bubbly fashion. Those two always made him laugh.

"That be good news, gal." Micah gave Ruth a lingering hug.

Martha's eyes grew wide, and her jaw dropped. She whispered something in Cora's ear while she kept one eye on the embracing couple, and Cora jiggled from head to toe.

One of the younger boys peeked inside the entrance and called to Ruth. "Pa say if you and Cora don't get on the wagon lickety-split, he gonna leave without you."

"You better hurry." Micah gave her a quick hug before she turned to leave.

She glanced over her shoulder and smiled at him.

Micah looked as if he was in another world, but Martha broke the trance. "Like I say before—Micah need a good wife." With a sly grin, she walked off. "But I just a mindin' my own business. Yessuh, I is."

CHAPTER NINE

The blacksmith's shop

Carrying a sack lunch that Mrs. Perky had thrown together for him, Timothy paused outside the blacksmith shop where Micah worked. He checked his pocket watch. Almost noon. Time for a break and a chat with Micah.

He opened the door and went in. Seeing that Micah was still working, he draped himself against the wall, crossed his ankles and waited.

The owner of the shop walked up to Micah. "What's bothering you? You're getting behind." The man lifted something from the shelf where Micah placed his finished work. "You're a million miles away."

Amused by that remark, Timothy stifled a chuckle. Micah's boss didn't know the half of it. A million miles away—and Timothy knew why. Were women really worth all that lovesick business? A pretty, as yet nameless nurse? A pregnant widow from New York? Why would any sane man want to put himself through all that? Pathetic.

"Sorry, suh." Micah picked up a grinding stone and chiseled away on his project. "Please don't take it out of Massa Roberts' share of my earnings."

The boss placed the item back on the shelf. "Mr. Roberts

hasn't had another setback, has he?"

"Oh no, suh. He near his normal self." Micah picked up a pair of forging tongs. "I aim to get all caught up this afternoon."

"Do you have Mr. Lipton's bench vise and calipers finished yet?"

"The calipers, they right here, suh." Micah pointed to the shelf. "I workin' on the bench vise right now. It almost done."

"Good work, Micah." His boss examined the new calipers and put them back. "I've been meaning to ask you something. How would you like to receive some training in farriery? You work very well with horses."

Timothy grinned as Micah's brows shot halfway up his forehead.

Using his dirty apron, Micah wiped away beads of sweat. "Yessuh! I be right glad to learn the trade."

"It's settled then. I'll talk to Roberts next week." The boss pivoted and walked away.

Micah put the bench vise next to the calipers on the shelf then grabbed his lunch bag.

"Micah!" Timothy flagged him over to the door. "Thought I'd stop by and eat lunch with you today. Let's go outside."

"Glad you came. I could use the company."

They took their usual places on the bench outside. Timothy fished a ham sandwich out of his lunch sack.

Leonard approached them and sat down next to Micah. "I hear you're hosting a social for your congregation at the farm Friday night."

"Word sure do get around." Micah wiped his hands on his trousers. "Can you come, Brother Leonard? Bring the missus and children, too."

"Don't think we can make it, but thanks for asking."

Micah looked at Timothy. "You coming, aren't you?"

Timothy swallowed a bite of ham. "I'll be there."

Micah bit into a hardboiled egg then unscrewed the lid from a water-filled mason jar. He turned to Leonard. "Can I ask you something?"

Leonard angled his head and lifted an eyebrow. "Certainly, but why are you whispering?"

"You won't tell a soul? Not even Gladys?" Micah chugged half the water from his jar.

"You're scaring me, Micah." Leonard looked at Micah with a kind of silly half grin. "My lips are sealed until you say otherwise."

Micah took a deep breath and blurted it out. "I want to ask Ruth to marry me."

Timothy landed a slap on Micah's back. "I knew it!"

"Hmm …" Leonard rubbed his chin between his thumb and forefinger. "I see."

Micah stared at Leonard for a few seconds. "That all you gonna say? Just 'I see'?"

Leonard leaned back and folded his arms. "Well, what's stopping you? Why don't you go ahead and ask her?"

"Don't know."

"Hmm …" A huge grin stretched across Leonard's face.

"You a lot of help."

"Well, my friend, like you said earlier, word gets around mighty fast, and I feel it's my duty to let you know that you and Ruth are all the buzz in the gossip circles." Leonard tossed a look to Timothy. "Am I right, Timothy?"

"Well, I wasn't going to say anything, but …" He burst out laughing.

Leonard punched Micah's arm. "Nothing bad, mind you—just that both of you have come down with a severe case of spring fever."

"Who say that?" Micah quirked his brow.

"My wife—Gladys. Who do you think?"

Micah screwed the lid back on the mason jar and set it on the boardwalk. "Where she hear that?"

"Oh, Micah, you have a lot to learn about women." Leonard shook his head.

Timothy had a lot to learn, too. How would he ever figure it out? Did he even want to?

Leonard slapped Micah's leg. "If you've prayed about it, then don't put it off. Ask her."

"If she say yes, will you marry us?" Micah's lunch bag slid off his lap, landing next to the mason jar.

Leonard bent over and picked up the bag. "You bet I will. Just tell me when."

ꕥ

The Delaney home

"Melia, is there anything you need me to do before I leave? I'll be spending most of the day at the camp meeting site."

Melia finished scribbling something on a piece of paper at the maple secretary and walked over to him. "Could you run to the grocer's first?" She handed Timothy the paper with her list of items. "I think that's everything."

Timothy glanced at the list. "Only three items? I can do that."

Brillie looked up from the table where she'd been practicing her reading and writing lessons with Alifair. "Miz Alifair looks sick, Miz Meely."

Melia pivoted and faced Alifair. "Oh, dear."

"Shush now, Brillie." Alifair frowned. "I'm fine."

"Then why were you massaging your temples like that?" Melia marched over and stood beside her. "Oh, Alifair, your face is all flushed." She put her hand to Alifair's forehead. "Gracious me! You're hotter than a firecracker!"

Alifair rested her head on the small table that served as Brillie's desk. "To be truthful, my head does ache terribly, and I have a slight cough. I thought it would go away."

"Alifair, you must never ignore this sort of thing, especially when you're pregnant." Melia faced Timothy. "Forget the grocery items for now. Go fetch Dr. Wright."

"I'm on my way." Timothy crossed the room to the foyer in a few long strides. He grabbed his hat and left through the front door.

About thirty minutes later, he returned—alone.

Melia greeted him from the top of the stairs. "I took Alifair to her room. Where's Dr. Wright?"

"I'm sorry, Melia, but the doctor was out making house calls this morning. The office clerk said she'd send a nurse over to the house as soon as one's available." Timothy hung his hat on the hall tree. "Should be any moment now."

"Oh dear. I guess that'll have to do." Melia disappeared into the upstairs hall.

Timothy waited in the parlor with Brillie, wondering which nurse would come.

Fifteen minutes went by, and a dark cloud hung low in the sky. Rain started to spit and within a minute turned into a steady downpour. Timothy watched from the window for a few minutes until the darkness lifted.

A knock on the door broke the monotony, and Timothy rushed to answer it, leaving Brillie in the parlor.

The swiftness by which he pulled the door open caused the young woman on the porch to gasp and drop her umbrella. She stooped immediately to retrieve it and so did Timothy. With a whack, their heads came together.

"Oh! I'm so sorry." He pressed his fingers against the knot forming on his forehead, but the nurse kept her gaze down as she rubbed her head. "Are you hurt, ma'am? I mean, I know it hurt. I'm such a clod. Please, allow me to get that for you."

The woman started to straighten up. "I'm fine."

He picked up the umbrella and lifted his head. In an instant, almond-shaped brown eyes converged on his blue eyes.

The nurse gawked. "It's you …"

"You're … you're the angel …" Timothy caught himself. What a dumb thing to say. "I mean, the nurse in the woods. You helped the boy with the injured leg."

"Yes, it's me." She straightened her nurse's cap and took her umbrella from him. "We meet again."

"Please, come in." He gestured with a sweeping wave of his arm. "You can put your umbrella here on the hall tree."

When she removed her bonnet, a few blonde locks worked loose from the ribbon behind her neck and framed her face. "Where's the patient?"

"She's upstairs with Mrs. Delaney." If only *he* could be the patient.

Melia appeared at the top of the stairs. "Oh, I'm glad you're here. Please come on up."

As the nurse picked up her bag and ascended the stairs, Timothy watched her from the foyer until she was about halfway up. *Fancy that.* He scurried across the foyer into the parlor where Brillie sat waiting.

He plopped down on the settee next to her. "Do you know her?"

With her chalk board on her lap, Brillie wiggled closer to him. "Who? The nurse?"

"Yes—do you know who she is?"

"That Nurse Haywood." Brillie grasped a piece of chalk in a writing position and wrote the letter "B" on her board.

"Nurse Haywood? What's her first name?" He slouched back and crossed one leg over the other.

"I dunno, Bro'er Tim." Brillie wrote the letters "r" and "i" on the board. "She just Nurse Haywood."

"What else do you know about her?" He folded his arms and watched her write the letter "l" two times.

Brillie gave him a quizzical look. "What you mean?"

"Well, for instance, is she married? Got a beau?"

Brillie giggled and punched him in the arm. "You think she purty, do you?"

"Shush, not so loud." He uncrossed his arms and legs and sat up straight. "Just finish writing your name."

"She ain't married, Bro'er Tim, and I don't know if she got a beau." Brillie leaned in, stretched her neck higher and cupped her mouth next to his ear. "You wanna take her courtin'?"

"I don't know. Maybe." He chuckled at Brillie's cuteness. "Is she a Christian?"

The child beamed. "Yessuh. Her daddy, he a country

preacher."

"Really?" Timothy switched his gaze to the stairs. "Hmm . . ."

Stunned by her encounter with the handsome man downstairs—the man she'd thought was a preacher—Haven felt like she'd been sucker-punched in the gut. What a foolish girl she'd been to allow a married man to visit her in her dreams. And now, here she was on a house call to care for that man's wife. What a lark! *Just wait till Sarah hears this.*

Haven followed Melia to Alifair's bedside. No sick room smell. Someone must have misted the air with perfume. She drew in a large whiff of the fragrance. "Is that jasmine?"

"Yes, isn't it lovely?" Melia picked up a dainty glass bottle painted with a gilt floral design from the bedside table. "Alifair brought this from New York."

"It smells wonderful." Embarrassed as she was about mistaking Alifair's husband for something he wasn't, Haven gave her a professional smile. After all, it wasn't Alifair's fault.

She lifted her wooden stethoscope from her bag and began the examination. Before checking Alifair's chest and abdomen for a rash, she took a look at her eyes and throat. "No rash, Alifair. I don't think it's anything serious like what we have going around right now."

"What's going around?"

"Scarlet fever cases are popping up. Nothing out of the ordinary for this time of year, though. Scarlet fever is dangerous, but I think you probably have a mild influenza. It should pass in a few days. Have you had any vomiting?"

Alifair scrunched up her nose. "No, not yet."

Haven tapped Alifair's arm. "You should be fine. Dr. Wright will come by later today." She faced Melia. "It's important she drink lots of water and other fluids. Some quince seed tea would be helpful."

"Thank you, Miss Haywood." Melia smoothed a blanket over Alifair, tucking it under her arms.

Haven closed up her bag. "I can show myself out, Mrs.

Delaney." Hopefully, she could avoid the patient's husband. If she ever saw that flirty face again, it would be too soon. Oh, the nerve of some men.

As soon as he heard footsteps on the stairs, Timothy hurried to the bottom landing and looked up. "How is she?"

A frown puckered Nurse Haywood's face as she paused midway on the stairs. "I think it's a mild influenza. Nothing to worry about."

"Thank you." Timothy stood starry-eyed by the landing as she opened the front door. Oops … he should help her. Smacking himself on the head, he ran to the door.

"I'm sor-sorry." His voice croaked. "How rude of me not to get the door for you."

"I'm perfectly capable of opening a door, thank you." The nurse tightened her grip on the knob and stepped over the threshold. She stopped and faced him. "But I forgot my umbrella. Would you get it for me please?"

"Of course." Timothy rushed to get her umbrella, ran back to the door and handed it to her. His hand inadvertently brushed against hers, making the skin on his arm prickle. He lingered there, but she snatched her hand away.

"Thank you very much." She snapped her head, and the heels of her shoes pounded across the porch.

Timothy stepped outside. "Is something wrong, Miss Haywood? Have I done something to—?"

"Why do you detain me, sir?" Her skirt swirled over her ankles as she turned back. "Shouldn't you be rushing to your sick wife's bedside?"

Timothy laughed before he could respond. "You think that—"

"Listen, Mr. Brooks, I fail to see any humor in this." She squared her shoulders. "Your wife is going to be fine."

"My name isn't Brooks, and—"

"Oh, I see." Nurse Haywood's brows shot up. "So you're not married to the mother of your child!" She turned her back to him in a huff and stomped away. "Good day, sir."

His jaw dropped. "Miss Haywood! You have it all wrong."

She glanced over her shoulder.

"My name is Timothy Locker. I met Mrs. Brooks a few weeks ago when she came here to live in her brother's house." He took a step toward her. "You see, I'm not from around here. I'm Mr. Delaney's guest, and Mrs. Brooks is a widow."

Her frown faded. "Oh my. I guess I assumed too much."

"Rather humorous misunderstanding, don't you think?"

"No, sir … I don't."

"Oh."

"What happened to Mrs. Brooks' husband?" The softer timbre of her voice put him at ease.

"Cholera."

She gasped. "How tragic." Awkward silence followed. "I must get back to the office now, Mr. Locker. Have a good day."

"Timothy … please call me Timothy."

"All right … Timothy." She smiled at him!

"It was nice to see you, Miss Haywood."

"Haven … my name is Haven." The way she walked down the porch steps—so graceful even with that cumbersome black bag and an umbrella.

"Haven." Her name purled through his head as she walked away.

CHAPTER TEN

The Roberts farm

Timothy kept his promise to Micah to be at the slaves' social on Friday night. When he arrived, he headed straight to the front porch of the farmhouse where Micah's master sat rocking away.

"Good evening, Mr. Roberts." He extended his hand for a handshake.

"It's a mighty fine, evening, Reverend. Micah told me you were coming." The farmer's old wooden rocker with the chipped white paint creaked in measured, percussive rhythm. He patted the arm of the rocker next to him. "Won't you sit a spell?"

"Thank you, but I really just came up to let you know how much I appreciate your letting Micah have these socials here." Timothy leaned into a porch post.

"Well, it's only twice a year, but Micah's socials always bring a smile to my face." Roberts puffed on his pipe. "Micah taught me about Jesus, you know."

"He's good at that." Timothy glanced out at the side yard where a group of members from Micah's church sat on simple, unfinished wood chairs and stools, laughing and talking. A bubbling brook ran along the edge of a grove of trees, winding on toward the back of the property. "Micah loves to talk about Jesus."

The screen door opened, and Mr. Roberts' wife stepped outside. Roberts patted the arm of the other rocker again. "Come on over and have a seat, Priscilla."

"Oh, John, must I?" She wrinkled her nose.

Roberts grinned at her. "Enjoy the cheery atmosphere for a change."

"If you insist." She looked at Timothy, hesitated a moment, then sat down in the matching white rocker next to her husband.

"Do you remember Micah's friend?" Roberts pointed to Timothy. "This is Reverend Tim—"

"I know who he is, John." Her rocker creaked just like his did.

Timothy doffed his hat. "Good evening, ma'am." He'd heard from numerous people that Priscilla Roberts wasn't the most pleasant person to be around. From what he could tell, she seemed downright rude. But Micah had never said an unkind word against her—only that he didn't understand why she treated him with such animosity.

Mrs. Roberts fixed her gaze on her husband. "I don't know why you always let Micah use our property for these wild get-togethers." Her rocking picked up speed. "There's all that hootin' and hollerin' all evening until well past midnight. Then they turn to singing those Negro spirituals, clapping and swaying and shouting. Doesn't sound Christian to me."

"Come now, Priscilla. Let 'em have some fun now and then." Roberts clamped his fingers over her arm. "Besides, how do you know what sounds Christian? You never go to church."

She harrumphed and jerked her arm free. "I would if I thought there was a reason to."

Roberts took a puff on his pipe and exhaled a smoke ring. "You should listen to Micah once in a while, dear."

"Oh, puh! What does he know?" She rolled her eyes, stopped rocking and leaned forward. Her frown bore right through Timothy.

Mr. Roberts stopped rocking, too. "I'm sorry you feel that way, Priscilla." He took another puff on his pipe. How could the man stay so calm?

Timothy pushed away from the porch post, leaving one hand on it for support. "Well, Mrs. Roberts, we have God's Word—the Bible. You see—"

"Ridiculous, if you ask me." She resumed her rocking.

"We didn't ask you, Priscilla." Mr. Roberts flashed a smirk to Timothy. "Have you heard? Tonight's a big night for our boy Micah. He's got something special planned."

Timothy winked. "I think I know."

"Oh?" Mrs. Roberts raised her brows. "What's so special about this social?"

Mr. Roberts hunched forward and looked her straight in the eye. "Micah says he wants to ask that gal named Ruth from the Trumbeaux Estate to marry him. Says he's gonna propose tonight. Asked for my blessing, so I gave it to him."

The creaking stopped. "John Roberts, how could you?"

"Why not?"

Frowning, Mrs. Roberts folded her arms. "Now what good could possibly come out of allowing him to do such a foolish thing as take a wife?"

"I've been asking myself that same question for years." The corner of Roberts' lip curled up, and Timothy surprised himself with a snort.

"John!" Mrs. Roberts wiggled in her rocker like a wet fish on a hook. "If you hadn't just had a stroke, why I'd-I'd—"

"You'd what, Priscilla?"

"Oh, never mind." She rolled her eyes. "What if Trumbeaux won't give permission for her to marry him?"

"Well, dear, I guess you haven't heard yet—Ruth's free now. All the Trumbeaux slaves are free. She can marry whomever she pleases."

Timothy's jaw dropped. Could it be true? "I didn't know that. So Ruth is free?"

Roberts nodded. "Just happened a couple days ago."

"Now why would Trumbeaux go and do a fool thing like that?" Mrs. Roberts' icy stare could have frozen Hades.

"Don't know."

If only Roberts did know. Wouldn't matter anyway—Mrs. Roberts was boss.

"I'll tell you one thing, John—I won't allow that wench to live on this property." She glanced at the slaves in the yard. "We've got enough bodies to feed and clothe as it is."

Roberts flipped his pipe over a tin can and tapped the ashes out. "I expect they'll find a way around it, Priscilla."

Timothy couldn't stop smiling. Ruth was free.

Mrs. Roberts stood up. "I'm going back inside." The old worn porch vibrated under her heavy gait as she plodded across, letting the screen door bang shut behind her.

Timothy straightened his back and massaged a kink out of a muscle in his arm. "Mr. Roberts, if you'll excuse me, I think I'll go, too. Time to join the party."

"Have a good evening, son."

Timothy found Micah engaged in small talk with Ruth. Had Micah asked the big question yet? Probably not. The lovesick man wasn't doing a very good job of hiding his uneasiness.

After watching his friend, Timothy tried to sort his own feelings about women and courting. Haven Haywood's pretty face flitted across his mind. Maybe he was ready to give it try. For her, anyway. Not Alifair. The widow could keep her sultry glances to herself.

Ruth left Micah's side to help the other ladies get the fried chicken and roasted pork set out on the food tables. The aroma wafted past Timothy's nose. "I don't know about you, Micah, but I'm ready to eat. Right now."

"Not me. I feel sick." Micah placed his hand over his stomach. "Haven't eaten all day."

Another symptom Timothy had no desire to deal with. "What are you waiting for? Just ask her and get it over with."

"After the meal. Timing has to be just right, you know."

"I wouldn't know."

Micah laughed. A nervous laugh, but still a laugh. "You'd best be workin' on that, Timothy."

"Like you said … timing has to be just right." He gave Micah a hefty slap on the back. "Hey, I just heard the news from Roberts about Trumbeaux freeing his slaves! That's wonderful for Ruth."

"Yes, she most fortunate. She gets to stay on with Miz Jeannette for pay." Micah pointed in the direction of the women. "Listen, Timothy … see those two gals over there walking together?"

"Cora and Martha?"

"Yes … those two." Micah leveled his eyes to Timothy. "Be extra careful you don't say anything about this here proposal in front of them. Neither of 'em could keep a secret if you put a lock on it and threw away the key."

"My lips are sealed, Micah." Timothy mock zipped his lips with his thumb and index finger.

After everyone had eaten their fill, the women did the cleaning up while some of the men separated into smaller groups. Timothy engaged in manly talk with them for the next hour or so while the children played games in the yard.

With everyone's attention focused on having fun, Timothy noticed that Micah and Ruth were nowhere to be seen. Had those two star-crossed lovers managed to slip away? He wished he could be a bug on a rock so he could hear Micah's proposal.

About thirty minutes later, when dusk was starting to fall, Micah and Ruth emerged from a grove of trees, grinning and holding hands. Timothy grinned, too. His friend must have conquered his fear.

"Listen, everyone!" Micah raised his hand high and waved. "Good news!"

A child's voice rang out. "You're not gonna preach to us, are you, Bro'er Micah?"

After the laughter died down, Micah draped his arm over Ruth's shoulders. "I ask Ruth to marry me, and she say yes!"

Cora and Martha hopped up and down like rabbits. What

a sight.

Timothy cupped his mouth and shouted. "When's the big day?"

Micah beamed. "This Sunday, after church. Brother Leonard say he gonna marry us."

"Sunday!" Cora bounced her way over to Ruth and wrapped her up in a big hug. "Can't believe it true. I gonna make you and Micah a cake. A mighty fine cake."

Confusing thoughts percolated through Timothy's head, making him so dizzy he had to sit down. Envy? He really did want a love like Micah's and Ruth's.

Did Haven Haywood ever think about him?

Haven Hill Farm

"Howard, have you seen my shawl anywhere? I've misplaced it again." Haven poked her head inside the doorway of the downstairs library where her brother sat reading a book.

Howard lowered the book to his lap and pushed his spectacles up. "If you're talking about the green crocheted one, I saw it on the table by the stairwell."

"Thanks. I seem to be misplacing things a lot today."

Shawls and other misplaced items ranked low on Haven's list of concerns. Timothy Locker had somehow managed to turn her independent, single lifestyle all topsy-turvy. Those eyes—those piercing, violet-blue eyes. She'd never forget.

She closed the library door, grabbed her shawl off the foyer table and went out to the veranda where her family had gathered. Thank goodness Ma had saved her a chair next to hers because, for some reason, Larkin Smith was out there, too. Mr. Smith and Uncle Brady sat directly across from her and Ma.

"Glad you could join us, darlin'. I was wondering where you were." Uncle Brady landed a hearty whack on Mr. Smith's leg. "Ain't she the purtiest thing you ever saw,

Larkin?"

Mr. Smith smiled as he squirmed in his chair, but he didn't say anything.

Haven squirmed, too. She wished Uncle Brady wouldn't embarrass people like that. He didn't mean to—that's just what Uncle Brady did. "Sorry I'm late, Uncle Brady. I had to look for something."

Ma patted Haven's knee in a way that meant she understood. Ma always understood. "Did you get much sewing done on your Easter dress?"

"Almost done, Ma." Haven scooted her chair back about six inches so her feet weren't so close to Mr. Smith's. "I'll start on Harmony's soon. I hope to get it done before she comes home."

As the evening wore on, Haven lost interest in all the family talk. Even Uncle Brady's tall Texas tales bored her. Why was Larkin Smith so creepy? She couldn't stay out there another minute.

All she could think about was Timothy Locker. Would she ever see him again?

The slaves' church

Sitting in Micah's church study, Timothy laughed with puckish delight as he watched Micah pace back and forth like a caged lion. "Are you going to keep that up until it's time for the ceremony?"

Micah stopped pacing and scratched his head. "Is Leonard here yet?"

"He'll be here. Don't worry. You told him two o'clock." Timothy reached in the pocket of his waistcoat and pulled out a pocket watch. "You still have twenty minutes. Now sit down."

Micah plopped into the chair by his desk. "Thank you for agreeing to stand up with me today, my friend." He kept making adjustments to his cravat.

"You're welcome." Timothy leaned over the desk and knocked Micah's hand away from his neck. "And will you stop doing that? I take it you've never worn a cravat before."

"Never."

Timothy redid the cravat. "There. That should feel better. The tailcoat Leonard let you borrow fits you perfectly." He walked over to the window and sat down.

"And these shoes, too." Micah raised his leg to show off the fancy footwear. As his foot fell to the floor, his countenance fell as well. He averted his gaze and hung his head. "What if I'm making a mistake? I don't want to disappoint Ruth. She deserves the very best."

Timothy rose to his feet. "What in the world are you saying, Micah? Where do you think Ruth would be right now if it weren't for you and all your love and support?"

Micah shook his head and shrugged. "What will she think when she sees the scars on my back?"

"I haven't known Ruth for very long, but from what I've observed, she's the kind of woman who will love you all the more. Besides, you've already told her what your previous master did to you." Timothy braced his arms on top of the desk. Had he heard Micah right? "I hate to say this, my friend, but I think maybe you're more concerned with your own feelings than what Ruth will think."

Micah dipped his head. "You're right. Forgive me."

Bear Brown tapped on the open door. "Brother Leonard here now."

Leonard burst into the study, beaming. "Are you ready, Micah?"

"Never been more ready!" Good thing Micah had gotten his concerns off his chest before the wedding.

Timothy swatted Micah's shoulder. "Let's do this."

After Leonard took his place on the platform, Timothy stood next to Micah. He dug deep into his waistcoat pocket and ferreted out Micah's homemade ring. Good … he hadn't lost it. His shoulders rose and fell with a deep breath.

Ruth looked beautiful in the dress Jeanette Trumbeaux let her borrow, and Cora was there to stand with her. Something about Cora always brought a smile to Timothy's face. Would she make it through the ceremony without bubbling over?

After praying for the couple, Leonard announced, "By the power invested in me by God and His Holy Church, I now pronounce you husband and wife."

Micah and Ruth gazed at each other. Such goofy expressions. Timothy wrinkled his nose. Was that what he looked like to Haven?

Leonard nudged Micah's elbow. "You may kiss the bride."

As the guests mingled in the churchyard, chatting and eating that cake Cora promised she'd make, Timothy overheard John Roberts telling Micah about a pass to stay with Ruth for a week.

"But don't tell Mrs. Roberts," John said. "And you must be at work on time every morning as usual."

Timothy wondered how Roberts would keep his wife from finding out. The thought of the woman gave him a shiver.

After Roberts left, Timothy gave Micah a good back slap. "I never in a million years would've guessed I'd be congratulating you on your wedding day!" He faced Ruth. "Ruth, you are a lovely bride, and Micah is a lucky man."

Ruth clung to Micah's arm and nuzzled her cheek against his shoulder. The smiles between them—pure bliss.

CHAPTER ELEVEN

Haven Hill Farm

Haven skipped breakfast and sneaked out of the house early. It was always a good start to her day when she could avoid Larkin Smith.

Big Joe had the carriage ready and waiting for her. She loved how he always greeted her with a warm, friendly smile. "Thanks for coming early, Joe. I'd like to pay a visit to Elias before you take me into town. I want to ask him about Sapphire. Haven't seen her out for weeks. Have you?"

Joe shook his head no and shrugged his shoulders.

"It shouldn't take long."

Joe nodded and helped her into the carriage. He took the lane that ran along the lake and waited by the carriage while Haven walked up to the front door of Elias's cottage and knocked.

Elias flung the door open, his eyes wide.

"Good morning, Elias." Reservations about this visit wormed their way into her conscience. She shouldn't have waited so long. "I hope I'm not interrupting anything."

"No, Miz Haven. Come in." Elias closed the door behind her. "What brings Missy here so early in the morning?" He glanced up at Anna who was peeking down from the loft, her face stone cold. "Is something the matter, Miz Haven?"

"Well, Elias, I was going to ask you the same question."

The sound of metal crashing to the floor at the bottom of the loft ladder rattled Haven, and she jumped. She and Elias both cast their gazes up to the loft.

"Sorry, Miz Haven." Anna's gruff voice carried across the room. The woman was obviously very unhappy. She hurried down the ladder, picked up the tin bowl and started wiping up the spilled mess.

With a hand to little Andy's shoulder, Elias nudged him to the door. "Son, I want you to fetch some water for the dishes." He faced his two younger daughters. "Ruby, Pearl, you go, too, and each of you draw a bucket of water. Your ma and me needs to talk to Miz Haven."

The children hurried out the door, leaving Haven alone with their parents. But where was Sapphire? Following an awkward silence, Haven spoke up. "I was concerned about Sapphire. I haven't seen her for a while."

Elias looked at Anna, but Anna said nothing. Tension hung thick between them.

"Well, where is she?"

"She be sick in bed, Miz Haven." Elias pointed toward the loft. "Please don't be angry with her. Anna gonna try and get her out to do some work today."

"Oh, Elias, don't be ridiculous. Why would I be angry with her for being sick?" Why would he even think that? "By all means keep her in bed until she's well. Did you forget I'm a nurse? For heaven's sake, why didn't you call on me? I'd like to take a look at her if you don't mind."

"All right, Miz Haven. She up in the loft." Elias walked with her to the ladder.

As they passed by Anna, Haven got a closer glimpse of Anna's callous face. She avoided looking down as she climbed the ladder. Anna was probably watching her.

"You been feeling out of sorts, Sapphire?" Haven sat by the girl's side and touched her arm.

Sapphire winced, squeezed her eyes, and rolled over on

her side. She yanked the blanket up over her head.

Haven tried to pull the blanket away from her face, but the girl held it there. "Hey, we're friends, remember?" Haven tugged on the blanket again, and Sapphire let it go. Haven felt her forehead. "You don't have a fever. Did you have one earlier?"

Sapphire shrugged her shoulders. Her hands clenched in a tight fist, grasping the edge of her blanket. She refused to make eye contact.

"Talk to me, sweetheart." Haven turned Sapphire's face toward her, catching a tear that trembled and dropped from swollen eyes. The touch seemed to have a calming effect. "What part of you feels sick?"

"My tummy. It better now." The girl's timid voice tore at Haven's heartstrings.

"You poor thing. It's probably that influenza virus." Haven stroked Sapphire's loose tendrils from her cheek and tucked them behind her ear. "Don't you worry about doing any chores until you're well enough to work."

"Is Massa Haywood angry?"

"No, silly. As a matter of fact, I don't think anyone besides me has even noticed that you've not been out." Haven tapped her arm. "And that's because I miss you. If Pa says anything, I'll tell him I told you to stay in bed."

As Haven descended the ladder, Anna stood at the bottom with her arms folded. She must have been listening. Her coldness left Haven perplexed.

Elias had waited by the door. "How she be, Miz Haven?"

"I think she'll be fine. She doesn't have a fever. That's a good sign. I told her to stay in bed until she feels better. And don't worry about Pa. I'll take care of it if he says anything."

"Thank you, Missy." Elias reached for the door latch just as the children approached with their buckets of water. He opened the door, and Haven stepped outside.

Elias watched her from his doorstep as Big Joe helped her into the carriage. Joe tipped his hat to Elias, and Haven waved. Elias waved back, but there was something unsettling about him, too.

As Joe drove her into town, Haven spent the time stewing over Elias and Anna's strange behavior.

ন

The Camp Meeting

Tuesday morning. Up before dawn. Timothy thanked God for the fair weather and prayed for His favor on the first day of the camp meetings.

The night before, he'd viewed the western horizon from the top of the hill where he'd pitched his tent, noticing the red hues of the sunset. "Red sky at night, sailors' delight. Red sky in the morning, sailors take warning." The old adage rolled off his tongue like a song. "The saying's true." He smiled as he ran his fingers through his uncombed hair.

Timothy trekked down the slope to the grove where the service would be held. What a perfect location—right at the edge of the woods by the Kentucky River. Everything appeared to be in good shape for the first service later that night.

Campers arrived throughout the day. The thrill of anticipation grabbed hold of him when Avery drove in with Brillie and Sylvia. Too bad Melia had to stay home with Alifair.

Later in the afternoon, Micah and Ruth pulled in with Mr. Roberts in the buggy followed by Bear, who drove the wagon with the rest of the Roberts slaves. What a pity Mrs. Roberts didn't join them.

"Thank you for coming out and bringing your crew." Timothy shook Mr. Roberts' hand.

"Almost didn't make it. We got some bad news earlier, and Priscilla tried to make me stay home." Roberts looked tired. Maybe he should be resting at home.

"Anything we can do to help?"

"Thank you, but no. It's all business related. The man

from the rigging company stopped by and said he had to reduce his hemp order from the factory by one-fourth. Seems the hemp industry is going down." Roberts coughed and cleared his throat. "They don't need as much cable for sailing vessels anymore because the steamships are beginning to take over. And since the steamships don't use sails, they don't need rigging. It's going to hurt us."

"I'm sorry to hear that."

"I'll have to work something else out." Roberts placed his hand on his chest.

"Are you all right?" Timothy waved Micah over.

"I'm fine." Roberts did not look fine. "Felt a little dizzy there for a second. It's gone now."

Timothy tapped Micah's arm. "You and Ruth better keep a close eye on him. He's not feeling well."

"That's what I thought." Micah braced the man's arm and walked him to the bench where they'd be sitting for the service.

What if Mr. Roberts had another stroke? Timothy lifted a prayer for him.

One hour before the service, Timothy slipped away from the crowd and took Danny Boy from the stable. He rode up the piney slope to his tent where he could pray alone.

He'd never been one to preach fire and brimstone. If anyone came looking for sensationalism, they might be disappointed. He dropped to his knees. "Lord, open their hearts and let them see the love and grace of Jesus Christ. Let them hear of your mighty power to save their souls by grace through faith in Jesus."

Almost seven o'clock. The sun began its evening descent, slowly fading below the tops of the trees. The beautiful strains of a musical call to worship made their way up the hill.

"How sweet the name of Jesus sounds
In a believer's ear!
It soothes his sorrows, heals his wounds,
And drives away his fear."

It was time. He mounted his horse and began the short ride down the hill to the clearing, singing along as he rode. The music would continue for thirty minutes or more, plenty of time to slip in from the side of the open-air tent to the platform.

A warm glow filled the dusky night around this part of the woods lighted by flickering pine-knot torches. He gazed at the big tent illuminated with its hanging lanterns, alive with worship.

While the last refrain was still winging its praise to heaven, he took his place on the stage to pray aloud. Then he read from Ephesians. "For by grace are ye saved through faith; and that not of yourselves: it is the gift of God, not of works, lest any man should boast."

For the next hour, Timothy preached the gospel of grace.

Thankful for a successful first night, he retreated to his tent nestled under a canopy of alders. A nearby beaver pond became the stage for a musical chorus, compliments of a few resident frogs and toads. *What a sense of humor our Creator has.*

Downtown Lexington

By Wednesday, things started to slow down a bit at Dr. Wright's office. Finally. Haven had a lot on her mind. Time for a leisurely lunch break to relax and sort things out.

She sure wished Uncle Brady hadn't brought his business partner with him. How much longer could she keep hiding from Mr. Smith and his creepy stares? Ma had pointed out that maybe he was extremely shy. Even so, it didn't make her feel any better.

"Did you bring your lunch with you today, Haven?" Sarah's question put a halt to her exasperating thoughts.

"No, did you?"

"No, I was thinking of having lunch at Millie's." Sarah

hung the "CLOSED" sign on the door. "Would you like to join me?"

"I'd love to." Haven grabbed her gray spring mantle from the wall hook so quickly it made Sarah laugh. "I feel like a bird let out of a cage!"

The two nurses strolled along the boardwalk, the dark gray skirts of their nursing uniforms rustling in rhythm with their footsteps. Haven stopped to admire the confections in the bakery window.

Sarah pulled on her arm. "Let's not linger here. I'm watching my waist, remember?"

They continued past a dentist's office, a meat market and a barber shop before arriving at Millie's Café.

A flyer tacked to the wall just inside the door caught Haven's attention. The heading said Camp Meeting. "Go on and be seated, Sarah." Haven focused on the ad. "I'll be right with you."

She read the rest of the information, repeating the name of the evangelist in a low whisper. "Timothy Locker." Her dream invader! Was he really holding a camp meeting?

"Are you all right, Haven?" Sarah's voice snapped her out of her trance. "We'd better order if we're going to get back to the office on time."

"Coming." Something stirred deep in Haven's gut. Something different than hunger pangs. She tried to tamp down the sensation by pressing her hand on her belly. As she seated herself at the table, Sarah gave her a weird look.

A teenaged black girl dressed in a green, yellow and brown plaid skirt and white blouse walked up to their table. "Special of the day is Millie's burgoo stew."

"Oooh …" The mere mention of Millie's burgoo made Haven's mouth water. "I thought that's what I smelled. Yes, please."

Sarah flashed a toothy grin to the waittress. "Me, too, sweetie."

The girl returned the grin. "I be right back."

After the waitress walked away, Haven's thoughts went

back to the flyer on the wall. "Sarah?" She flicked her gaze to the flyer and back to Sarah. "Have you ever been to a camp meeting?"

"Once, a long time ago." A few stray chestnut curls dangled over Sarah's cheek. She tucked them behind her ear.

"I've never been to one. What was it like?" Haven leaned in for the reply. Did it really matter what Sarah had to say?

Sarah puffed her cheeks. "A little too much excitement for me."

"Hmm …" Intriguing. How could Timothy Locker stir up excitement? Surely not him.

"Why the sudden interest in a camp meeting?" Sarah spread her napkin over her lap.

"That flyer tacked to the wall over there where we came in. It says camp meetings are going on this week not too far from here." Haven stretched her arm across the table and planted her hand in front of Sarah. "Guess who the evangelist is."

"I don't know. Who?"

Haven tapped the table. "The minister you've been teasing me about for weeks."

"No! Are you sure?"

"I think so. Same name … Timothy Locker." Haven hadn't told Sarah the story about that house call for Alifair when she'd thought Timothy was Alifair's husband. Mercy sakes … how Sarah would have teased her if she knew.

Sarah winked. "Why don't you go to the camp meeting and see for yourself?"

Haven rested her chin on the palm of her hand. "I might just do that, Sarah."

A herd of wild horses couldn't keep her away.

CHAPTER TWELVE

Haven Hill Farm

Haven had just sat down to supper with her family and their guests when a telegram from New York arrived. She squeezed Harrison's arm. "I bet I know who it's from."

Pa pushed his chair back and stood up. A playful grin ripped through his beard. All eyes turned his way as he flicked the note and cleared his throat. "Where shall I begin?"

"Frank!" Ma's outburst triggered a wave of laughter.

Giving a wink, Pa positioned his reading spectacles. He cleared his throat one more time and read aloud: "WILL BE HOME THURSDAY 21 APRIL. GOOD TO BE IN AMERICA. LOVE TO ALL. HARMONY."

A burst of applause filled the dining hall. Caught in the moment, Haven ignored Larkin Smith's stares and clapped her hands.

Pa said grace, and the head cook, Lena, rolled in a serving cart. Two platters of fried chicken, large mounds of mashed potatoes, biscuits, a silver bowl overflowing with mixed fruit, and a large stoneware dish steaming with seasoned green beans, all crammed onto the two cart shelves, released an irresistible aroma.

As the Haywood boys dug in, Haven avoided eye contact

with Mr. Smith like the plague. Having sagely seated herself between her two older brothers, she tapped Harrison's arm. "What would you think of taking me to a camp meeting either Saturday or Sunday night? Or maybe both?"

"I've been hearing about a camp meeting. Be happy to escort you on Saturday." Harrison slathered thick honey on a biscuit. "I'm afraid I won't be able to spare the time on Sunday, though. Pa needs me at church."

"Thanks. Saturday's good." She positioned her knife across the edge of her plate and turned to Howard. "What do you think, dear brother? Could you take me on Sunday night?"

Howard finished chewing on some chicken and swallowed. "I'd be happy to, sis. Actually, it sounds like fun."

"Sunday it is then." She smiled at one brother and then the other, thankful neither one asked why she wanted to go to a camp meeting. Dare she tell them? Heaven forbid. "Thanks, fellows. You two are the best."

After dinner, a stroke of good fortune allowed Haven the chance to spend a few moments alone with Uncle Brady. Since Pa had taken Mr. Smith into the library to discuss business deals, she figured that would most likely take care of the creep for the rest of the evening. She had a few questions to ask her uncle.

She found Uncle Brady on the veranda, sitting alone and gazing off into the western sky. Dusk had settled, but a storm loomed on the horizon, causing darkness to fall early.

She wrapped her shoulders with a shawl as she approached him. "Uncle Brady?"

He looked her way. "Hey, gorgeous. Haven't seen much of you at all since I've been here." He pulled up a chair next to his. "Here, have a seat."

She eased into the chair. "I wanted to talk to you about something—or somebody, rather."

"Shoot away, gal. I'm all ears." Uncle Brady always had a big Texas smile for her.

"I'll get right to the point." She took a deep breath. "I wanted to ask you about your business partner."

"Larkin? He's a good guy." Uncle Brady quirked a brow. "You interested in Larkin?"

"No, not at all. I think he's interested in me, and I don't like it."

Uncle Brady sat up straight and stiffened his spine. "Has Larkin done something inappropriate? Why, if he has, I'll—"

"No, Uncle Brady. He hasn't done anything. He hasn't even said anything."

"You're confusing me darlin'." He rubbed the back of his neck.

"This is silly, now that I think about it." Haven blew air through her lips. "Mr. Smith stares at me a lot. It gives me the willies."

"Well now …" Uncle Brady stroked his beard. "Can't say I blame the fellow much for that offense." He looked her straight in the eye. "Men are like that, sugar. They recognize beauty when they see it. And, Haven, you've been blessed with a Texas-sized share of it, you know."

"Aww … thank you, Uncle Brady. I'll try not to let it bother me."

If Mr. Smith would only go back to Texas.

The camp meeting

Timothy chuckled to himself as the last drenched sinner walked up the bank of the river. The baptismal waters had begun to stir around noon on Saturday, continuing for nearly two hours—thanks to several strategically timed lightning bolts and thunder claps during Friday night's altar call. Did the Almighty's humor ever cease to amaze?

After supper, he saddled up Danny Boy for the trek up the slope. Time to be alone with God. From the corner of his eye, he saw a man on horseback slowly coming his way.

Stephen—a contact for the Underground Railroad.

He rode Danny Boy at a slow walk until Stephen caught up with him. "Good to see you here. New passengers?"

"Just one." Stephen kept his voice low. "His wife and two children died before they could make it to Kentucky."

Timothy flinched. "I'm so sorry. Where's the station?"

"Lexington."

Timothy scanned the area. Good. No one watching. "Address?"

Stephen discreetly slipped a small piece of paper into his Bible and closed it up. "Obadiah." He handed it to Timothy. "I'll retrieve my Bible tomorrow."

Timothy nodded. "Tuesday around midnight. All right?" He came to a stop at the bottom of the hill.

"Perfect. I'll let them know." Stephen stopped and turned his horse to face the opposite direction. "The next station is Ironton, Ohio. Look for Mr. Douglas. Our passenger has other family waiting for him there."

Timothy pressed the Bible against his chest. "Lord willing." As Stephen rode away, Timothy clicked to Danny Boy to take the slope.

Haven and Harrison arrived at the campgrounds late in the afternoon. Harrison parked the carriage, helped her get down and walked with her to an old oak tree near the big tent.

"Wait for me here, sis. I'll get the horses taken care of then I'll come back to get you."

While Haven waited, her eyes scanned the large and growing crowd. Timothy Locker had to be there somewhere. She recognized several people from town, but they only knew her as Nurse Haywood. Where could Timothy be?

Was that the banker, Mr. Delaney, walking away from a parked carriage with his daughter and the little black girl who lives with them? And over there, outside the back of the open-air tent—her pa's slaves. They clustered together on the front row of roughly hewn benches. She spotted Elias. No Anna, though. Sapphire must still be sick.

Harrison sneaked up behind her. "Ready to find a place?"

"You startled me!" Haven laughed at herself as she took his arm. "I'm ready."

"Where would you like to sit?" He guided her to the tent.

"It's filling up fast." Haven looked up and down the rows. "Doesn't look like we have much choice."

About halfway down the center aisle, they found a bench with room for two more. Harrison asked the people if they'd mind scooting over, then he ushered Haven in. "Who's preaching anyway? Do you know?"

"His name is Timothy Locker." She turned her face away from Harrison.

"You said that as if you know him." Harrison tugged on the sleeve of her light blue taffeta dress. "Do you?"

She wiggled and sat up straight. "No."

"Haven?"

"All right, I've met him, but that's it. Honest." She couldn't tell her brother that the preacher had been coming to see her every day—in her dreams.

"So now that we're here I find out you have an ulterior motive for wanting to attend a camp meeting." Harrison laughed. A little too loud. "I should have known."

"That's not entirely true." She chewed her lower lip and met his gaze. "Does that bother you?"

"Course not, sis. I wanted to come."

For what seemed like eternity, Haven stretched this way and that, craning her neck. Where was the evangelist? The singing began. Still no Timothy Locker. Could there be another preacher with the same name? She supposed it was possible.

The song leader's rich tenor voice filled the night air with the call to worship. Haven got so caught up in the music that, for a while, she almost forgot about the preacher she'd come to hear.

As the last song of praise ended, Timothy entered from the side and stood center stage to pray.

Haven's heart did a strange flip—or two. Maybe three. She

quickly stifled an involuntary gasp. *It's him.*

A sharp jab of her brother's finger on her arm gave her a jolt. Harrison sported a mischievous look, but Haven refused to acknowledge it with a reaction. No way would she give her impish brother that satisfaction.

Her cheeks burned, and she immediately bowed her head for the prayer. The temptation to sneak a peek at the handsome preacher nearly overwhelmed her, but she dared not look up until the prayer was over.

"I gather that's him?" Harrison kept his pokey fingers to himself. Good for him.

"Yes." Her eyes stayed riveted to the young preacher on the stage.

Before Timothy began his sermon for the evening, he spoke about the many people who'd come forward the night before during a storm. He called it the "Thunderbolt Altar Call."

Haven giggled as a few chuckles droned through the tent. "Funny."

Now that he had disarmed their defenses, Timothy focused on the cross of Christ. He opened his Bible and read from Isaiah 53, verse 5: "'But he was wounded for our transgressions, he was bruised for our iniquities; the chastisement of our peace was upon him, and with his stripes we are healed.'" He placed a bookmark on the page.

Timothy looked out across the sea of faces. "Those words from the prophet Isaiah were written seven hundred years before Jesus went to Calvary's cross."

About three-quarters of the way through his message, a rude outburst bellowed from the lot off the side of the tent where the wagons and buggies were parked. A heckler.

Timothy kept on preaching even though Leonard Thompson and Pastor Sam Watson had gotten up and headed in the heckler's direction.

No stranger to scoffers, Timothy had learned how to deal with such types. He grinned when Thompson and Watson returned with the young, bedraggled troublemaker pinned between them. The kid wore a look of uttermost sorrow. Probably sorry he got caught.

"Excuse me, ladies and gentlemen, it seems we have an unexpected guest speaker with us tonight." As people snickered, he zeroed in on the boy, his lips stretching into a huge grin. He waved the kid up to the stage. "Don't be shy. You had something to say a while ago, so come on up here and share with us." Why shouldn't he make the guest speaker feel welcome?

Leonard and Pastor Watson walked him a few steps forward. As soon as he started to buck, they lifted him up between them.

Timothy laughed at the kid's dangling feet. "What's your name, young man?"

When the boy didn't answer, a few more snickers popped up here and there.

"We want to hear what you have to say. Speak up. You weren't having any difficulty earlier." Timothy almost felt sorry for him. Almost. "Seems our guest speaker has come down with a case of laryngitis."

The boy's knees were knocking together.

"Tell you what … we have a special seat just for you. Don't we, Brother Leonard?" He pointed to Leonard's wife and their children. "Maybe the Good Lord will give you your voice back soon."

With that episode taken care of, Timothy wrapped up his message and extended the invitation with an analogy of Noah's ark. "And so I close with that thought. Let those who are ready to enter the ark, come now."

A line formed before he could catch his breath.

Thirty minutes later, the crowd had dwindled to a dozen people or so. He listened to the last confession of faith and heaved a lungful of air. Another successful meeting and only one more night left.

Then his eyes landed on the nurse. *She came.* He almost didn't recognize her without that gray uniform. And her hair!

Flowing tresses like spun gold spilled over her shoulders. A torrent of collywobbles swept through his gut.

He started to wave when she smiled his way, but some man put his arm around her waist and moved her along to the back of the tent with the other people who were leaving. Who was she with?

Timothy's heart sank.

CHAPTER THIRTEEN

The campgrounds

After the Palm Sunday morning service at the campgrounds, Timothy joined the campers for a huge picnic. They had plenty of fresh game to roast. The host family and some of their neighbors had prepared more food than he'd ever seen in one place.

So many new people to meet. So many old friends to catch up with. If only it could last a few more days. But tonight he'd wrap up a successful week … Lord willing.

He slipped away to his place of solitude on the hill. This time he walked up the slope alone and left Danny Boy with a member of the stable crew. The old horse needed to get in some exercise time.

Once he reached his tent, he stood beside it for a few moments, taking in the view from the top of the hill. Awestruck by the beauty of God's creation, he drew in a deep breath. Ah … the fresh spring air. He savored the sweet smell of the pines and wildflowers.

He dropped to his knees by a large rock. Time to pray. As he bowed his head, an unwanted image from the night before penetrated his mind. *No, not now!*

Squeezing his eyes, he rubbed his temples. Why wouldn't

it go away?

He wished he'd never met Haven Haywood.

Haven entered the back of the open-air tent with Howard. She gaped at the jam-packed benches. So much for sitting closer to the front this time. She should have known all the good seats would be taken earlier since it was Palm Sunday. *And* the last night. The back row would have to do.

"Which one is he?" Howard leaned toward her but kept his gaze straight ahead.

"Who?"

"You know perfectly well who." Smirking, Howard poked her arm just like Harrison had done on Saturday night. What was it about brothers anyway? "Harrison told me why you suddenly wanted to attend a camp meeting."

With an indignant flair, Haven folded her arms. "Now that's simply not true." She turned her head away and harumphed. "Brothers!"

Haven put her worldly thoughts aside. What would Timothy preach about tonight?

As Timothy read from the Bible, Haven mouthed the words with him. "'For I know that my Redeemer liveth, and that he shall stand at the latter day upon the earth.'" She'd memorized that scripture from Job 19 a long time ago.

When the "hallelujahs" rang out, she surprised herself with her own "hallelujah." And all Timothy had done so far was quote a scripture. Impressive.

It surprised Timothy to see the young heckler from the night before sitting in the front row with Leonard and Gladys. The kid actually looked happy. God sure did work in mysterious ways.

He'd prayed for hearts to be open to the gospel, and with Easter being one week away, he focused on the Resurrection. At the close of his message, he raised his arm high, lifted his head upward and prayed for lost souls to come forward.

With the song of the crickets pulsing through the night air, dozens poured to the front. God had answered his prayers.

Would God be so gracious as to spare him the torment of seeing Haven Haywood with her gentleman friend? He could only hope.

But when the last few folks were leaving, that's when he caught sight of her for the first time that night. Could it get any worse? That nurse was with yet a different man than the one who'd escorted her the night before.

That did it for Timothy! His stomach soured. There would be no more ridiculous romantic fancies of ever getting to know Haven Haywood. Ever.

God would show him the right woman at the proper time.

He'd wait.

~

Downtown Lexington

Eleven o'clock. Not the kind of Monday morning Timothy expected following a week of camp meetings. After crashing on his cozy bed in his apartment in the middle of the night, he'd tossed and turned for hours before finally falling asleep. He should have slept like a baby, but that nurse wouldn't let his mind rest. How had he slept so late?

He splashed water on his face then threw on his clothes. After a quick cup of coffee in Melia's house, he excused himself to head downtown.

With a determined gait, he walked along the boardwalk, past the banks and offices and the shops on his way to the blacksmith shop to see Micah. His emotions ran the gamut from heartfelt gratitude for the camp meetings to extreme self-pity for allowing himself to think Haven Haywood was something she was not.

He glanced across the street and saw Micah coming out of the shop. Micah had his lunch bag. Good. Perfect timing for one of their bench chats.

Before he could even make it to the corner where he

needed to cross to the other side, he saw his worst nightmare heading straight toward him. The other nurse walked beside her—the taller one. *Great.*

As the women got closer, he averted his gaze and looked across the street at Micah. He waved, and Micah waved back. Maybe if he kept his head low and his eyes on the boardwalk, Haven wouldn't notice him.

"Timothy!" Ugh … Haven's voice. She slowed her pace.

He saw the two gray skirts and lifted his gaze for a split second. One split second. "Good day, ladies." He kept right on walking, never slowed down and didn't look back.

Less than a minute later, he found himself approaching Micah. "Hello, my friend." He nudged Micah's arm. "Scoot over, will ya? I could use some advice."

"You asking me?" Micah laughed and made room for him on the bench. "Sit down and tell ol' Micah what this all about."

Timothy rested his elbows on his knees and looked down, rubbing his face and temples.

Silence.

Micah took a bite of his sandwich, chewed and swallowed. "Wonderful camp meeting." He took another bite.

"Thank you. God blessed it all week." Timothy stared at his boots.

More awkward silence.

Micah lowered the sandwich to his lap. "Well, you gonna just sit there or you gonna tell me what's eatin' at ya?"

Timothy locked eyes with Micah but still couldn't bring himself to speak up.

"It sure do seem like you in some kind of pickle. I'd like to help you out, but you gotta tell me what it is first." Micah wrapped up the remainder of his sandwich in a cloth and put it back in his lunch bag. "Don't reckon you need my advice on preaching, but judging by what I just saw across the street, it probably has something to do with the ladies."

Timothy gritted his teeth and looked away.

Micah nodded. "Aha … struck a chord, did I?"

"Ladies! Humph!" Timothy gave Micah his best if-you-only-knew-what-I-know stare. "I'm not so sure about her."

"Who? Nurse Haven? Why, she be a fine lady." Micah's brows furrowed. "You got some fancy for Miz Haven?"

"No!" Timothy's hands smacked against his lap. "I mean … not anymore."

Micah settled back against the bench, put his lunch bag down beside him, and folded his arms. "I got fifteen minutes left on this here break. Better talk fast and tell ol' Micah what's ailing ya, boy. Then I tell you what I think."

"All right, it's like this … I only met her a couple of times before. She helped me with an injured boy—maybe even saved his life." Timothy paused to calculate his words. "She's beautiful, even in that nurse's uniform. She seemed so nice, so thoughtful, so willing to do anything to help."

"Yessuh, that sure do sound like Miz Haven. She be as kind as she be purty."

Timothy palmed his forehead. "Then, to my surprise, she showed up at the camp meeting on Saturday night and again on Sunday night."

"Yessuh, I saw her there, too." Micah shrugged. "So what be wrong with that?"

"She didn't stay to talk or anything. She was … she had …" Timothy's jaw twitched.

Micah flicked Timothy's arm. "Speak up, boy."

"Each night she had a different fellow to escort her. It's like she was flaunting it to get my goat." Timothy ignored Micah's laughter. "It was like the devil showed up just to try and make me stumble."

Micah laughed even harder.

"This isn't funny! What's wrong with you?" He started to stand up. "Some help you are!"

Micah grabbed his arm and pulled him back down to his seat. "I sorry." His laughter subsided. "The devil done got you goat for sure, but not like you think."

"What do you mean?"

"I saw Miz Haven both nights. With her brothers!" Micah

punched Timothy's arm. "First one brother then the other. Jumpin' to conclusions sure cause you a lot of unnecessary grief."

Timothy gaped. Could he feel any more embarrassed? "I-I don't know what to say. I've been such a fool."

"Nah. I know what them kind of feelings do to a man." Micah picked up his mason jar of water. "We think we so strong and then we come undone in an instant—all because of a woman."

Timothy chuckled. "Yes, I remember how ridiculous you acted before your wedding."

Micah chugged water from the jar. "All I know is Ruth the best thing ever happen to me."

"I think you're right about that." Timothy shifted his body at an angle and draped his arm across the back of the bench. "Tell me … what's the latest on Roberts? I noticed he didn't come back to the camp meetings after that first night."

"Not doin' very well. Miz Cilla say he have another mild stroke."

"I'm sorry to hear that. He seemed quite concerned about the hemp crop. It's hard these days."

"Did you know that Trumbeaux left this morning for a business trip down south?" A hint of expectation seasoned Micah's voice. "He promised Ruth he'd search for Lottie and say he willing to go all the way to Natchez if he have to."

"Trumbeaux's a good man, Micah. Pray for the Lord's blessing on his journey and don't give up hope." Timothy looked him straight in the eye. "Never forget the parable of the widow and the judge. She continually came to the judge with her request until he wearied of it and granted her what she asked."

"I promise we gonna weary the Lord praying for Lottie until Trumbeaux find her."

"That's what I like to hear." Timothy put a hand to Micah's shoulder.

Micah closed up his lunch bag. "Break's over, but if you really want my advice, I say you apologize to Miz Haven and give her another chance. The Lord, he let you know if Miz Haven be the right gal for you."

"Apologize? For what?"

"For not speaking to her when she call out your name a while ago. I saw how you ignore her and walk right by. Very rude."

Timothy huffed. "But I did speak to her. I spoke to both of them. I said, 'Good day, ladies.'"

"I didn't see you tip your hat." Micah shook his head. "A gentleman always tip his hat to the ladies."

"You're right, Micah. That was rude of me."

"Miz Haven a fine Christian woman." Micah picked up his mason jar and gulped some water. "But they is one thing you should know—her pa, he a slave owner, and he feel strongly about it. Mighty strong."

"I figured as much."

"As for Miz Haven, well, I reckon I don't know how she feel about her pa's slaves." Micah got up from the bench, flicking crumbs off his trousers. "I do know she treat everybody real nice."

Timothy stood and faced Micah. "Thanks, friend. You've been very helpful. I've got some deep thinking to do."

Haven Hill Farm

Haven barely spoke a word to Big Joe on the drive home from work. She usually had a story to tell about one of the patients in Dr. Wright's office or at least something to brighten Joe's day. But not this time. Too much brooding over Timothy.

Why had he brushed her off like that?

Joe brought the carriage to a stop in front of the house. Elias and Anna had just come into view at the far side of the lawn. It looked like they were unloading supplies from a small wagon.

Haven waved to them, and Elias waved back. But Anna snapped her head the other way.

"Did you see that, Joe? What's wrong with Anna?"

Joe shrugged his shoulders before helping her down from the carriage. Had Joe noticed the change in Anna, too? "Thank you, Joe. I'm sorry I wasn't better company. I'll see you in the morning." She waved as Joe tipped his cap to her.

Joe drove off, and Haven watched Elias and Anna's wagon going down the trail in the opposite direction. She sure did miss the way Anna and her girls used to greet her—always eager to talk about this, that, or the other.

Haven trudged up the steps to the veranda, weary from a hard Monday at the office. Timothy's snub at noon added a ton of weight to her depression over Anna.

She looked up and saw Molly—the woman who'd been her mammy from the day she and her twin sister were born—waiting at the front door. At least Molly had a big smile for her.

As Haven passed the library on her way to the staircase she noticed the door was open. Voices drifted from the room. She glanced inside and saw Pa talking to Larkin. Pa smiled at her and waved. She waved back and hurried past the door.

No wave from Mr. Smith. Just the usual stare. If it weren't for her sweet dreams about Timothy Locker, she'd probably have nightmares about Larkin Smith every night.

She stood in the hall outside the library door facing Molly, indicating silence with her finger to her lips. What was that Mr. Smith just said to Pa? Had she heard him correctly? Ears perked, she managed to catch Mr. Smith's next comment.

"I've spoken with a man from Louisville by the name of Kerrick," she heard him say. "He's asked me to spend two or three weeks at his farm. I want to look over some of his stock, and he says he has some other business he'd like to discuss with me. I'll be leaving tomorrow."

Sweet music to her ears … she stifled a squeal. Was God looking out for her after all?

CHAPTER FOURTEEN

Downtown Lexington

Maybe Micah was right. Timothy walked the streets of downtown Lexington Tuesday morning, tossing the pros and cons of an apology to Haven around in his head.

Who am I kidding? There are no cons.

One foot in front of the other … he had to keep moving. Why was this so hard? What a pathetic bundle of nerves he was.

Minutes away from Dr. Wright's office, he shook off his fears and crossed the street. By the time he reached the end of the block and rounded the corner, he found himself gliding along like a sailboat in a gentle breeze.

But when he got to the block where he'd passed Haven the day before, every nerve in his body broke into a twitching frenzy. His heart quickened, and he stopped dead in his tracks.

I can't go through with this.

Contemplating a U-turn, he noticed a young couple, arm in arm, as they rounded the corner. The two lovers smiled at him with that same goofy look on their faces like he'd seen on Micah and Ruth. The young man doffed his hat. "Lovely day, isn't it?"

"Yes … it is." Timothy returned the smile. "Quite lovely."

They seemed so happy and so very much in love. How did they get that way?

The freeze that had paralyzed him a moment ago began to thaw. He lifted his hat, combed his fingers through his hair and, feeling light as a feather, walked on.

I'm going to do this.

As he approached the office, he slowed his pace, cleared his throat several times and practiced his well-prepared greeting. Pounding his fist into his palm, he set his mind to stay the course. Straight to the doctor's door.

A "CLOSED" sign hung in the window. Lunchtime. He must have just missed her. Undeterred, he decided to wait outside until Haven came back from her break.

Five minutes went by. A discarded copy of *The Kentucky Statesman*, or at least a portion of it, flapped about in the wind and landed near his feet.

He stooped to pick it up, and a man's voice called to him from behind. "Say there, young man … I see you've found my missing paper." Dr. Wright stepped outside and closed the door behind him.

"Uh, yes … I believe I did." Timothy held the paper out to him. "Here you go, sir."

"Thank you. The wind blew it right out of my hand as I was walking back to my office." The doctor checked to see if it was all there. "Didn't notice until I got inside that two pages were gone."

Not sure what to say next, Timothy flashed an awkward smile and stuffed his hands into his pockets.

Dr. Wright stood there, skimming over his paper. "Is there something I can help you with?"

"Oh, no, sir." Timothy raised his shoulders. If they'd swallowed up his head, that would have been perfect.

"Are you ill?"

"No, sir, not at all. Thank you, sir." Definitely nothing he'd care to share with the doctor.

"I see. Well, if you don't mind my asking, why are you

standing in front of my office?"

"I-I was just waiting for Nurse Haywood to return from her lunch break." Why was the doctor being so nosy? "I was hoping to talk to her."

"Well, why didn't you say so? She's inside." The doctor palmed the door knob. "Is she expecting you or something?"

"No, sir." Maybe he should run home. Now would be a good time.

"And your name is?" Dr. Wright had him on a hook.

"Timothy Locker. Reverend Timothy Locker." He cleared his throat. "I met you once before at Avery Delaney's house the night you made a house call for his sister."

"Oh yes … I thought you looked familiar. Are you the evangelist who did the camp meeting last week?" The doctor tucked the newspaper under his left arm and stepped up to Timothy.

"Yes, sir."

With his free arm outstretched, Dr. Wright gave Timothy's hand a lively five-pump shake. "Wonderful! I've heard a lot of good reports, Reverend Locker. I regret that I couldn't make it to the meetings." He opened the door. "Listen, the girls brought their lunches with them, and they're eating in the back room right now. Won't you come in? I'll let Haven know you're here."

Timothy followed Dr. Wright into the waiting room. The doctor went on ahead, turned into a hall and left him standing there alone. No backing out now.

Footsteps faded down the hall followed by a rapping sound and a door creaking open. Women's voices—giggling, talking—and unmistakable clarity on every word.

"It's the honest truth, Sarah. I've been wanting to tell you this crazy story for weeks, but I feared you might use it to torment me. I seriously thought he was Alifair's husband."

Timothy's ears perked.

"When we both realized the misunderstanding, I was able to look at him a little easier. That's when I got a real good dose of those dreamy eyes."

"Dreamy, Haven? I've never seen you like this before. I love it!"

One of them giggled. Or maybe it was both. Female giggles all sounded the same to him.

"I don't mind telling you now after what happened yesterday. He's clearly not the least bit interested in me. So go ahead and torture me more if you wish."

Timothy winced. Maybe he should run. Now would be good. But his legs felt like jelly.

"Dr. Wright!" Haven shot to her feet so fast her leg bumped the table. How long had her boss been standing at the door?

"Sorry to disturb you, ladies, but you have a visitor, Haven." Dr. Wright pursed his lips.

"Me? A visitor?" Why was he giving her that playful look?

"Reverend Timothy Locker."

Haven flicked her gaze to Sarah, who'd covered her lips with her hand. *Funny Sarah.* She followed Dr. Wright into the waiting room.

"If you'll excuse me, Reverend Locker, I'll be back in my study." The doctor pivoted and headed down the hall.

Haven turned to face Timothy. "What a surprise to see you here." How much of her conversation with Sarah had he heard? She couldn't bring herself to smile.

Timothy bowed slightly. "Haven, I've come to apologize and to—"

"Apologize for what?" Hands on her hips, she squared her shoulders. "Eavesdropping? Hasn't anyone ever told you how rude that is?" The many times she'd been an eavesdropper herself buzzed through her mind like stinging bees. Why did conviction have to be so painful?

"But I wasn't—"

"You should make your presence known when you enter a room!" She aimed her best icy glare at him, ignoring the stings.

"But you weren't—"

"Furthermore, whatever you overheard you may totally

disregard. It had nothing to do with you." Not true at all. How could she say that with a straight face?

"But Dr. Wright invited me to come in. I didn't even know you were—"

"I'll thank you to leave now, Reverend Locker." Is that what she really wanted?

What's wrong with me?

"Yes, ma'am." Timothy made a sharp turn on his heel and headed for the door. "Sorry to have disturbed you, Nurse Haywood." It was forced politeness, she could tell. He looked crushed, and she regretted her temper. He cast a quick glance over his shoulder before leaving.

As soon as the door closed, Sarah stormed into the waiting room, striking at Haven like a lightning bolt out of heaven or a flaming torch from hell—Haven couldn't tell which.

"What on God's green earth do you think you're doing?" Fire blazed in Sarah's eyes.

"I don't appreciate having my personal conversations spied upon. It's most unsettling." There was that annoying sting again.

"What you just did is most unsettling, Haven Haywood! That poor man wasn't spying on you, nor was I." Sarah's nostrils flared. "Didn't you hear what he said? He said he came to apologize for something, and I don't think spying was his intent. How rude can you be?"

"Was it that bad?"

"Yes!" Sarah took a step forward and pointed a finger so close to Haven's nose it made her eyes cross. "Admit it—you jumped to conclusions and took your embarrassment out on that poor preacher!"

"You're right." Haven's heart swelled. "I was embarrassed, and my reaction was most impertinent."

"Go find him and hurry." Sarah pushed her toward the door. "Or I'll fire you!"

She shot Sarah a girlfriend kind of smirk. "You can't fire me."

"I know." Sarah smacked her arm. "Now hurry!"

Haven looked up and down the crowded block several times. No Timothy Locker anywhere. She'd never be able to find him with so many people everywhere. After the way she'd treated him, he probably didn't want to see her again anyway.

She randomly picked a direction and started walking. She couldn't even remember what color his coat was. Black? Brown? Was he even wearing a coat?

When she reached the corner, she turned herself around in a complete circle and threw her arms up. Where could he have gone?

A two-seated buckboard made its way down the street, and the young driver resembled Timothy. Could that be him? She had to get a closer look. Walking faster, she strained to turn her head toward the passing buckboard. As she fixed her gaze on the driver, she smacked head-on into a customer exiting the hardware store. The impact landed her face down on her hands and knees.

Crash! Plink! Plink!

A small wooden box lay open on the boardwalk next to a man's boots, spilling out its contents of what seemed like a million nuts, bolts, screws, washers, rivets and nails. Great. How many more things could she do wrong in one day?

"Mercy me … what a mess!" She started picking up as many of the tiny items as she could, putting them back in the box, and the ill-fated customer did the same. Afraid to look up, she worked at it feverishly. "I'm so sorry. I wasn't paying attention to where I was going."

Then he spoke.

"Are you all right?" His voice.

She tossed a handful of nails into the box and slowly raised her head. Her eyes locked with the dreamy eyes of her victim. "I-I'm fine. I was looking for you."

"You certainly found me."

"I did indeed." Any closer and their noses would touch. "Timothy, I'm truly sorry for the way I spoke to you. I don't know what got into me."

"Apology accepted." Timothy scooped up more nuts and bolts. "Now it's my turn. I'm sorry that I rushed by you in such a hurry yesterday. It was rude of me. I was hoping to make up for it today."

"Apology accepted." Haven's hand brushed his as she picked up the last of the hardware. A prickling sensation crept up her arm.

"Are we even now?" He got up from his knees and extended his hand to her.

"Even-steven." She reached out, and he pulled her to her feet. "What are these things for anyway?"

"I need to replenish my repair kit for my rig every now and then." He bent over and recouped his box. "I'm leaving to go on another trip tonight so I thought I'd best take care of it today. Heading north to Ohio. I promised my parents I'd be home in time to preach at my home church in Greenville for the Easter service."

"Oh." She hoped that didn't come out sounding too disappointed. "Tell me, how is Mrs. Brooks doing?"

"She's fine now."

"I'll have to pay her a visit." Haven swiped a loose strand of hair off her forehead. "How long before you come back to Lexington?"

"About three weeks."

"Oh." She did it again.

"I saw you at the camp meeting Saturday and Sunday." So he *did* know she was there. "Thank you for coming."

"I'm glad I went."

Beads of sweat formed on Timothy's forehead, and Haven wanted so badly to wipe them away with her own hanky. The nurse in her almost did it, but he beat her to the task.

"Haven, I was wondering …" Scratching the side of his neck, he averted his gaze.

"Yes?" The heart flips doubled. No, tripled. Out of control.

He turned those captivating eyes back to her. "I was wondering if I might have the … uh … honor of calling on you when I return."

"I'd like that." Was this one of her dreams or was this really happening?

He tapped the side of his hardware box. "Good. I'll see you in three weeks."

"Three weeks." Such a long time.

From the corner of her eye, Haven spotted Sarah in front of the office talking to a mother and her two small children. "Timothy, I have to get back to work now." She took a step back.

"Careful now." The way he raised his brows—so cute. "Better watch where you're going."

A rush of heat spread through her neck and cheeks. "Thank you for coming to see me." Hard as it was, she walked away.

"Remember … three weeks."

She glanced over her shoulder. "I'll see you then!"

Timothy jaunted straight to the blacksmith's shop, hoping to catch Micah on a break. When he found himself on the opposite side of the street, he couldn't even remember how he'd gotten there.

But a disturbing clamor coming from the direction of Cheapside brought his romantic fancies to an abrupt halt. The grim reality of the midnight appointment he'd made to transport a fugitive across the river manifested itself in a coffle of slaves winding around the courthouse. A guard led them to a slave pen.

Timothy's eyes stung. He watched until the gut-wrenching sight left his view, and a dispirited feeling washed over him like a mighty ocean wave.

CHAPTER FIFTEEN

The Landry Mansion
Lexington, Kentucky

The stars shone in their full celestial glory just before midnight as Timothy approached the house where Stephen told him to meet the fugitive slave for transport. He slowed Danny Boy down to an easy trot and stopped in front of the house.

The gated residence on the outskirts of the city rose from the shadows like an intimidating colossus. Such an eerily beautiful house with the outline of its numerous gables backlit by the midnight glow of the moon. A shudder flitted through him. Was it this foreboding of a structure in the daylight?

Engraved numbers gleamed from a bronze plate fastened to the stone wall bracing the gate. He squinted his eyes. Pulling out the small scrap of paper he'd found in Stephen's Bible, he checked to make sure he had the right address. The numbers matched up with Stephen's note.

Stuffing the scrap of paper into his pants pocket, he climbed down and walked over to the entrance. The gate was locked. How strange. Why hadn't Stephen been more specific? What was he supposed to do now?

"Grrr! Grrr!" Two demonic-looking dogs lunged at the gate, barking.

He tumbled backward and landed on his hind side. Shivers racked his body. He backed up double-quick in a crablike crawl as Danny Boy whinnied and pounded his hoof into the dirt. Timothy shot to his feet and grabbed the reins. The last thing he needed was for his horse to take off down the road and leave him there alone.

"Caesar! Nero! Off!" A man's shout brought the long string of ferocious barks to a halt.

The man, dressed in a night watchman's uniform, peered at Timothy through the rails of the gate. "Excuse me, sir, what brings you to the Landry residence at this hour?"

Landry residence? Stephen had written down the address but not a name. "Uh, I think I have the wrong house, sir. If you'll excuse me …"

"What is your name?"

"Must be some mistake. I'll just be on my way." He hurtled back into the rig.

"If you have the correct password, I can unlock the gate for you." The watchman lifted a lantern with one hand and jangled some keys in the other. "I'm sure Mrs. Landry would be glad to discuss this matter with you."

Password? Timothy looked at the house and saw some lights still on. "I'm afraid I don't know any password." Stephen hadn't said anything about a password. Or had he?

Timothy jumped down. "Wait, sir." He tied the reins to the post and approached the watchman, fishing Stephen's note from his pocket. "Obadiah." He unfolded the note and showed the watchman.

The watchman grinned. "Welcome, Reverend Locker. Mrs. Landry is expecting you." He proceeded to unlock the gate.

"But what about those dogs?"

The man winked. "Harmless as puppies as long as you're with me.

Timothy followed the watchman like a shadow. As they

neared the steps, the eyes of a grotesque-looking gargoyle projecting from the gutter above appeared to have its eyes on him. Illuminated by a moonbeam that spilled its silvery light on one side of the beast's head, the haunting sculpture sent chills up and down his spine.

Once inside the mansion, a butler introduced him to the elderly Widow Landry. She looked quite elegant in her navy blue dress with ivory lace trim and the high collar with a cameo brooch pinned in the center.

Timothy removed his hat. "Thank you for your help, Mrs. Landry."

"And thank you, Reverend Locker." The widow escorted Timothy to a third floor secret passageway that led to a hidden room on the other side of a well-disguised fireplace. In this room, Timothy met his charge for the trip to Ironton.

Mrs. Landry gestured to a man seated in a wing chair. "This is Marcus, Reverend Locker."

Marcus stood up and nodded. His tall stature, sturdy build and broad shoulders reminded Timothy of Big Joe.

"A pleasure to meet you, Marcus." Timothy proffered his hand.

Marcus hesitated then reached out for a hearty handshake.

Mrs. Landry faced Timothy. "I shall be back in thirty minutes. In the meantime, my livery hand will lead your horse to the stable and prepare him for the journey." She left and closed the door.

Timothy sat in a wing chair facing Marcus and explained everything the fugitive needed to know for a successful escape.

"Yessuh, the Lord watchin' over me, but my wife and daughter, they too weak to survive the hardships of our journey." Marcus pointed a finger to heaven. "I came close to givin' up, but the Lord give me strength."

"I'm so sorry about your family, Marcus, but I'm happy to hear of your faith." Another lift for Timothy's spirit. Not all his charges knew about Jesus.

Mrs. Landry returned and escorted them by candlelight

through the long, dark corridor. The lamps in every downstairs room had been extinguished, and her butler stood waiting with a candle in hand to guide them to the back door. The widow stayed in the house while the butler took them to the stable.

With his precious cargo tucked safely away, the midnight ride began. Timothy lifted his gaze to the silver light of the moon—perfect for night travel.

As he drove along, every shadow that crept across his path kindled disturbing images of the men he'd seen earlier that day, trudging along like chained oxen. If only he could take them all with him.

Haven Hill Farm

Haven held up the peach-colored silk dress that she'd stitched for her sister to wear for Easter. "All done, Ma. How's this?"

"It's absolutely lovely dear. Harmony's going to love it." Ma spread the full gathers of the swagged skirt with both hands and carefully arranged it over the back of the settee next to Haven's pale green dress. "My girls will be the most beautiful maidens in all of Lexington."

"Thank you, Ma. You're so sweet." Haven kissed her ma's cheek. "I can't believe it's Thursday already. She'll be home any moment now! I can't wait to hear her stories."

"I'll help you clean up the mess and put away your sewing notions." Ma started picking up scraps of fabric, lace and thread that lay strewn on the carpet around the Singer.

"I hope she gets here before Uncle Brady has to leave. Be a pity if they just miss each other." Haven put the last of her sewing notions in a basket.

A whiny voice sounded from the foyer. Hank? What was he doing? She followed Ma out of the room to the grand hall.

"But I don't want you to go, Uncle Brady. Please stay longer. Ple-e-ease." Hank pushed Uncle Brady's trunk away from the front door.

"Can't, little colt. Gotta get back to my ranch." Uncle Brady put both hands to Hank's shoulders. "I got a Texas-sized achin' in my heart to see your Aunt Karen and my kids. Besides, I'm sure I've done wore out my welcome around here, anyway."

"You most certainly have not!" Ma put her hands on her hips and walked over to Uncle Brady.

"That's right, Uncle Brady." Haven followed Ma and gave her uncle a big hug. "You know you're welcome here anytime."

Uncle Brady patted her back. "Thank you darlin'. You know I'd stay if I could."

Screams sounded from the kitchen, and a few seconds later a barking gray cloud on four legs blurred past Ma. Ma's hand flew to her mouth, and Hank took off to chase the cloud.

Haven and Uncle Brady burst out laughing.

"Scratch! You come back here, you dumb dog!" Hank's hand swiped at the dog and missed. "Ma's gonna skin you alive if you go tearin' through the house."

"Oh, mercy." Ma shook her finger at Hank. "So help me, Hank, if you don't catch that mangy mutt, that's the last you're gonna see of him. You hear?"

"No, Ma!" Hank ran in circles after the dog. "And he ain't no mangy mutt neither!"

"He isn't." Ma blew out a blast of air, making a funny sound with her lips. "I mean, he is, but … oh, fiddlesticks, Hank, you know what I mean."

Uncle Brady cut Scratch off at the foot of the stairs and grabbed the dog by the scruff of his neck. "This mutt ain't got a lick of sense. Why, if brains were made of leather, he wouldn't have enough to saddle a junebug!"

"Ain't true!" Hank shot back.

Haven glanced at Ma. "I'm sure going to miss having Uncle Brady around."

With Scratch out of the house, Haven and Ma joined the

family on the veranda where they'd gathered to wait for Harmony. As soon as the carriage came into view, everyone jumped from their seats and hurried down to the circular drive.

A weird feeling got the better of Haven, and she trailed behind the others. She should be excited about seeing her sister—not apprehensive. It had been over a year. What was wrong with her?

The carriage came to a stop, and her sister waved through the window, beaming. The driver opened the door, and Pa raced over to help Harmony. "Hey, beautiful." Was Pa gushing? He swung Harmony around before her feet met the ground.

"Pa!" Harmony threw her arms around him. "Ma!" She turned and hugged their mother.

Uncle Brady grabbed Harmony's arm. "Hey, good-lookin'!"

"Uncle Brady! What a surprise. I didn't know you'd be here."

"Give me a hug, darlin'." Uncle Brady wrapped Harmony up in a big embrace. "Wish I could stay longer, but I gotta head on home today."

"I'm glad I got here in time to see you." The way Harmony talked seemed different. Not warm like Kentucky. Perhaps too stiff. Had she picked up a British accent?

Haven studied her sister, paying scrupulous attention to everything. Not the same Harmony who'd left Kentucky to study Equestrian Arts in England. She had an air about her that Haven wasn't sure she liked very much.

That dress and hat must be the latest style of Europeans. Haven wrinkled her nose. Whoa … that neckline! A little lower than Ma and Pa had ever allowed.

Aware of her own jealousy, she remembered the old Proverb, "Envy is but a chasing after the wind."

Making a noble resolve to simply enjoy watching her sister receive all the attention that rightfully follows a year of being away, Haven squeezed between her brothers to take her turn.

As soon as she made eye contact with Harmony, a lifetime of conflict seized her thoughts.

She forced a smile and hugged her. "Glad you're home. It's so good to see you, Harmony. You look wonderful."

Harmony pulled away. "I know. I love the fashions over there." She fingered the rim of her bonnet and curtsied in a kind of show-off way. That wide purple ribbon … the purple dress. Who did she think she was? Royalty?

Ma cupped Haven's elbow. "Why don't you girls go on upstairs? Haven, you can help Harmony put things away in her room.

"All right, Ma." Haven took her sister by the arm and started walking with her to the house. All those misgivings she'd had a few moments earlier calmed as she engaged Harmony in sisterly small talk.

Then Harmony rattled on and on about herself. Nonstop. Never once did she ask about Haven. Daydream thoughts of Timothy came to her rescue, helping her block out the monotony of Harmony's voice.

"We need to get back downstairs, girls." Thank goodness Ma came in. "Uncle Brady will be leaving shortly to catch the stage."

"Yes, Ma." Harmony stood in front of the cheval glass, turning this way and that as she gazed at her image. With one tug on the already low-cut neckline and a quick lift of her bosom, she turned and faced Ma. "Ready."

Haven gritted her teeth. Why did she allow Harmony to ruffle her feathers like that?

She slipped her hand through the crook of Ma's left elbow as Harmony took the right. Together they descended the stairs.

"Well, if that ain't a sight for sore eyes." Uncle Brady beamed a toothy grin at the women from the bottom of the staircase. "Frank, if I didn't know better, I'd think I'd died, and heaven's purtiest angels were coming down to carry me away."

Pa looked proud enough to bust his buttons. He walked

up to Brady's side, giving a sweeping wave of his arm. "The three most beautiful women in all of Ken-tuck."

The sisters said their good-byes to Uncle Brady before Pa took him into town to catch the stage.

Haven couldn't wait to show Harmony the new Easter dresses. She nudged her into the sewing room, and Ma followed them. Haven had draped the dresses side by side over the back of the settee so her sister would see them.

Harmony noticed them right away. Whipping out a dainty, floral-printed fan from her sleeve, Harmony began fanning herself as she strutted around the settee. "What are these dresses for?"

"Those are our Easter dresses." Haven raised hopeful brows at Ma.

Harmony lifted the sleeve of one of the dresses. "Our Easter dresses?"

"Yes. Do you like them?"

"Well, I-I …" Harmony skewed her lips.

"The peach one is yours. I just got it done before you came." Haven held the mint green dress up in front of herself. "What do you think?"

"It's … it's …" Harmony tilted her head to one side and then the other like she was giving the dress an evaluation. "It's very *you*." Her nose disappeared into a scrunch.

Ma walked over and stood between them. "Haven worked very hard to get your dress done before you got home, dear. You said you like peach, didn't you?"

"Yes, I do, but—"

"But what?" Ma gathered up the dress and held it in front of Harmony. "How's this?"

Harmony fingered the lace on the bodice. "It's very well made, Ma."

Haven smiled, and so did Ma.

"But I bought a new dress from a London shop for Easter." With a flick of her wrist, Harmony pushed the peach dress away. "It's much more fashionable."

Haven's mood crashed.

"Oh, I see." Ma carefully placed the dress back on the settee. Silence followed. Was that all Ma was going to say?

Harmony turned her back to the dresses, gazed out the window and whipped out her fan for the second time. "I'm sure I'll find occasion to wear that peach dress some other time."

"Of course." Haven pivoted and stalked to the front of the settee, frumping down on the cushion. She hoped Harmony would smack herself in the face with that ridiculous frippery.

Harmony flung her head back like some arrogant princess and sashayed out of the parlor.

Narrowing her eyes, Haven folded her arms. *And to think I took the day off for this.*

Ma sat down beside her and whispered something in her ear—something about patience.

CHAPTER SIXTEEN

Easter Sunday, April 24, 1859
Haven Hill Farm

On the way home from church, Ma sat between Haven and Harmony in the carriage. That smile on Ma's face looked so peaceful. Was it because Haven and her sister had actually engaged in friendly conversation and hadn't argued all morning? Or maybe it was Pa's Easter message. Why couldn't every day be like this?

Haven rested her head on Ma's shoulder, sleepy from another restless night dreaming about Timothy. Just the thought of his promise to call on her gave her goosebumps. That day couldn't get here fast enough.

Arm in arm, Haven and Harmony entered the front door of the house. Haven's mint green dress rustled against Harmony's peach dress. Haven didn't know why her sister changed her mind and wore the peach dress. Best not to ask. A grin teased her lips. Probably a little "persuasion" from Pa.

After dinner, the twins joined their ma in the parlor. Haven and Harmony sat in the wing chairs facing the chaise where Ma stretched out for a short nap.

Harmony straightened her back and folded her hands on her lap. "Tell me, Haven, how many suitors have called on you this past year?"

"Well, one … I think."

"You think?" Harmony snickered in the most annoying way. "How does one not know if she has a suitor or not?"

"Well, he only asked to call on me once so far." Haven glanced at Ma, who appeared to be asleep. But she knew Ma was really awake and listening. That was fine with her.

"And how did it go?" Harmony sure could be persistent. "Do you like him?"

"Yes, I do like him." Haven averted her gaze for a second. "All right, Harmony, here's what happened. He asked if he could call on me when he gets back from a trip. So I told him he could."

There—she'd spilled the beans. To be sure, her sister would have fished it out of her if it was the last thing she did.

"Is that it? Only one suitor all year while I was in England?" Harmony's knack for being condescending ranked right up there with her ability to be persistent.

"Well, now, let's see. There's that fellow who came to visit with Uncle Brady. I know he likes me, but he's not my type." Haven caught Ma lifting her head a little and turning her face toward them. "I stayed as far away from him as I could."

"I didn't see anyone here with Uncle Brady. You're making that up." Harmony's brows furrowed.

"I'm not making it up. He left here and went to Louisville." Haven folded her arms. "But he's coming back. Then you'll see that I didn't make it up."

"Really?" Harmony's eyes twinkled. "He's coming back?"

Ma made a strange noise that sounded a little bit like a snort.

"Yes, but I'm not sure exactly when." Haven pursed her lips. She'd about had it with her sister's interrogation. "And what about you, Harmony? How many suitors did you have?"

"Quite a few, actually." Harmony wiggled in her seat, holding her head up high like a pompous queen.

Ma's body jerked and her eyebrows flew up. One eye opened a sliver.

Haven narrowed her gaze. "Quite a few, huh?"

"You sound jealous."

"I'm not jealous. Why would I be jealous?"

"I just said you sounded jealous. I didn't say you were."

"Well, I'm not!" Haven stomped her foot on the carpet.

"You don't need to shout!" Harmony mimicked Haven's stomp.

"I'm not shouting! You're the one who's shou—"

"Girls!" Ma shot straight up, shoulders squared. "That's enough, you two. You're both behaving like little children. Gracious me! Even Hank and Andy don't argue like that."

"Sorry, Ma." Haven spoke first.

"Sorry, Ma." At least Harmony had the decency to apologize.

"Now, I want you both to go to your rooms and take a nap." Ma rose to her feet. "You need your beauty sleep."

The sisters spoke in unison as Ma started for the door. "Yes, Ma."

"And remember what day this is. This is the Lord's Day—Easter Sunday. Now come here, both of you." Ma stretched out her arms. "Give your ma a hug."

Haven nestled into Ma's open arms. How many times was she going to allow her sister to bring out the worst in her?

The Locker farm
Darke County, Ohio

Timothy had just finished eating one of Mama's delicious Easter meals before he joined his two brothers and Pop on the front porch. The Locker men sat in their pine wood rockers enjoying the lovely spring weather. So good to be home.

He rubbed his full belly. In all his travels as a circuit rider, he'd not met anyone who'd even come close to cooking up a meal as good as Mama's.

"I believe your Easter sermon went well this morning, son." Pop rolled the toothpick he'd been chewing to the other side of his mouth. "The people love it when you come home to preach. Nothing against Pastor Schmidt, of course. It's just nice to hear a fresh voice share the Word now and then."

"I think so, too." His older brother, Nick, leaned forward in his rocker. "We're all real proud of you."

"Same here, Timothy." His younger brother, Nathan, who sat next to him, reached over and poked his arm. "Besides, Pastor Schmidt is getting on in years. He may retire soon, you know. You'd be perfect for the position."

"Something to think about, I suppose. And I appreciate the encouragement. Thank you." Looking out over the fields, Timothy noted the contrast between the never-ending flatness of the land before him and the luscious rolling hills of Kentucky. As much as he loved his home in Ohio, he sure did miss the Bluegrass State—especially a pretty little nurse named Haven.

He sagged deep into the chair, stretched out his long legs, crossing them at the ankles, and pulled his hat down over his face. Breathing in the country smells of the farm, he closed his eyes.

Haven.

He hadn't told any of his family about the girl he'd met. Not even Mama. Maybe he should tell Mama. No … better not. She'd be sure to tell Pop. Then Pop might slip up and tell his brothers. Lord, have mercy if his brothers found out. Nope—they were all going to have to wait.

A few more weeks and then …

Ahh … Haven.

All conversation faded into the background. He could fall asleep right there dreaming about that pretty nurse. He pulled his hat down a little bit more to hide whatever smile his lips might have formed. Life was good.

Haven Hill Farm

Here it was May … the weeks had been long for Haven, waiting for her traveling evangelist to return. How did she ever allow herself to fall so hard for Timothy Locker? Answers to the mystery of her infatuation simply didn't exist. And there seemed to be no cure.

Butterflies. Dreams. More butterflies. A never-ending cycle. Ma told her it was pointless to try and fight it—just let it run its course. If it was the real thing, she'd know soon enough.

While Harmony exercised her prized stallion around the paddock closest to the main house, Haven sat alone on the veranda, sipping lemonade as she read *The Scarlet Letter.* The book belonged to Ma, and Ma had pulled it from its hiding place in a hat box for the first time since she'd read it herself several years ago.

Ma stepped outside, walked over to her and placed her hands on Haven's shoulders. She sported an impish grin. "Remember, you have to give the book back to me later today before your pa comes home. He wouldn't like it if he knew his wife had such a scandalous novel in her possession."

"I promise, Ma. It's good so far. I'm sure I'll finish it in one sitting."

"All right, dear. I'll leave you to your reading." She walked to the front door and turned to face Haven. "Harmony should be done with Solomon shortly. She's supposed to have tea with me. Would you care to join us?"

"No, Ma, but thanks for asking. You two enjoy your mother-daughter time. I'll stay here and read."

Ma winked and closed the door behind her.

Haven resumed reading until she heard a wagon coming down the lane. She quickly slipped the book under the folds of her shawl and watched the wagon for a few seconds. It was only Elias with a wagonload of supplies from town. He stopped his team next to the paddock and waved to Harmony.

Dressed in a riding habit, her sister looked very sharp and professional atop her steed. Her long blonde ponytail, tied below her black cap with a matching ribbon, bounced up and down in synchronized fashion with the bobbing of Solomon's tail. She stopped the horse and looked toward Elias.

Elias hopped down and walked over to the fence. "Miz Hominy!" He waved her over. "Messenger a comin', Miz Hominy!"

Harmony dismounted and walked over to Elias. Haven wished she could hear what they were saying. She saw her sister wave Elias away.

After Elias drove off, Harmony rode over to the gate where Molly sat in the grass. "Open the gate, Molly! We're coming out."

"Yessam, Miz Hominy." Poor Molly. Such a sweet woman.

After Molly opened the gate, Harmony rode out into the lane and stayed there. Molly followed her on foot.

The messenger pulled up alongside Harmony and stopped. He reached in his satchel, pulled out an envelope and handed it to her. As he rode off, Harmony opened the telegram.

Who'd be sending Harmony a telegram? Oh well … it was none of her business. She had a book to finish.

Flipping through to the page where she'd left off, she glanced once more toward her sister. Harmony cast a scornful look at Molly. *What's she scolding Molly about now?* Haven raised an eyebrow as Molly picked up her skirts and bounded toward the veranda.

Haven bowed her head and returned to reading.

By the time Molly reached the veranda, Haven could see her intense frown. Molly's cheeks jiggled like jelly as she tromped by. "The devil done got hold of that girl, sure enough. Mm, mm, mm—just ain't right."

"What's that you're saying, Molly?"

"Nothin', Miz Haven. I ain't sayin' nothin'." Molly kept her gaze straight ahead until she reached the side of the house and rounded the corner, out of Haven's sight.

Haven sighed. She knew all too well how vexing Harmony could be.

No time to worry about those two. In less than a minute, Haven found herself lost in another century among the Puritan settlers of Boston. A growing empathy for Hester Prynne and little Pearl soon took control of her emotions. How could those settlers be so mean to that young mother? Where was forgiveness? Where was grace? These people were heartless.

The pages turned faster and faster. No wonder Ma said Pa wouldn't like it.

CHAPTER SEVENTEEN

Haven Hill Farm

When Timothy turned his rig into the lane of Haven Hill Farm, anticipation sent his heart racing like a thoroughbred. Three weeks had never seemed so long.

Their first date. What on earth was he doing?

"Take a look at the size of that house on the hill, Danny Boy." He slowed down and came to a complete stop. "What do you think of those beautiful pastures and regal looking stables?"

Danny Boy snorted.

"Is that so? You're just jealous." Timothy glanced at the time on his pocket watch. Two o'clock. It would be ungentlemanly to arrive too early. He was exactly on time. The watch slid back into his pocket.

"Time to go on up to the house, Danny Boy." He tapped the reins.

One of the slaves stopped him as he got close to the drive in front of the house and directed him to a parking area.

He made his way up the veranda steps and rapped on the front door. Gawking at the intricate carvings on the wood, he jumped when a servant pulled the door open. "Good afternoon! My name is Timothy Locker. I'm here to call on

Miss Haven."

"Is Miz Haven expecting you?"

"Yes, sir. I sent her a telegram two days ago to let her know." That same jittery feeling Timothy had when he went to talk to Haven at the doctor's office returned, only worse.

"Miz Haven upstairs. I'll send her mammy up there to tell her she has a visitor. Come in and wait here, suh." The man left him alone in the grand hall and disappeared somewhere toward the back of the house.

Except for a few house servants passing through while doing their chores and men's voices coming from a room not too far down one of the halls, it was as though he were just another fixture.

What if she didn't want to see him?

Haven rolled over on her bed and stretched her arms. Sometimes she wished Ma wouldn't make her and Harmony take naps on Saturdays. But Ma insisted they needed their beauty rest.

She glanced at the white porcelain clock on the mantel. A quarter past two. She'd been sleeping over an hour. Ma always said the nap had to be at least one hour.

Harmony must have gotten up early. She could hear her sister in the powder room—the room that connected their bedrooms. Why was she singing? Strange. Haven threw on an everyday muslin dress and shuffled toward the powder room door.

She walked in and found Harmony primping. "What's this? Why are you dressed to the nines today?" Haven sat on the stool next to her sister in front of the ornately framed vanity mirror and started brushing her hair.

Harmony pinched her cheeks and bobbed her upswept hair with the palms of her hands. "Must a girl have a reason to look her best?" She adjusted a hairpin, got up and walked toward the door to her room. "Why are *you* wearing that simple dress?"

"Why not?"

Harmony flashed a wicked grin. "I'm going downstairs now."

Haven got up and followed her. "Wait … I'm going with you."

"Suit yourself."

Molly met them near the bottom landing. "I just on my way up to find you, Miz Haven. You have a caller waiting. He say his name is Timothy Locker."

"What?" Haven snapped her gaze toward the front of the grand hall, and sure enough, there he was—looking right at them. Why hadn't he let her know what day he'd come to call?

Stunned, Haven watched Harmony whip out her dainty little fan and walk down the last two steps to the marble floor.

Wait a minute … what's going on?

A surge of rage shot through her body. *She knew! That telegram!* Her fists clenched, and her cheeks burned.

Harmony glanced up at her from over her shoulder. Oh, that wicked grin. "Aren't you going to introduce me to your gentleman caller, Haven?"

Haven wanted to scream for Ma. But not in front of Timothy. It would be rude to go back upstairs to change her dress after he'd already seen her. And she dare not leave her sister alone with him. Lord only knows what Harmony might do. Gritting her teeth, she took the last two steps, pasted on a smile and made her way past Harmony over to Timothy. She could feel the blasts of tepid air on her arm coming from that stupid little frippery. Must her sister fan herself so close behind her?

"Hello, Timothy." One look in his eyes calmed her nerves. A little bit. "I'd like you to meet my sister—Harmony." She faced her sister. "Harmony, this is Timothy Locker. *Reverend* Timothy Locker." She hoped the little bit of emphasis she put on the word "Reverend" grabbed Harmony's attention.

"Pleased to meet you, ma'am." Timothy looked nervous as a mouse cornered by two cats. "You're … um … twins."

"Timothy, I didn't know you were coming today or I would have dressed in better fashion." She glanced down at her sprigged muslin dress.

"But I sent you a telegram."

Haven flashed a scowl at her sister and somehow managed to quell a fire of fury. She had to maintain self-control.

Vengeance is mine … saith the Lord. The reminder came just in time.

Harmony folded her fan. "Oh dear … I meant to give it to you, Haven. Silly me … I must have laid it down on my dresser and forgotten about it."

If Ma hadn't stepped out of the small parlor at that very moment, Haven might have snatched that fan out of Harmony's hand and smacked those insolent lips right off her face.

Ma walked over and stood between them. "I didn't know we had company, girls." She curtsied to Timothy. Graceful Ma—always so polite. "I'm Rebekah Haywood, the girls' mother."

"Ma, this is Timothy Locker." Haven slipped her hand through Ma's elbow. "Apparently, Harmony forgot to pass along Timothy's telegram to me." She held out the skirt of her simple dress. "As you can see, I didn't know he'd be here today."

Timothy bowed to Ma. "My pleasure to meet you, ma'am."

Ma faced Harmony. "I'm sure it was just a simple oversight. Right, dear?" Ma didn't really believe that, did she? "Why don't we all go to the parlor, and I'll let Pa know we have a guest. I'll have Lena make us some lemonade, too." Ma led the way, nudging Harmony along by the arm. Maybe Ma *did* suspect foul play.

Haven's heart fluttered when Timothy extended his arm to her. She slipped her hand through the crook of his elbow as they followed Ma across the grand hall toward the parlor.

He leaned close and whispered in her ear, making every hair on her neck stand on end. "You look very pretty."

Those four words! He thought she looked pretty, and he didn't even give Harmony a second glance. Haven's mood lifted like quicksilver. It felt so good to be back on that cloud she'd been dreaming on for weeks.

Timothy sat in one of the two matching armless chairs next to Haven facing the settee where her parents had sandwiched her sister between them. Something about that girl seemed to create an unspoken tension with Haven.

He narrowed his gaze at Mr. Haywood. The curly red hair. The big belly. Him again—that same man that always rankled Leonard.

So that's Haven's pa? Maybe he should hightail it out of there. Now.

Mr. Haywood took a large swig of lemonade and set his glass on the serving tray. "Haven tells me you're an evangelist—a circuit rider. Is that right?"

"Yes, sir, I am." Timothy tossed a glance to Haven. Oh my, that smile of hers. "I travel quite a bit, hold camp meetings, preach at revivals and so on." *Not to mention I transport fugitive slaves.* He picked up a glass of lemonade. "I understand you're a preacher, too."

"Yes, a country church right down the road." Mr. Haywood seemed like a nice enough gentleman. "You probably went by it on your way here."

"I did. I remember seeing it." Timothy drank some lemonade, gulping when a young boy barreled into the room.

The kid careened around the settee, shouting "Ma!" over and over before tripping over Harmony's crinolined skirt. Amid female shrieks, his body hurled into Mrs. Haywood.

While Harmony smoothed her skirt, Mr. Haywood pulled the boy to his side of the settee. "Hank, don't you see that we have company? Haven has a caller today." He gestured toward Timothy. "My apologies, Mr. Locker. This is our youngest son, Henry. We call him Hank."

"Sorry, sir." Hank grinned and pouted at the same time. "Didn't see you."

"It's all right, Hank. My name is Timothy, and I'm happy to meet you." Timothy wondered how many more Haywood brothers he'd meet.

Hank walked right up to him and shook his hand. "Are you going to marry my sister?"

"Henry Colton Haywood!" All three women shot to their feet, shouting in unison. Such scarlet cheeks.

Cute kid.

"I gotta go, Timothy." Hank started backing up toward the parlor entrance. "Harrison's waiting to take me riding." He pivoted and zoomed out of the room.

Haven wilted into her chair, squirming like a wiggly worm. "I am so sorry, Timothy. I've never been so embarrassed in my life."

"No worries." Timothy rather enjoyed the break in the ice. "I like Hank. He reminds me of my own younger brother at that age."

"Again, my apologies." Mr. Haywood sunk down into the cushion, squishing Harmony's lavish dress. "Harrison is my oldest son. He and I pastor the church together. Small church, you know—around thirty of us. He also co-manages the farm with me."

Timothy leaned forward, resting his elbows on his knees. "You must be very proud of him, Mr. Haywood."

"I am, indeed. And please … call me Frank."

"Yes, sir … um, Frank."

Mrs. Haywood got up from the settee, and Harmony wiggled a few inches away from her pa, pressing the wrinkles from her skirt for the second time. Mrs. Haywood steepled her fingers together. "If you'll excuse me, I have a few things to oversee." She faced Harmony. "I need your help, dear."

Harmony's arrogant manner faded into a petulant sulk as her ma gave her a stern look. What was that girl's problem?

Mrs. Haywood walked over to Haven and leaned over her shoulder. "Haven, dear, why don't you show Timothy around the land, maybe go down to the lake, visit the stables and see some of the horses?"

Timothy rose from his chair. "I'd like a tour!" Should he have waited for Haven's reply?

"I'll get Big Joe to drive you." Mr. Haywood winked.

Timothy remembered Big Joe from that day in the woods. He wasn't nearly as intimidating this time. Joe actually smiled at him.

Once seated next to Haven in the carriage, Timothy filled his lungs with a deep breath, exhaled, then smiled at her.

"Timothy, I'm so sorry for my sister's behavior." Haven's frustration with her sister was obviously a sore spot.

Joe glanced over his shoulder with a nod. The gesture made Timothy laugh. Her twin sister must be quite a character.

"Ooo … the more I think about it, the angrier I get." Her knuckles whitened from a tight fist.

Timothy placed his hand on top of hers. "Then don't think about it anymore." As she relaxed, he caught her gaze. "Now tell me about Haven Hill Farm."

When they reached the lake's shore, they took a leisurely stroll, catching the warmth of the sun's rays. A gentle May breeze whispered fanciful notions to Timothy's heart.

His gut instinct told him he should get the slavery issue out in the open right away, but his romantic inclinations convinced him otherwise.

Before he knew it, Joe was taking them up the hill to the house. Why did the afternoon have to end so soon?

Leonard Thompson's parlor

"Leonard, I've met a girl." Timothy walked with him across the hall to the parsonage parlor. "I need to ask you something about her father."

"What a nice surprise, son. Here, have a seat." Leonard indicated the wooden chairs at a small, round table in the corner. "Now tell me—how is it that I would know something about this girl's father?"

"I met her family this afternoon. Her father is the same man you argued with at Cheapside the day Lottie was sold." Timothy leaned forward, resting his chin on the palm of his hand. "And you got into it with him again at the tavern that night I went with Avery."

"Ah, yes." Leonard shook his head. "So you went and fell for one of Frank Haywood's daughters, huh?"

"That's him—Frank Haywood." Timothy averted his gaze to the paisley design on the rug. This was more awkward than he thought it would be. He looked at Leonard again. "Tell me about him."

"He's a slaveholder, son." Leonard pressed his back against the slats of his chair and rested his ankle on his knee. "You know that, don't you?"

"Unfortunately, I do." Timothy sat up straight and flattened both palms on the table. "What had he done to upset you, Leonard? I have to know."

"Well, it's mostly what he didn't do. He's in ministry—like us. He could have helped save Lottie. He knew her circumstances." Leonard uncrossed his legs, allowing his boot to fall on the rug with a thud. "But he chose not to."

"I see." Timothy leaned back and folded his arms. "His daughter doesn't strike me as that type."

"I was about your age when I started courting Gladys. Been married almost nineteen years now—best thing that ever happened to me." The twinkle in Leonard's eyes proved he meant it. "So which one of Frank's daughters has your head all up in the clouds?"

Timothy ignored the sudden rush of heat to his head. "It's Haven. What do you know about her?"

The timbre of Leonard's voice switched back to normal. "Haven's a fine Christian girl. Hardworking, polite, caring."

"I've heard that from several people. It's been my observation as well."

"She has a twin sister. I've heard that one can be a real

spitfire. I think her name is Harmony." Leonard breathed a chuckle. "The name rather contradicts her personality."

"I met her today." Timothy laughed with him. "I'll tell you this—what you've heard is true."

"Well, son, my advice to you is to be upfront with Haven from the beginning. Let her know where you stand." Leonard extended his arm across the table top and tapped his index finger down hard. "And listen—this is important—never, ever compromise your beliefs that slavery is wrong. Let the Lord lead from there."

"Thanks, Leonard. I needed to hear that."

CHAPTER EIGHTEEN

Downtown Lexington

If Haven had counted the days once, she'd counted them a hundred times. Now here she was with Timothy on their second date. A lunch break, but still a date.

Her breath caught as Timothy helped her position her chair at the cozy table for two in the corner of the restaurant. How could the mere brush of his arm against her shoulder make her feel this way?

Timothy seated himself across from her. "I'm glad we get to spend some time together before I leave on my trip." He hooked his umbrella on the back of his chair.

"How long will you be in Lexington?"

"Saturday morning. I have two camp meetings coming up back to back starting next week. I'll probably be gone a month."

"That's a long time." She lifted her gaze, and her eyes met his. Oh, she could stay there forever.

"I know. It is a long time." He held her gaze.

Was he as disappointed as she was? She broke eye contact and stared at the white tablecloth.

With one elbow on the table, he rested his chin in his palm, tilting his head to one side and then the other.

"What are you doing? Is something wrong?" She dabbed her lips and cheeks with the corner of her handkerchief. Had something unsightly attached itself to her face?

"Nothing could be more right." He put his hand down and sat up straight. "You're beautiful … even in your uniform."

"You make me blush, sir." The sudden clinking and clanging of dishes from the back of the restaurant nearly drowned out her voice.

He tapped the table and winked. "It's the truth, Haven."

Hearing him speak her name charmed her as much as if he'd sung a love song. This man was a treasure. Not only a dream to look at, but a gentleman as well. She liked that. She liked him.

He cleared his throat and reached across the table. His fingers slid beneath her hand.

She sneaked a peek at his thumb caressing her knuckles. A tingle crept up her arm.

"I'd like to see you again as soon as I get back to Lexington." He gave her hand a squeeze.

"I-I'd like to … that." Great. Now she couldn't even talk right.

"I'll be done with my commitments in time for Independence Day." A glimmer of expectancy sparked in his eyes. "I'd be honored if you'd celebrate it with me."

Stomach butterflies fluttered out of control. "I'd like that more than anything, Timothy."

The way Haven said his name filled Timothy with a longing he'd never experienced before. He'd never felt like that around Alifair. With Haven, he had to be careful.

He gave her hand a quick but gentle squeeze and drew back, relaxing into the slats of the chair. "Then it's a date. I'll pick you up the morning of the Fourth, and we'll spend the entire day together."

"Are you ready to order?" The waiter's voice spoiled the moment.

"Yes. I believe we're ready." Timothy picked up the menu and nodded. "After you, Haven."

"I'll have a fresh vegetable plate." She looked so cute.

"I'll have the ham and bean soup." Timothy handed him the menu. "With cornbread, please."

"I'll be back in a moment." The waiter smiled, pivoted and maneuvered his way through the dining hall to the kitchen.

"Are you all right?" Timothy noticed Haven had become very quiet and seemed to be distracted by the other diners. Had he done something wrong already?

She met his gaze. "Oh, I was just thinking. I'm fine."

"Good thoughts, I hope."

"Of course." She smiled and unrolled the white linen napkin, spreading it over her gray skirt. "Timothy, I want you to know I appreciate how important your work is. What I'm trying to say is, I'm sorry I won't see you for so long, but I understand why."

"That means a lot to me, Haven." This time he took both of her hands in his. Could she be any more perfect? If she knew everything about his work, would she still feel the same? "I appreciate the encouragement more than you know."

By the time they finished eating, the hour had all but vanished. He walked with Haven to Dr. Wright's office. In the rain. Normally, he wouldn't like being out in the rain, but this time it gave him the perfect excuse to hold Haven closer under his umbrella. If only she didn't have to go back to work.

They stood in front of the office door, and she slipped her arm out from his. "Will I see you again before you leave?"

He must have done something right. "Lunch tomorrow?"

She beamed. "I'd love to."

"I'll be here." His eyes strayed for a brief moment to her lips, the urge to kiss her good-bye almost too strong to resist.

Sarah Goolsby cracked open the door of the office and stuck her head out. "Are you coming back to work, Haven, or are you going to stand out here in the rain all afternoon?"

"Coming, Sarah." She kept her gaze on him as Sarah let the door close.

"I guess this is good-bye." He opened the door for her. "Until tomorrow."

He closed the door behind her and walked down the boardwalk, his head spinning. Was this love?

The blacksmith's shop

After winding up his errands for the day, Timothy headed over to the blacksmith's shop where he found Micah sitting on the bench for an afternoon break. "Glad the rain finally stopped. Scoot over." He slid in next to him. "I have to tell you—things are starting to look up for me and Haven. We had a lunch date today, and I think she likes me, Micah!." He drew in deep breath. "I've never felt like this before."

"I can see that." Micah's glum reply surprised Timothy.

"What's wrong, Micah? Aren't you happy for me?"

"Sorry, Timothy. Of course, I happy for you." Micah gave Timothy a slap on the back, but was that smile a thin disguise for a heavy heart? "It about time you start getting serious about finding the right woman."

Timothy studied Micah's face. "Something's bothering you. Are things all right between you and Ruth?"

"Why you ask that?" Micah drew back. "Couldn't be better. She my rock, and I thank God every day for giving Ruth to me."

"Then it's something else." He studied Micah's expression. "Care to share?"

"Ah, no, Timothy." Micah palmed his face and pressed his fingers hard against his temples. "Don't want to spoil your happy day."

"I won't leave here until you tell me." He tapped Micah on the leg. "I want to pray about whatever it is. We always pray for each other, remember? Tell me what's ailing you."

"All right." Micah straightened up and rubbed the back of his neck. "I overheard Massa Roberts and Miz Cilla quarreling about me. I'd gone to the house to turn in Massa's share of my wages and tell him I got my first farrier work lined up. Lucy let me in like she always do, but when I get to the parlor entrance, I hear Miz Cilla yelling at Massa."

Timothy looked away. "I can hear her voice in my head already. Not pleasant."

"She sayin' things like she didn't know Massa let me keep some of my wages and telling him to make me pay back every penny. She all upset because they had to sell some of their land to make ends meet, and she blame it on me."

"Oh, Micah." Timothy shook his head. "What did Mr. Roberts say to her?"

"First he tell her to sit down 'cause she makin' him dizzy. Then he tell her it's his medical expenses that cause the hardship and not me, and she get even angrier." Micah placed his hand over his heart. "But when she say awful things about my wife, then it really hurt."

Timothy gaped. "Oh no, Micah. She doesn't even know Ruth. What did she say?"

"I can't repeat what she say about Ruth. But she accuse us of building a nest egg while she and Massa be forced to sell they land piece by piece. And she also say awful things about Massa being a Christian." Tears swam in Micah's eyes. "Break this preacher's heart."

"Mine, too. I don't know what to say." Timothy slumped.

"When her tirade be over, I tap on the entrance to make my presence known. Massa invite me to come in, and Miz Cilla get mad about that, too."

Timothy shook his head. "What did she say to you?"

"She just scowl." Micah's eyes grew wide as silver dollars. "And you should see her face when Massa ask her to leave the room so he can talk to me alone."

Micah's expression made Timothy laugh out loud. "I'm glad I didn't see it. The image in my head is scary enough."

"Me and Massa get it all worked out, though. He say he

aim to remedy the situation when he get his health back. Besides, Ruth makes a fair wage from Trumbeaux. We be fine."

"Is everything else all right?"

"No suh. Haven't you heard? Trumbreaux back from his trip, but he not find Lottie."

"No, I hadn't heard. When did he get back?"

"Yesterday. Ruth say he travel all the way down to Natchez." Micah unscrewed the lid of his water jar. "I have a long talk with Ruth. She be a strong woman, I tell you. We cry together, and when she ask me why the Lord not help Trumbeaux find Lottie, I have to say her husband not have all the answers."

Timothy put a hand to Micah's shoulder. "Maurice won't give up."

"I hope not." Micah slanted his gaze to Timothy. "Well, I guess I ruin your happy moment with all my bad news."

"Nonsense, Micah. I'm glad you told me so I know how to pray for you."

"I very happy for you and Miz Haven. That lightens my heart today." Micah chugged some water, screwed the lid on the jar then got up from the bench. "But now I have to get back to work before the boss come out here and drag me inside."

Timothy stood up, too. "I have a lot of travel ahead of me, Micah. A couple of camp meetings and several other stops in the mountains where they want me to preach. I covet your prayers."

"May the Good Lord be with you, my friend. Come see me when you're back in town."

Haven Hill Farm

As soon as Big Joe pulled the carriage into the lane, Haven noticed Harmony in one of the paddocks exercising

Solomon. As usual, Molly stood in her place by the gate.

"Looks like Harmony has had a good day, Joe. I've had a very good day, too." Haven leaned forward to make sure Joe could hear her. "I got to have lunch with Timothy Locker. You remember, Timothy, don't you?"

Big Joe glanced back over his shoulder, nodded and smiled.

"He wants to see me again. Makes me happy, Joe." Haven's joy bubbled over and came out in a giggle.

Joe stopped the carriage in front of the house and helped her down. She waved good-bye and skipped up the stairs to the front door. Before she could close the door, she saw a coach making its way down the lane toward the house. *Who could that be?*

She hurried on in the house and dashed to the front parlor. It wouldn't do to be seen in her nursing uniform. Standing off to the side of the window, she peeked out. The coach stopped in the drive, and along came Harmony—right on cue—riding Solomon to greet the visitor.

Haven opened the window a crack so she could hear what was going on. A man dressed in western attire emerged and brushed some dust off his pants while Harmony circled the coach. The man paid the hackman and picked up his trunks. As the coach left, the man took one step and turned, facing the house. *Larkin Smith?*

Oh, this was going to be good.

Mr. Smith stared at Harmony. She stared right back.

"Welcome to Haven Hill." Harmony stared him down for several seconds. He said nothing. No surprise there.

Solomon reared his head, sidestepped and snorted.

"Whoa, boy." Harmony used her softer voice. "Easy now."

"I haven't been gone that long, have I, Miss Haywood?" Larkin Smith smiled for the first time. "You've never spoken to me before. To what do I owe this great honor?"

Haven palmed her cheek and smirked. "He thinks she's me."

"Oh, so you've been to Haven Hill before? My name's Harmony Haywood."

The confusion about her sister's identity tickled Haven's fancy to no end. "I'm Haven's twin sister."

A huge grin stretched across Mr. Smith's scarlet face. "Please forgive me, ma'am. I knew Haven had a sister, but no one told me you were twins." His grin gave way to laughter. "You look exactly like her."

"So we've been told." Was Harmony blushing, too?

This was better than Haven anticipated.

Mr. Smith put the trunks down on the brick walkway and removed his hat. "I'm Larkin Smith. It's a pleasure to meet you, Miss Harmony Haywood."

"Thank you, Mr. Smith."

"Larkin—please call me Larkin."

"Larkin." Harmony actually gushed when she said it. "I like that name."

Could this really be happening? Her sister had a weird look on her face. A silly and ridiculous look.

"I have to get back now. I'm afraid I've interrupted Solomon's routine." She turned the horse and looked back over her shoulder. "I'll see you later, Larkin. If you get a chance, come out to the track."

Mr. Smith cleared his throat. "Thank you. I will." He raised his hat to her as she tapped the stallion's reins.

As soon as Solomon trotted off with Harmony, Haven backed away from the window, darted out of the parlor, made a sharp right and headed straight for the stairs. She had to get to her room fast. If Mr. Smith came in and caught her spying on him … perish the thought!

Did Harmony and Larkin Smith really like each other? Maybe he would stop staring at her and start staring at her sister instead. One could only hope.

CHAPTER NINETEEN

July 4, 1859
Downtown Lexington

The downtown boardwalk was teeming with excited people by the time Timothy and Haven arrived for the Independence Day celebration. With Haven on his arm, Timothy soaked it all in—bright sun, blue sky, children playing, and festivities abuzz in every direction.

He'd never seen Haven so happy. Her infectious laughter spilled over in bubbly spurts.

They reached the end of the block, stood on the corner and gazed up and down the boardwalk. He gave her shoulder a squeeze. "What shall we do first?"

"I hear the band!" Haven jumped up and down like a loose spring, pointing cater-cornered across the street at the park gazebo.

He grinned and took her hand. "The gazebo it is then!"

Lively songs of Stephen Foster and the American Revolution filled the air. A chorus of birds among the shade trees yielded a cheery contrast to the rhythm of the drums and the boldness of the brass.

"Yankee Doodle went to town a ridin' on a pony"—Haven burst into song as they approached the gazebo.

"Stuck a feather in his cap and called it macaroni!" Timothy tipped his hat to a rust-colored fox squirrel as it darted in front of them before scampering up the nearest poplar tree.

After finding the perfect spot to spread their quilt, he helped Haven ease onto it first.

"Timothy!" A young girl's voice called his name. Was that Brillie?

A short distance away, next to a large number of parked carriages and buggies, the Delaney family filed out of Avery's carriage. They waved, and Timothy waved back as Sylvia and Brillie ran off to play.

He cast his gaze down to Haven. The gathers of her white cotton skirt covered his left boot. Somehow, he managed to sit down without stepping on her dress. He could be so clumsy sometimes.

A minute later, the conversation of the Delaney family got very loud. Timothy turned his head in their direction and saw Melia spreading a quilt on the lawn. Where was Alifair? She probably didn't come. Before he could say anything to Haven, he heard Melia mention Alifair's name.

"Avery, dear, do you really think it was wise to bring Alifair? It's just not proper, you know." Melia sounded perturbed. "I mean, haven't you noticed? She's about to—"

"Melia, I can hear you!" Alifair's very pregnant belly filled the opened door of the carriage. "I wish you'd relax, Melia. I never missed an Independence Day celebration in New York, and you're not going to make me miss this one."

Timothy laughed, and Haven covered her grinning lips as the melody of "Camptown Races" filled the park. He watched as Avery placed his hands under his sister's arms and lifted her to the ground.

Alifair continued to babble over Melia's *tsk tsk*. "Besides, this baby's not due for at least another three weeks." She opened a lace-trimmed parasol.

"Well, it's inappropriate, that's all." Melia reached into her reticule and retrieved a small fan. "Women in your condition should stay home, no matter what. I would have been glad to stay home with you."

"My condition, huh?" Alifair twirled the parasol until it came to rest on her shoulder. "You make it sound as though I have some dreadful disease."

"Ladies, please!" Avery opened the rear compartment of the carriage, lifted out a folding bench and brought it to his sister to sit on. "There … that should do."

Timothy locked eyes with Haven, and they both burst out laughing.

Haven clapped her hands when the band played "Oh! Susanna"—great way to drown out the quibbling Delaney family. She elbowed Timothy to join her. They sang and laughed, having so much fun she wished it would never end.

Children skipped about on the lawn, trundling large rolling hoops with their dowels. She noticed some little girls playing a Game of Graces. A childhood memory flashed through her mind of when she used to play that game with Harmony. The girls tossed colorful, ribbon-bedecked flying hoops back and forth as each one tried to catch the rings with a catching wand. Laughing inwardly, she remembered Harmony's tantrums whenever Haven caught the most rings.

"Looks like fun, doesn't it?" When Timothy didn't answer, she turned her head back to face him. Those gorgeous eyes, less than a foot away. He looked lost. Had he heard a single word she'd said? "Timothy?"

"Hmm?"

"Nevermind."

"Let's take a stroll down the boardwalk." Without waiting for her to respond, he rose to his feet and reached down to help her up.

Halfway down the first block, a man cranking a barrel organ on wheels entertained a small crowd. A cute little monkey frolicked on his shoulders. They watched for a while and moved on.

Harmony and Larkin approached them from the opposite

direction and stopped to chat. Those two had been seeing each other regularly—ever since their first encounter at Haven Hill. No more stares from Mr. Smith. No more willies!

"Larkin has decided he's not going back to Texas." Harmony held on to Larkin's arm like he might fly away if she let go. "He's going to settle in Louisville."

Larkin gazed at Harmony with a goofy, twitterpated, schoolboy smile. *Sickening.*

"Timothy!" Hank bolted out of nowhere, blindsiding him. "Isn't this grand?"

"Henry Colton Haywood!" Haven grabbed her brother by his arm. "No need to be running around like some wild mustang in a crowd like this!"

As Hank stuck his tongue out at her, Timothy tapped him on the shoulder. "Grand as can be, Hank!"

Haven bent over her little brother. "Why aren't you with Ma?"

"Ma and Pa are right there." Hank pointed a few yards down the boardwalk. "See?"

"Say, Hank? How would you like some ice cream after the parade?" Timothy shot a glance to Haven as if asking for her permission.

"Yee haw! I love ice cream." Hank ran off, happy as a pup with two tails.

Timothy cupped Haven's elbow and grinned. "C'mon … there's more to see."

Clasping Timothy's hand, she said good-bye to her sister. The day was still young, and they had lots more to enjoy. She supposed she could sacrifice one stop at the ice cream parlor with Hank.

On the way back to the park for the afternoon concert and picnic lunch, they stopped for a moment to watch the Lexington Rifles engage in a bayonet drill. Haven pursed her lips at all the young women who'd gathered there as spectators. Silly girls—swooning over Captain John Hunt Morgan like that. He wasn't near as handsome as Timothy.

A cacophony of notes blared from the gazebo, and she

pulled Timothy away. "We'd better hurry or we'll miss the concert!" She started running, dragging him along. They made it to the park lawn just in time to sing "The Star-Spangled Banner."

The land of the free. The words echoed in Timothy's head long after the music switched to "Jeanie with the Light Brown Hair." He took a bite of his ham sandwich, watching Haven sip her lemonade.

The land of the free.

What did it mean to her? He caught her gaze, and she smiled. Oh, that pretty face. Those blushed cheeks and those brown eyes. She looked so lovely in that summer white dress with the big red sash. But what were her thoughts?

"Was your sandwich good?" Haven whisked some crumbs off her skirt. "I brought an extra one for you, in case you're still hungry." She reached into the poke that held their lunch and fished it out.

"Mmm, yes … delicious." He took the sandwich and bit into it. "I was starved."

Haven patted her lips with a red and white checkered cloth and stuffed it back into the poke. "I think Lena and Molly made enough food to feed the whole town."

Timothy froze.

Lena and Molly. Slaves had made his lunch so that he could enjoy a picnic on a day that celebrated freedom.

"Timothy? Is something wrong?"

"No … I mean yes." He put the sandwich down. "I mean … it's just that …" His shoulders slumped.

"What happened, Timothy?"

He turned his face away. He couldn't keep putting it off. Leonard had warned him. Facing her, he held her hand. "Haven, we need to talk."

She immediately recoiled, drawing her hand away. "Did I do something wrong?"

"No, you didn't." God help him. He didn't know what to say. "It's just that … you see …" He drew in a deep breath and exhaled. "It's just that we come from completely different backgrounds in regard to slaveholding."

"And?" Haven straightened her back. Puzzled eyes peered at him from under the brim of her white bonnet. "Why did you choose this particular moment to bring that up?"

"Can't you see the irony of it? The lyrics we sang a little while ago—'the land of the free'—that statement doesn't ring true when one considers that slaves aren't free." There … he'd finally said it. "Am I right?"

"Why, I've never thought about it, Timothy." Haven looked away. After a long, awkward silence, she faced him. Her brows dipped. "Are you an abolitionist or something?"

"Yes, Haven … as a matter of fact, I am." *Never, ever compromise your beliefs that slavery is wrong.* Leonard's counsel spoke to his heart. "I thought you knew."

"How would I know?"

"The first time we met … remember? The woods? The injured boy? You made a promise that you wouldn't speak of it to anyone."

"Yes, I remember now that you mention it. What became of him anyway?"

"I'm not at liberty to discuss the details, but please know that your help that day was invaluable." He hoped the encouragement would soften the blow. "You saved his life."

"I'm so thankful he's all right. I won't ask any more questions, Timothy, but I want you to know that I abhor the mistreatment of slaves. My pa has never abused anyone."

"But it goes far beyond that, Haven. It's a question of morality." How was he supposed to approach this tactfully? Maybe this wasn't the right time. He tilted his head upward as a still small voice whispered otherwise. "It's simply immoral for a human being to own another human being in the same way he owns property."

"So, now you're saying my pa is immoral?" She scooted away and folded her arms. "I don't have to sit here and listen to this. Pa's a good man. He treats his slaves like family, and they love him. Who do you think you are, telling me that my pa is immoral?"

"Haven, please." He hated to see her so upset. "I reckon the issue isn't your pa, but rather you. What about you, Haven?"

"Well … since you asked, I'd have to say it doesn't really matter to me one way or the other. I don't need anyone to do anything for me." Her dark eyes flashed.

"I know you're very independent, Haven." Placing his hand on hers, he gave it a gentle squeeze.

"Don't!" She yanked her hand away and buried both hands in the folds of her skirt.

"Haven, please listen to me. I didn't mean to upset you." With a finger to her chin, he turned her face toward him. When she tried to turn away, he cupped her face. "Look at me, Haven. You're very special, and I'm glad you shared your thoughts. But I need to ask you one more thing. I have to know. Now that I've told you how I feel about slavery, are you willing to continue seeing me?"

Silence.

"Haven?" He waited. "I'm willing, Haven. Are you?"

"Do you condemn my pa?" Her frown—so intense.

"No, Haven, of course not. I denounce the institution of slavery, but I condemn no man. That's not my place. I never said your pa wasn't a good man." He tugged on his collar. Was he making any sense? "Can you accept that?"

"I think so." One hand slid out of hiding, then the other. "I mean, I'd like to try."

"Good." When he touched her hand, she didn't flinch. "That makes me happy."

As the band played the last refrain of "My Old Kentucky Home," Haven's pretty smile replaced that scary frown. "I think it's time for the parade, Timothy."

"You're right. We'd better hurry." He helped her up from the quilt. "And then ice cream with Hank, don't forget."

Haven laughed when Timothy mimicked the way Hank licked his lips as he caught drips of ice cream with his tongue. She loved the way he interacted with her little brother. The boy had taken to Timothy like a bear to honey.

The door to the ice cream parlor flung open, and Harrison bolted over to their table, out of breath. "Haven … Pa said I'd find you in here."

"What's wrong, Harrison?"

"A woman has gone into labor in a carriage close to the gazebo." Harrison pressed his palms to his temples. "I forgot her name already. But I was nearby when I heard Melia Delaney call for help. She couldn't find Mr. Delaney, so she asked me to find you. She needs to get that woman home quickly."

"Alifair!" Haven squeezed Timothy's arm. "She's having the baby!"

"We're on our way." Timothy handed Hank over to Harrison. "Look for Mr. Delaney and tell him Haven and I took his wife and sister home."

The Delaney home

Timothy sat in the armchair next to the grandfather clock. *Tick, tock, tick, tock.* In the empty silence, the rhythmic ticking of the bothersome thing dominated the whole room, growing louder with each swing of the pendulum.

Why wasn't Avery home yet? He twiddled his thumbs, waiting, waiting, waiting.

The front door flew open. "Is it here?" Avery started for the stairs.

"You're not allowed up there." Timothy stood in the parlor entrance, his hands in his pockets. "The baby's not here yet."

"Oh." Avery faced him. "An Independence Day baby. Imagine that."

"Come … let's wait in the parlor." Timothy was glad for the company.

A few minutes later, the lusty cries of a newborn filled the house and sent them both racing toward the staircase landing. They waited like gentlemen at the bottom until Melia appeared at the top, a wrapped bundle in her arms.

"It's a boy, and mother and baby are fine."

Avery parted his lips, but no words came out.

The reality of a new little life was a lot for Timothy to process, too. And to think Haven—the woman who'd captured his heart—had a hand in helping the baby into the world.

Finally, he broke the silence and whacked Avery on the back. "Congratulations, Uncle Avery!"

Melia brought the baby downstairs, allowing them a quick peek.

"He looks like Alifair." Avery made a silly face and touched the baby's chin with his index finger.

"No he doesn't." Melia tilted her head and pursed her lips. "He's the spittin' image of William."

Timothy leaned in for a closer look. "Does he have a name?"

Melia broke into the biggest grin. "Alifair said since today is Uncle Sam's birthday, she's naming him Sam. Samuel William Brooks. It's a fine name."

Timothy clapped his hands. "Perfect! Reckon you could say he's a real 'firecracker' baby!"

Avery slapped his palm to his forehead and groaned. "What a day."

Melia started up the stairs. "I'm taking this Yankee Doodle Dandy back to his mother."

CHAPTER TWENTY

The Delaney home

At ten in the morning, the glaring sun promised another hot and humid August day—not exactly ideal weather for running errands. Timothy closed the door to his apartment, adjusted the rim of his hat to shade his eyes and braced himself for a walk downtown.

The moment his boots hit the brick walk outside his apartment, the loudest baby wail he'd ever heard blasted from the open windows of Avery's house.

"Timothy!" The kitchen door flung open, and Alifair stood there bouncing a very fussy six-week-old Sam. "Are you getting ready to leave?"

"Yes, as a matter of fact I am." He could barely hear his own voice over Sam's. "Not very happy today, huh?"

"No, he's not. I think it's the heat. He can't be hungry because I just fed him. And his diaper's clean." Alifair took to swaying and patting, but nothing soothed Sam's cries. "Could I ask a favor of you?"

"Of course, what is it?" His body tensed. Now, why did he say that?

"I've been trying to write a letter to my friend in New York, and I could use a little help with Sam. I was wondering if you'd mind holding him for me so I can finish it."

"Uh ..." How was he going to get out of this? "Have you tried playing the harpsichord for him?"

"Tried that. Didn't work."

"Well, I reckon I could hold him. How long will it take?"

"Not very long. I'm almost finished." She tried to shush Sam with nuzzles and kisses.

The next thing he knew, a wiggling, wailing infant held him prisoner in the warm, muggy house while Alifair sat down at the maple secretary to finish her letter.

"Nothing wrong with his lungs, huh?" Timothy patted Sam's back.

"Sorry." Alifair smiled like he'd said something funny.

"Where is everybody?" He knew it was Mrs. Perky's day off, but no one else seemed to be around.

"Melia's at the grocer's, and Avery and the girls took the dog for a stroll."

This is not good.

Alifair resumed her writing, glancing at him now and then.

Timothy continued pacing, bouncing and patting. Didn't she say it wouldn't take very long? It was taking forever. Feeling a little dizzy from the ringing in his ears, he gently braced Sam at his shoulder, pushed aside Alifair's copy of *Godey's Lady's Book*, and sat down on the chaise.

Slumping back against the cushion, he reclined with one leg extended straight out and one foot planted on the floor. With Sam tummy-side-down against his chest, he caressed the infant's back. Just like that, the cries diminished into weak mewls, and Sam fell fast asleep.

Alifair looked up from her writing. "Amazing. You're a natural, Timothy."

Hesitant to move for fear of disturbing Sam, he kept his gaze still. But he could see Alifair from the corner of his eye. After what seemed like an eternity, he saw her fold the letter, slide it into an envelope, and press a seal on the flap.

Then she got up. But for some reason, she just stood there, torturing him with her eyes while he lay there helpless on the chaise with her sleeping baby snuggled against his chest.

"He's sound asleep." How was he supposed to get up without waking Sam?

Alifair tiptoed quietly toward him. "I know." Her whisper voice sounded a little too flirtatious.

Trapped. How on earth had he gotten into this predicament? What if Avery walked in right now? Or Melia? He swallowed the thick lump lodged in his throat. Such a compromising situation. Alifair should never have asked him to help with Sam. She could have waited until Melia got back. His cheeks burned.

As she stood there looking down at him with her skirts pressed right up against the chaise by his leg, it suddenly dawned on him that he'd never seen her in a fitted dress. A simple, everyday tarlatan, but she looked good in it. All that pregnancy weight had certainly vanished.

Her auburn hair shone with radiance in the sunlight that streamed through the window. She held his gaze with those seagreen eyes that sparkled like glass.

Lord, have mercy.

He held his breath as Alifair slipped her fingers under little Sam's belly, and his abdomen tightened at the touch of her hands. As soon as she'd lifted the infant away, Timothy sat upright, watching her place Sam in the cradle and pat his back.

Maybe if he tiptoed across the room while she had her back to him, he could make it to the front door. Worth a try.

But Alifair's footsteps caught up with him.

"Timothy?" Her voice—almost seductive. "Thank you."

"You're welcome. Glad I could help." He'd made it to the foyer. Was she searching his eyes? Backing away, he reached for his hat on the hall tree, mystified by her enchanting smile.

"Would you please mail the letter for me while you're downtown?" Her flawless skin glistened in the humidity.

"I'd be happy to." He took the letter. As soon as he could get it mailed and finish his errands, he'd be on his way to see

Haven.

"Wait." She snatched the letter from him. "I forgot the postage. Be right back."

Watching her as she climbed the stairs, he turned his head away when she looked back over her shoulder. That alluring expression of hers trifled with his thoughts. Surely he was imagining things.

He opened the front door all the way and waited right there until she returned. The sweet scent of jasmine wafted past his nostrils as soon as she reappeared on the stairs, letter in hand. He stayed put at the opened door, keeping one foot on the threshold.

"Here it is, Timothy—stamped, scented and sealed."

Timothy slid the letter into the inner pocket of his waistcoat. "I'll see that it gets mailed." He doffed his hat, taking one step out the door.

"Are you going to see *her* today?"

Timothy froze. "Her?" Another lump. Another gulp.

"That nurse."

Was Alifair jealous?

"Uh … yes, I am. After I'm done with my errands."

He'd been looking forward to spending time with Haven, though it seemed they'd done nothing but argue since Independence Day. Did Alifair know about that?

"Wh-why do you ask?"

"Just wondered." Alifair flicked her gaze to his hand on the doorknob. "Thank you for helping me, Timothy. You were wonderful with Sam." She took a step closer.

He took a step back. "You're wel—" His voice did that croaking thing again. "You're welcome … again."

Their eyes locked, creating a mesmerizing effect. God help him, he had to walk away. Fast. The sound of a carriage passing by the house undid the spell.

He tripped over the threshold. "Oops … sorry."

Alifair giggled as the door closed. "Good-bye, Timothy."

He drew a deep breath and never looked back.

&

Haven Hill Farm

Sweat trickled down Haven's face. She wiped it away with a hanky. A cool breeze drifted in from Lake Harmony, and she lifted her face to catch it. For the past hour, she'd been trying to strike up a conversation with Sapphire while helping the girl pull weeds by the lakeshore.

As she knelt beside Sapphire in one of the gardens, pruning and pulling weeds and tossing them into a basket, Sapphire's mother and sisters worked in other gardens within her view. Every now and then Haven caught a stony-faced Anna keeping a watchful eye on Sapphire.

Haven slipped the hanky back into her sleeve. "Sapphire, why don't we take a break for a few minutes? I'd really enjoy a walk with you so we can chat for a while. What do you say?"

"I not feel like walking, Miz Haven." Sapphire yanked on a stubborn weed.

"That's fine. I understand. But I sure do miss the way we used to laugh together." Haven thrust a spade deep into the earth. "You're not sick anymore, are you?"

"No, Miz Haven, I not sick no more." Sapphire kept her gaze downward.

"Got your appetite back?"

Sapphire clenched a weed in her hand. "Yes, Miz Haven. I eat good." She gave the weed a forceful toss, missing the basket.

Haven picked up the stray weed. "That's good, Sapphire, but you don't seem very happy. I miss your pretty smile. I wish you'd talk to me."

Saying nothing, Sapphire repositioned her wide-brimmed straw hat then yanked another weed.

"Sapphire?" Haven picked up the shears and pruned a dead blossom.

"I happy, Miz Haven." Sapphire sounded agitated.

"If you say so, sweetie." At least she'd tried.

Haven pushed herself up to her feet and swiped her hands together several times, removing as much soil as possible. She didn't have much time to get cleaned up before Timothy arrived. "I have to get back to the house now, Sapphire. Maybe we can talk again another day."

"Good-bye, Miz Haven."

Haven took in the view of the floral landscape around the lake. The hills dotted with deep red, late-blooming azaleas, the magnolia trees in bloom, dahlias everywhere—all because Sapphire's family worked so hard. She caught Anna looking her way. Had Anna been watching her the whole time?

Haven untied her horse, taking note of the dirt under her fingernails. She couldn't let Timothy see her hands looking like that. She rode the mare fast up the hill to the house. The wind felt good against her sweaty face.

If only she and Timothy wouldn't argue today. Men could be so remarkably pigheaded sometimes.

Timothy rapped on the front door of the mansion, and the house servant invited him to step inside. His breath caught when he saw Haven waiting for him in the grand hall—not the least bit sullied by the oppressive heat.

"Hello, Timothy." With a carefree air, Haven extended her hand for a kiss.

His skin prickled at her touch. "You look beautiful." He lifted her hand to his lips only to be taken aback when she snatched it away. "What's wrong?"

"Timothy." Her voice deepened with a throaty timbre. "Might I have a word with you outside on the lawn, please?"

He backed away, impaled by her scowl. What on earth just happened? In a matter of seconds and with no explanation, he stood face to face with her on the lawn where he found himself on the receiving end of a flurry of verbal daggers.

"How dare you come to charm me after you've … you've …" Haven sucked in an abnormal amount of air and held it. Suddenly, she spewed out an endless string of accusations against him.

"What?" His brows shot up, and his voice took on a higher pitch. "What did I do? I don't understand."

"Don't play innocent with me, you … you …" She pointed her finger straight at his face, shaking it with every "don't" and every "you" and every other angry word that escaped her lips.

"What has gotten into you?" He threw his hands up over his head in surrender and did a half-turn away from her. This was ridiculous.

She continued to rant. "All those letters saying how you thought of only me all the time. And now this!"

"And now what? I meant every word of—"

"Don't lie to me, Timothy Locker! Do you think I'm foolish enough to believe you now?"

"Now? Haven, I don't understand."

She stomped her foot. Twice. "It certainly takes a lot of nerve for a fellow to come calling on a lady straight out of the arms of another woman!"

"What?" He widened his eyes. "How did you get such a preposterous notion as that?" His mind flashed back to Alifair. Sure, he'd been tempted. But … how in the world …?

"There's nothing wrong with my sense of smell, Reverend Locker." Haven's incendiary temper added several degrees to the already sultry day. "There's no mistaking that jasmine scent all over your waistcoat. I know who wears that fragrance. You've been in the embrace of Alifair Brooks!"

"No, Haven, you've got it all wrong." He slapped his hands to his cheeks in disbelief. It all made sense now. How could he have been so ignorant as to put that scented letter in his pocket?

"I'm no fool, sir. Why else would your clothing reek of her perfume? I'll thank you to please leave. I'll not be lied to and trifled with." Her eyes misting, she walked away.

"Haven, please. There's a perfectly logical explanation for this." On second thought, he wasn't sure he'd believe his story either.

Haven turned and faced him, glaring.

"Please … listen to me." He touched her arm, flinching when she smacked his hand away. "Let me explain."

"I'm waiting." Her arms locked into a fold, and her foot tapped like a thumping rabbit on the grass.

"You see … Alifair asked me to mail a letter for her, and I carried the letter in my waistcoat. I never dreamed that—"

"Well, aren't you 'Mr. Johnny-on-the-spot'? How quickly you concocted that tale!"

"Haven!"

"Please go! Hurry back to Mrs. Brooks. Maybe she has another letter for you to mail." This time Haven ran, leaving him alone on the lawn.

Now what was he going to do? He couldn't go back to Avery's house. How humiliating would that be? He certainly didn't want to be around Alifair. In fact, he didn't want to be around people at all.

He untied Danny Boy and prepared the horse for a long ride in the woods. Yes, the woods. He'd spend the day with God. They had some talking to do—he and God. He tore off the offensive waistcoat and hurled it to the back of the rig before heading out.

Why had Alifair asked him to mail that letter?

She did that on purpose!

The Trumbeaux Estate

Twilight had settled in around Ruth's tiny cottage. Micah propped himself up on one elbow, leering at his grinning wife beside him on the bed.

Ruth giggled as she met his gaze.

"For certain?" He searched her eyes. "Ain't no chance you be mistaken?"

"Sure as the sun rise ever' morning and set ever' evening." She tapped on his nose.

Micah let his head fall back onto the pillow. He'd never been more stupefied in his life.

Ruth propped herself up on her elbow and leaned over him. "Well, husband, how you feel about being a daddy?"

Slipping his hand behind her head, he pulled her face to his and kissed her lips. As she eased away, he stroked her cheek. "I the happiest man in the whole world, Ruth." One more kiss. Long. Passionate. Overflowing with irrepressible love.

"You're the first one to know, Micah." She rested her head on his chest.

"When this baby gonna get here?" If only he could stay the night so they could be together like a real family—Ruth, their unborn child, and himself. But he had to get back to the Roberts farm before Miz Cilla found out Massa had given him a pass.

"I figure it be February, just over six months." With her finger, she tenderly traced the line of a scar on Micah's side. "This child gonna be born free."

CHAPTER TWENTY-ONE

Haven Hill Farm

A month of separation and exchange of missives had passed, and Haven still felt the pangs of remorse over what she'd done to Timothy. If only she hadn't been so irrational—sending him away in a fit of rage over something she later realized never happened.

She collapsed across her bed, exhausted from a morning out with Ma. They'd just gotten home from a luncheon hosted by Jeannette Trumbeaux for the September meeting of the Orphan Society of Lexington. Time for her Saturday nap.

Ma opened her door a crack and peeked in. "You still awake?"

"Yes, Ma. Come on in." Haven rolled over on her side. "I thought I'd catch a few winks before Timothy arrives."

"Good idea. I'm glad you two made up. I just wanted to thank you for going with me to the meeting. I'm pleased the ladies voted to have the Holiday Charity Ball at the Phoenix Hotel."

"Me, too. It was unanimous." Haven's head fell back on her pillow. "I can't wait until November!"

"I'll leave you to your beauty rest." Ma kissed her cheek

and left the room.

Closing her eyes, Haven fancied herself dancing the evening away—a princess with her handsome prince in their magical kingdom. Timothy. Goosebumps sprouted across her arms like itty bitty pearls as his image appeared majestically on the back of her eyelids.

Restless, she sat up in bed, propping several pillows behind her, and gathered up a small bundle of Timothy's missives from her bedside table. A thin scarlet ribbon held them together.

She ran her finger across the name on the return address and plopped back onto her pillow. "Timothy Locker"—her arms prickled again at the mere whisper of his name. With a wistful sigh, she slid the latest missive from the stack and began to read:

My dearest Haven,

Your letter came to me as healing oil, a balm of Gilead, for I'd felt within me a wasting away of my spirit since we last parted. How grateful I am that you reconsidered your allegation in regard to a certain female acquaintance. I feared I'd lost your favor forever, but I've since discovered the sweetest comfort knowing I'll see you again. Haven, you possess all the desirable attributes of Christian character and, despite our differing backgrounds, I've concluded in my heart that it's you with whom I long to pursue a lasting relationship. Unless I hear from you otherwise, I will arrive in the late afternoon of the third of September.

All my love,
Timothy

"I'm sorry, Timothy." Haven spoke to the parchment as if it could hear. With his letter in her hand, she rolled over and stared out the window, amused by the playful antics of two chipmunks frolicking on her balcony. Her eyes grew heavy. Still time for a short nap.

Wham! A downstairs door slammed.

Haven bolted upright as the sound of heavy footsteps echoed through the house.

"Becky! Haven!" Pa's gravelly voice bellowed up the stairs. "Harrison! Howard!"

Why was Pa angry? She rolled out of bed and crammed Timothy's letter back in the drawer. Frantic, she slipped into her house shoes and flew out the door, catching up with Ma at the top of the stairs. They hurried down together.

Harrison and Howard emerged from the parlor, headed toward Pa.

Pa cleared the house of everyone but the Haywood family, and he made Hank's mammy, Ella, take Hank outside. What had Pa so riled?

"This got something to do with Harley, Pa?" Howard pushed his spectacles up.

"No, nothing to do with Harley. It's Sapphire. I was riding down by the lake when I noticed her carrying a bucket of water. She turned away immediately, but there's no mistaking what I saw."

Haven's throat tightened. "Wh-what did you see, Pa?"

"I'm afraid there's a woods colt on the way. And soon!" Pa turned his fiery eyes on Haven. "You know anything about this?"

"No, Pa. I didn't know." Haven remembered that day in August when Sapphire refused to take a walk with her. The girl must have been trying to hide her belly.

Pa faced Harrison and Howard. "Boys, take the carryall and bring Sapphire back here with her parents. I won't tolerate that kind of behavior, and I'm gonna get to the bottom of this." Pa turned to Ma. "Becky, you and Haven go wait in the parlor."

About thirty minutes later, Harrison and Howard returned with Elias and his visibly shaken wife and daughter. No doubt about it ... Sapphire was pregnant.

The two families faced each other—Pa at the forefront of his and a trembling Sapphire forced to step forward in front of her parents. Haven wanted so badly to wrap the girl in her arms.

"Sapphire!" Pa spoke a little too sternly, sending a shiver through Haven. "How long did you expect to hide your shame?"

The girl gave no response. She kept her head bowed.

"Sapphire, answer me!" Pa's thunderous voice made them all jump.

"Dunno, Massa."

"Who's the father?" Pa waited. "Confound it, Sapphire, I asked you a question. You cannot escape the judgment of Almighty God, you promiscuous harlot! You must repent. Now answer me!"

In silence, Sapphire hung her head, but Anna glared, narrow-eyed, head held high. She looked as though a rushing river of emotion would explode from within her at any moment. Haven had never seen Anna like that.

"Sapphire, I'm trying to stay calm. Now tell me who you've been with. Was it one of Noah's boys? Some buck from another farm?"

Sapphire's lips quivered.

"Answer me!"

Elias put his hand on his daughter's shoulder. "You gots to tell Massa now he know you with child. The truth be found out soon enough."

Sapphire lifted her head. "It … it …" A tear trickled down her cheek.

"Out with it, girl!"

Brushing her hand over her wet cheek, Sapphire looked right at Pa. "It Massa Harley, suh. He rape me."

"You lie! You little wench!" Pa lifted his hand to strike her, but Harrison grabbed his arm. Struggling to break loose, Pa continued his rant. "You'll burn in hell! I'll have Edwards take you to be whipped!"

"No, Pa!" Haven shrilled so high it scratched her throat.

"Please, Pa, no!"

"Elias!" Pa jerked his arm free of Harrison's grip. "What do you have to say about this?"

"It true, Massa." Trembling, Elias took a step forward. "Massa Harley, he powerful drunk that night of the fire. Yessuh, Massa, he grab Sapphie when she comin' back from the outhouse—it be after midnight—and he take her into that barn where he be put up for the night."

"Are you just taking Sapphire's word for it?"

"Yessuh. He tear her dressing gown." Elias pulled a scrap of fabric from his pocket and held it out for all to see. "I be keeping it all this time."

"That rag is just trash." Pa swatted at the scrap with a flick of his wrist. "Don't mean a thing."

"He's telling the truth, Pa." Harrison took the scrap from Elias. "I saw this in the barn when Haven and I rode out there the morning after the fire."

"Me, too, Pa." Tears swam in Haven's eyes as she took the cloth from Harrison. "I remember picking it up, and I thought Harley had torn his own shirt. The barn was a ramshackle mess. It all makes sense now."

"Take them home, boys. I've heard enough." Pa waved his hand with a snap and headed for the door. "I need to think."

Haven ran to her room. She tried cleaning her eyes, but the tears kept coming, and she finally gave up. Her eyes were already too puffy, and Timothy could arrive any minute. Leaning over her wash basin, she threw up. Why did things always go wrong?

She had to get out of the house, away from her family. Maybe if she went out to the lane to wait for Timothy there, she could avoid Pa.

Timothy pulled his rig into the lane of Haven Hill, and his heart did all those crazy things like the first time he'd called on Haven. Wait … was that her running toward him? He grinned and jumped down, rushing to meet her.

"What's this? You're shaking like a leaf." He lifted her

chin. "Haven, you've been crying."

She threw herself at him, wrapped her arms around his neck, and buried her head against his chest. "I got your letter. I'm so glad you came." As she pulled away, his hands slid down her arms. "Oh, Timothy, it's been dreadful here."

He drew her into another embrace. "Come, let's take a ride and you can tell me all about it."

Haven spilled the whole sordid tale. As they jaunted down the lane, she steered him away from the house and in the opposite direction of the lake. No wonder she wanted to avoid everyone.

Under a canopy of honey locust branches, he drove along the winding lane, waiting for Haven to calm down. What else could he do? While shadows dappled with sunlight played among the leaves, he held her close with his arm around her shoulder.

How could the picturesque beauty of Haven Hill's rolling bluegrass pastures abide such turmoil? How could the mares graze and the young foals nurse? What stark contrast.

Haven lifted her head for a moment and smiled. It took his breath away. The love in his heart for this woman frightened him.

"Miz Haven! Massa Timothy!" The frantic voice startled them from behind.

Timothy brought the rig to a stop as Noah's boy raced toward them on horseback.

"Miz Haven! Oh, Lawd o' mercy!"

"Sammy!" Haven squeezed Timothy's hand. "What happened?"

"Oh, Miz Haven, you gotta come quick! It that slave woman, Mary, from the Weaver farm. She need tendin' to right quick. She be beaten bad. Come see, Miz Haven."

"Where, Sammy? Where's Mary?" Timothy wondered how much more Haven could endure.

"Behind you house, Miz Haven." Sammy pointed. "Her boy, he drag her over the field on a cowhide. Jeb Weaver, he done beat her mightily, and the blood run till she faint. Her boy say Weaver deep into the moonshine, and he done pass out. Hurry, Miz Haven!"

Timothy flicked the reins. "We'll follow you, Sammy." He pressed Danny Boy onward to keep up.

The scene in the yard by the slave entrance of the mansion tore at his heart. He'd witnessed a lot of abuse cases, and this ranked among the worst. A young mother, naked from the waist up and covered with a blood-soaked sheet, lay unconscious on the makeshift stretcher jury-rigged by her son. The boy stood off to the side, watching.

Nearby, on the back steps, the woman's little girl sucked her thumb as Molly rocked and coddled her.

"Molly, take the child into the house." Haven knelt down by the other women to examine Mary's wounds. "This is worse than the last time."

"The last time?" Timothy fell to his knees next to Haven. "You mean this has happened before?" Anger seethed from every pore of his skin. "May God have mercy on the monster that did this."

Haven sluiced water from a bucket over some cloths. "Last time it was because she accidentally scorched his shirt with an iron."

The young boy inched a little closer. "This time Massa not like the stew she make. He throw it to the floor and make her clean it up while he go after the whip. Then he into his whisky and beats on my mama." The boy sobbed and wiped his eyes. "He start tearin' at her clothes and he beats her some more. Massa Weaver … he crazy."

Frank rode up on horseback with Harrison and Howard right behind him. "What's going on here?" He dismounted and walked toward Haven.

Haven glanced at her pa then continued with the compresses. "Jeb Weaver beat Mary again, Pa. She's unconscious."

Frank stood behind Haven, peering at Mary. "Why, that good-for-nothin', worthless heap of manure. Looks bad. She gonna make it?"

"Don't know, Pa. She's lost a lot of blood."

Timothy got up and faced Frank. "I know some folks who can help her. I can take her there."

"All right … sounds good. Take her, get her mended and bring her back." Frank shot a fleeting glance toward the little boy. "I'll worry about getting her and the children back over to Jeb's sometime tomorrow. I doubt he'll be comin' to before then anyway."

"No!" Timothy took a step closer to Frank, stopping a mere six inches from his frizzy red beard. "I'll not allow them to go back to that beast!"

Frank threw his shoulders back and stiffened his spine. "Just who gave you the authority to make a decision like that? And where do you think they're gonna go? They can't stay here. Weaver'll have the law on us like a pack o' wolves."

Timothy looked down at Haven, but she kept working on Mary's wounds. He turned back to Frank and looked him square in the eye. "My God-given conscience won't allow me to return this helpless woman to such a sorry excuse of a man. Look at her, will ya?"

"Please, Pa! She's running out of time!" Haven's plea revealed her caring heart.

Timothy kept his eyes riveted on Frank. How could there possibly be any question about this?

Frank glanced at Harrison, whose face reflected compassion for Mary. He turned back to face Timothy. "Take her then!" His brackish voice lacked any hint of compassion. "And take the children. Do with them as you will. I wash my hands of it all." He waggled a finger at his slaves. "Not one word of this to anyone—ever! Do I make myself clear?"

Big Joe and Noah helped Timothy lift Mary into his rig after Haven finished applying the last compress.

Timothy touched Haven's arm. "I could use your help. Will you go with me?"

Haven worried her lip, snapping her gaze to her pa.

"She'll do no such thing!" Frank flashed a stern look to his daughter, mounted his horse and rode off, spurring the horse into a full gallop.

"Haven?" Timothy hoped she'd exercise some of that independent determination. He needed her to stand with him now.

"I can't go." Haven walked over to Harrison, still crying. "I've done all I can do."

"Very well." A stinging sensation burned Timothy's cheeks. "I thought you cared more than that."

Harrison put an arm around his sister's shoulder. "She does care. But Pa said—"

"She's old enough to make her own decisions!" Timothy shouted louder than he'd intended.

"That *is* my decision, Timothy!"

Why was he wasting time arguing with these people? Maybe Haven did have some of her pa in her. Why had he thought she was ready? He'd been such a fool.

"I'm really sorry to hear that, Haven." Mustering every ounce of restraint he could, he took a step closer to Harrison. "I need another horse, please. I have a double hitch—just get me another horse."

Once everything was ready, Timothy climbed into the rig and shot one last disappointed look to Haven. Clearly, she cared about Mary, but Frank was a stubborn, confused man.

Haven. His heart ached for her.

CHAPTER TWENTY-TWO

The road to Shaker Village

For fifteen agonizing minutes, Timothy drove slowly, trying to keep Mary from being jostled about before the Shakers could treat her wounds.

The image of Haven's face when she said she couldn't go with him lingered in his mind. He glanced over his shoulder at the young boy sitting next to his mother and the little girl curled up sleeping.

Heavy clatter from a horse gaining on him from behind sent a panic creeping into his bones. He'd purposely not used the secret trap because of Mary's condition, nor could he risk going any faster. God help him. Timothy's stomach twisted into a knot.

"Timothy! Wait!"

Two voices—male and female.

Timothy slowed the rig to a stop as the horse, bearing two riders, halted beside him. If his heart pounded any harder, it would surely burst through his chest.

"I'm going with you." Haven … thank the Lord. With Harrison's help, she slid off the saddle and rushed to the rig.

Timothy leaned over and stretched out his arm to pull her up beside him. No time for formalities. "This means more to me than you can imagine, Haven."

Harrison handed over Haven's medical bag. "I'm sorry. You're absolutely right about everything you said. Pa has blinders on or something. I just don't understand him sometimes." He bade them farewell and rode off.

Haven crawled to the back with Mary. "She's still breathing."

"Keep praying." Relieved, Timothy clicked to the team.

Haven comforted the boy and tended to Mary. She'd brought fresh cloths to change the blood-soaked dressings. "Where are you taking them, Timothy?"

"To Shaker Village. Haven, we need to talk."

"All right, Timothy." She finished putting the clean dressings on Mary then crawled up into the seat beside him.

"I have something important to tell you, Haven." Was this the right time to tell her everything?

"I think I've figured it out, Timothy."

He lifted a silent prayer, took a deep breath then shared the secrets of the Underground Railroad with Haven. Did she really understand the tremendous challenge that lay before them? Would she be able to separate her upbringing from her new awakening?

The evils of slavery were plentiful. Later that very night, in spite of the medical care of the Shakers, Mary died, and Timothy and Haven witnessed together the heartbreak of the little boy and girl who lost their mother.

Heavy-hearted, they left the children there until Timothy could return to transport them north. What a comfort to have Haven by his side on this mission. Her love and support made all the difference in the world.

As they headed back to Haven Hill, the songs of crickets and katydids chirping in the thickets filled the balmy September night. He wished he didn't have to take Haven back to her family, especially after everything she'd told him happened that day and what he'd witnessed of her pa's fiery temper.

If only he could whisk her away and marry her right now.

❧

Haven Hill Farm

October had been the longest month. Timothy had been riding the circuit and leading revivals, and Haven hadn't seen him for weeks. She'd been miserable without him.

He'd picked her up at Dr. Wright's office to take her home after work, and here they were, back at Haven Hill. Together at last. She could hardly take her eyes off him.

"I hope you know how hard it was for me to concentrate at the office today knowing you were in town." She playfully tugged on his sleeve as Danny Boy ambled along the lane up to the house.

Timothy peered down at her from the corner of his eye, flashing a quirky smile. "Would you believe I was tempted to feign illness just so I could come see you at the office?"

He could be so funny sometimes. One of many reasons to love this man.

The clippety-clop of Danny Boy's hooves kept time with the rolling wheels of the rig. About halfway up the hill, Haven remembered a burning question she'd had on her mind all week regarding a big news story.

"Timothy, I've been wondering … were you involved in that raid with John Brown on Harpers Ferry?"

"No, but I did know two of the men. When I learned of Brown's plan to attack a federal arsenal, I finished my circuit and came straight here. And that's the truth, Haven."

"I believe you, Timothy. It's just that earlier this week, when we heard about some abolitionist who'd assembled a group of men and arms for a raid at Harpers Ferry—something about a slave rebellion—I thought about you."

"I understand, Haven."

"And then I got your letter postmarked from Virginia and all. You were so close to it."

"I would have been concerned, too, if I were you. I'm just

thankful I had enough sense to stay away from it."

"I know. I won't say another word, but Pa's a little suspicious, as you can imagine." She leaned in closer to him.

"I'm not surprised." He slipped his arm across her shoulders and gave her a quick squeeze before bringing the rig to a stop. He gazed up the hill. "Look at your family's house up there. I don't think I've ever seen it looking so gorgeous."

"It is beautiful, isn't it? I love this time of year." Haven took in the scenery as the afternoon sun spilled its light on the colorful trees, highlighting the vibrant red and gold hues of the autumn leaves. Busy woodland critters scurried from tree to tree, chattering noisily as they foraged for their winter store.

Closing her eyes, she breathed in the crisp fall air, but the warmth of Timothy's breath suddenly caressed her cheek. She opened her eyes and there he was, inches from her face. She melted into his embrace as his lips found hers for their first lovers' kiss.

For the next few moments, she danced on a cloud with her handsome prince. Nothing else in the world mattered.

Timothy eased away and looked all around. "It's so quiet around here."

She nestled her cheek against his chest, smiling because his heart was beating so fast. "I don't think anyone saw us, if that's what you're worried about."

"No, that's not it." He kissed her forehead. "Look around. There's not a soul in sight."

"You're right. A little too quiet if you ask me. Something must be—"

"No-o-o!" A woman's scream echoed from up the hill, somewhere close to the house, but she couldn't see anyone.

"It must have come from the far side." Timothy flicked the reins and raced toward the house.

As they neared the top of the hill, a sided wagon suddenly appeared, coming right at them. Had something happened to Ma? Harmony? Where was everybody?

Timothy pulled over to let the wagon pass. "That's a police wagon." He flicked the reins again.

"No, no, no!" Tears spilled down her cheeks. "I'm so sorry, Timothy."

A gathering of slaves had assembled at the side of the house. Her family was there, too. A woman wailed from somewhere within the crowd.

Haven narrowed her eyes. Anna—struggling to break free from the restraining clutches of Big Joe and Noah. What happened to her?

Noah's boys held little Andy's arms as he fought them, kicking and screaming. "Bring back my pa!"

"Lord, have mercy. No!" Haven stood up as soon as Timothy stopped the rig. "Not Elias. It can't be!"

"Surely not." Timothy helped her down from the rig.

Harrison walked over to them, his horse in tow. "Another crazy day, sis."

Haven pointed toward the slaves. "Why is Anna crying, and why is Andy calling for his pa?"

"Harley came home." Harrison's brusque answer confused her even more.

"Who was in the police wagon?"

"Elias."

"I don't understand, Harrison." She glanced over at Anna.

Timothy took Haven's hand. "I'm not following this either."

"I don't know where to begin." Harrison rubbed the back of his neck. "Edwards—that's our overseer here," he said to Timothy, "he was riding by the old tool shed this afternoon and heard a man calling for help from inside." Harrison's eyes darted back and forth between her and Timothy. "So he went in and found Harley on the ground, all bloodied and bruised with two big gashes in his head. He'd been left for dead, but we think he's gonna make it."

Timothy's brows knit. "So you think Elias attacked Harley because of what he did to Sapphire?"

"Absolutely. No one else has a motive like that." Harrison

faced Haven. "So Pa had the sheriff arrest him."

"Sweet, gentle Elias?" Haven couldn't imagine anything more out of character for him.

"I know." Harrison lifted his hat and raked his fingers through his hair. "Hard to believe."

"How's Ma? Is Howard with her?" Haven squeezed Timothy's hand as she braced for Harrison's answer.

"Ma's in a bad way. Pa and Harmony are with her." Harrison gave a tug on his horse's rope. "Howard's not home from Louisville yet. He sent a telegram saying he'd be home later."

Haven's eyes drifted to the pathetic scene at the side of the house where Anna and Andy sat on the grass, sobbing.

"I'm really worried about Pa, too." Harrison hooked a thumb on his pants pocket. "I don't like the changes in his behavior. It's frightening."

"What did he do now?" Did she really want to know?

"Well, sis … he attacked Elias when Edwards brought him to the house. We had to pull him off."

"Oh no!" Haven slumped into Timothy's arms. "Please, no."

"He's calmed down now. Been waitin' for you to get home to sit with Ma so he can go see Harley at the hospital." Harrison mounted his roan-coated horse and turned the animal sideways. "I'm headin' out to the shed. Gonna have a look around."

Haven leaned on Timothy as they walked up the front steps, through the great hall, and up the staircase to her parents' bedroom. She went inside, but Timothy waited in the hall by the door.

"Thank God you're here." Pa rushed over to her, stopping before she could give him a hug. "What's *he* doing here?" He flashed a scowl at Timothy.

"Timothy brought me home, Pa, to visit for the evening."

Harmony got up from her chair by Ma's bed and marched across the room. Her glare impaled Haven. "It's about time you got home! Ma needs your help. Where's her laudanum?"

"I'll get it for her." Haven gritted her teeth. *Patience.* She walked to the medicine chest, unlocked it and pulled out the coveted solution. Sitting next to the bed, she stroked Ma's hair. "Ma, please don't cry. I've got your medicine. All right?"

As soon as Ma fell asleep, Pa kissed Ma's forehead then started for the door with Harmony right behind him. Haven followed them, but Pa turned to face her. "I'm going to the hospital. Check on your ma now and then. She'll probably sleep through till morning."

When they stepped out into the hall, Harmony huffed away to the stairs, and Pa confronted Timothy. Scowling, he stood ramrod straight. "It seems you've brought a wretched curse upon my house, young man!"

"Pa!" Haven raced to Timothy's side. "How can you say such a thing?"

"Every time he comes near here, terrible things happen."

Timothy eyeballed her pa. "With all due respect, sir, I believe it's the other way around."

Haven frowned. "He's right, Pa."

Pa rubbed his temples and shook his head. "Sorry. Don't know what got into me. I must get to the hospital now."

"It's all right, Frank. I understand."

Haven and Timothy followed Pa down the staircase. As soon as they reached the grand hall, the front door opened, and Harrison burst in.

"Pa, I think you need to take a look at this." Harrison paused to catch his breath.

"Look at what, son?"

"I just came from the tool shed where Edwards found Harley today. I was walking around with a lantern when I kicked up some straw and found these." He reached in his pocket and pulled out a mangled mess of metal and broken glass speckled with dried blood.

Haven gasped, throwing her hands over her mouth.

Pa leaned in for a closer look. "Those look like Howard's spectacles. But that's impossible. He's not even here."

"I know, Pa, but that doesn't mean he wasn't here during

the night." Harrison handed the spectacles to Haven. "What do you think, sis?"

"They sure look like Howard's." She handed them back to Harrison. "But why would he scuffle with Harley?"

"Wait a minute … hold everything." Timothy crossed his arms. "Are you saying Elias probably didn't do it after all?"

Harrison nodded his head. "That could very well be the case."

"Then you need to get him out of that jail immediately!" Timothy turned to Pa. "I've seen the way they treat slaves in jail."

"Come on, Pa." Harrison started for the door. "Let's get to the jail before it's too late. Timothy, you come with us. We'll go to the hospital after we get Elias out."

Before Haven could blink an eye, Timothy kissed her forehead, and the three men rushed out the door. She walked over to the staircase and collapsed on the bottom step. What was wrong with her family? Why Howard? How could he? She needed another good cry, but she had to get back upstairs with Ma.

Why was God allowing her family to fall apart like this?

Outside a Lexington hospital

Timothy waited outside in the wagon with Elias while Frank and Harrison went in to see Harley. They'd posted bail until the charges against Elias could be dropped.

"How quickly people jump to conclusions. Right, Elias?" Timothy remembered his own habit of doing the same.

"I thank the Good Lord for leading Massa Harrison to those spectacles in time." Elias had the most wonderful, forgiving heart.

"Me, too. And since Frank probably won't apologize, I apologize for him."

"Oh, I not blame Massa. I know how things look." Elias

also possessed great wisdom.

Timothy smiled and gave him a slap on the knee.

Almost an hour went by before Frank and Harrison returned to the wagon. They both wore solemn faces. Had Harley told them what happened?

Timothy hopped down so they could talk. "How's Harley?"

"He was awake when we walked into his room." Harrison undid the tether ropes as he spoke. "He had a difficult time speaking, but he told us everything. I was right—it was Howard."

"Where do you think Howard is now?" Timothy had only met Howard once, and he'd never met Harley at all.

Frank shrugged. "We don't know. I'm not too worried about him, though. Howard knows how to take care of himself."

"Did Harley tell you what the scuffle was about?" Timothy wondered how Haven's siblings could have such different personalities.

Frank adjusted the harnesses. "He said Howard was angry with him for coming home drunk, and he was tired of Harley's lack of respect for their ma. Harley confessed he took the first swing at Howard, and that's how it all got physical."

Harrison tossed the ropes in the wagon. "He said Howard started yelling at him about what he did to Sapphire, too. Apparently, things escalated from there."

Frank climbed up to the driver's seat. "He says he feels bad about his behavior and wants to get help. That should make his ma happy."

Timothy puffed his cheeks and put a hand to Harrison's shoulder. "At least something good came out of all this."

Picking up the reins, Frank looked down at Timothy and Harrison. "Hop in, boys. Let's go home."

CHAPTER TWENTY-THREE

Downtown Louisville

Haven drew a deep breath of cool, crisp November air as the scent of fallen leaves filled her nostrils. Perfect weather for traveling and sightseeing. She could barely contain her excitement. Louisville … what a fine city. She squeezed Timothy's arm and gazed out the small window of a closed cab.

Larkin and Harmony sat facing her and Timothy from across the cab. Larkin had invited them to visit as long as they brought Harmony with them.

"Louisville is really growing." Haven found the bustling city more fascinating than she'd imagined. Had it been that many years since she'd been there? "My, how it's changed."

"I thought so, too." Harmony peered out the window on her side of the cab. "I was amazed at the changes when I came back here for the first time after my return from London."

"It's a beautiful riverfront town." Larkin eased back into his seat and pulled Harmony closer to him. "I really like living here—especially when Harmony comes to see me."

"Do you think you'll stay in Louisville, then?" Timothy's interest in Larkin's plans amused Haven. She'd never told

Timothy how she used to loathe the man.

"I'm almost certain I will." As the cab continued along Second Street, Larkin cast a dove-eyed glance at Harmony. That silly expression rather softened his rugged, western complexion.

The driver turned the corner onto Main Street, and Haven nearly sprung from her seat. "There's the Galt House Hotel!" She leaned back so Timothy could see. "Isn't it grand?"

Timothy chuckled. "Indeed, it is."

The cab came to a stop in front of the Louisville Hotel, and Larkin rose from his seat. "This is where we get out." He took Harmony by the hand. "I made reservations for us to eat dinner here."

While Larkin paid the hackman, Timothy whispered in Haven's ear. "This must be why Larkin insisted that I borrow this dandy suit today."

Haven tapped his nose. He could be so cute sometimes. "I think so."

A waiter seated them at a table for four near the back of the dining hall and placed a menu in front of each guest. He bowed and left their table, returning a few minutes later with pencil in hand. "Are you ready to order?"

Larkin spoke first. "My lady and I love the salmon here. We'll have the baked salmon with Madeira wine sauce, and I'll have rice with stewed carrots, and the lady will have rice with sweet potatoes."

The waiter turned to Timothy. "And you, sir?"

"Hmm …"

Haven nudged his arm and whispered in his ear.

Timothy cleared his throat. "We'll have the same, please."

Haven put forth her best we-got-through-that-part smile as the waiter collected the menus and excused himself.

"So, tell me, Larkin, how's business at your new tack shop?" Timothy took a sip of water.

"Very good! Everything's going so much better than I expected. I'm seriously considering going into this full time."

Larkin's interests matched her sister's a hundred percent.

Maybe Harmony would be a little less self-centered now. One could only hope.

The small talk continued until dinner was served. About halfway through the meal, a startling clink on Timothy's plate turned all eyes toward him, but Timothy gazed in the direction of the open double doors of the kitchen.

"What is it, Timothy?" Haven placed her hand on his arm. "You look as though you've seen a ghost." Everyone turned their heads toward the kitchen. "Timothy?"

He pushed away from the table and tossed his napkin down beside his plate. "Excuse me a moment." With no explanation, he left his party.

"Timothy, what's wrong?" Haven called after him, but he didn't answer.

Larkin and Harmony shot puzzled glances at her. She shrugged her shoulders as they all watched Timothy approach the open doors.

Timothy made it to the kitchen entrance, but the proprietor promptly stopped him. "Excuse me, sir, but you can't go in there. Is there something I can get for you?"

"I saw a girl in there—a black girl."

The man stood straight and stiff, looking sharp in his black tail coat and pants, a crisp white shirt and white spats. "Yes, sir, there are several girls working in the kitchen for their owners."

"I recognize one of them." Timothy's pulse picked up. "Can you tell me her name?" He strained his neck to see around the proprietor, catching another glimpse of the girl. "I need to know her name."

The man quirked a brow. "I'm sorry, sir, but I can't divulge that information. You'd have to ask the man who owns her." As he spoke, someone closed the double doors.

Timothy turned to find Haven standing right behind him.

"What are you doing? People are staring at you." Haven folded her arms. "Will you please tell me what this is all about?"

Another man walked up to the proprietor and stood next to him. He wore a fancy suit and white spats, too. Both men kept a close watch on Timothy.

"Shhh … all right." Timothy lowered his voice. "But not a word of this in front of Larkin or Harmony." His shoulders rose and fell. Then he continued in a whisper. "I think I saw Ruth's daughter—you know, the girl Trumbeaux's been looking for. She's working back there in that kitchen. I'm positive it's her."

"Do you mean the Ruth who's married to your friend Micah?"

"Yes." He shot a glance toward Larkin and Harmony, who still had eyes on him. "I was at Cheapside that day, and I recognize her face."

"Oh, Timothy, you must let Mr. Trumbeaux know you found her. If only we could get away from my sister and Larkin for a while, we could go to the telegraph office so you could send him a message."

Timothy shook his head. "No, Haven, that would be too risky for security reasons. I think the best thing would be for you to deliver the message to him yourself when you get back to Lexington Thursday night."

"You mean you won't be going back with us?" Her lower lip thrust forward.

"I can't, sweetheart. Not now. I need to stay here to check this out. If that girl really is Ruth's daughter, I must help Mr. Trumbeaux with a rescue mission." He knew she'd be disappointed. "Besides, you'll have Harmony with you for a traveling companion. I hope you understand."

"I … I guess I do, but—"

"Haven, there's no other way."

There went that lower lip again. "But the Charity Ball is Saturday night. Will you be back in time for it?"

Timothy cupped her cheeks and kissed her forehead. "Mr. Trumbeaux and I will do our best. You know I want to go to the ball with you very much. But right now, this is more important. I'm sure Trumbeaux will agree with me."

"Of course. I understand."

"Good. Now let's get back to our table." He took her hand and placed it on his arm. "I think I've stirred up enough angst already."

Timothy seated Haven and began an explanation for his behavior to Larkin and Harmony. *Mercy … those glaring stares!*

He forced a grin. "I thought I saw somebody I know."

Harmony leaned forward. "And who might that be?"

"Ahem …" Larkin patted Harmony's forearm while smiling at Timothy. "You two should finish your dinner before it gets too cold."

"Of course." He picked up his fork. "It's delicious. Don't you agree, Haven?"

"Absolutely divine." Haven spread her napkin over her skirt.

Timothy did his best to mask his concern, but he couldn't get his mind off the girl in the kitchen.

A hotel room in Louisville

Early Saturday morning, Timothy awoke to rain drumming against the window of the hotel room. He sat on the edge of his bed waiting for Maurice to finish getting dressed. The previous day, Maurice had taken the first Friday morning train from Lexington to Louisville after reading the message Haven had personally delivered to him.

Timothy and Maurice planned to lie in wait for the girl who'd be arriving at her restaurant job for the morning shift. Timothy had already staked out the alley behind the restaurant, and he'd found the perfect place where they could lie in wait for the girl to arrive for the morning shift. He'd also taken note of her driver's fancy barouche.

While he waited for Maurice, Timothy reached in his waistcoat pocket and pulled out a rose-scented missive from Haven that Maurice brought with him. He slipped the pretty linen paper out of the envelope and angled it toward the kerosene lamp by his bed. He'd read the letter earlier, but he wanted to read it again.

My beloved Timothy,

Please know that I am praying for you. Micah has chosen to keep this from his wife, regretting his lack of faith but fearing her frailty in her sixth month. I realize, as does Jeannette Trumbeaux, that you and Mr. Trumbeaux might not be back in time to attend the Charity Ball Saturday evening. While I would be deeply disappointed should this be the case, it is of secondary importance to the business that keeps you in Louisville. I must not be selfish but am truly grateful for the days we spent together this week, and I think of you every waking moment that we are apart. May the Good Lord protect you and bring you safely home.

Love always,
Haven

Haven. He closed his eyes, and his heart did that strange little flip.

"Are you ready to do this, Timothy?" Maurice donned his hat and hooked his umbrella over his arm.

Timothy snapped back to the present and folded the fragrant letter. "Yes, I'm ready."

❧

A back alley, downtown Louisville

The early morning rain dwindled to a light drizzle as Timothy and Maurice waited in a rented carriage on the side street next to the restaurant's alley. Each time a carriage turned into the alley, a surge of adrenaline pulsed through Timothy, and his heart slammed against his ribs.

His eyes scanned the area continually. The morning sun was up full, and a distant clock tolled eight.

Another carriage approached.

"That's it!" He pointed to a fancy barouche as it passed by. A uniformed black man wearing a stovepipe hat was driving from an elevated front seat.

Maurice started to tap the reins, but Timothy grabbed his arm. "Wait a minute. There's a man inside with her. He wasn't there yesterday." Timothy watched as the barouche turned into the alley. He glanced at Maurice from the corner of his eye. "Did you get a good look at the girl?"

"No, my eyes fail me at this distance. I must get closer." Without waiting for Timothy's reaction, Maurice tapped the reins and turned the horses into the alley, following close behind the barouche. When the barouche stopped, Maurice pulled over, and they waited.

The driver of the barouche got down first and helped the girl, and the young, rich-looking white man stayed inside. The girl walked toward the back door of the establishment.

A strong wind skimmed the morning shadows of the alley, loosening the girl's bonnet. As she spun on her heel to shield herself from the cold gust, her hand flew up to catch her bonnet. For that brief moment, her head tilted toward the light of a lamp by the rear entrance, illuminating her face.

"That's her!" Maurice tossed the reins to Timothy and jumped down. He rushed toward the girl just as the barouche took off. She froze as if frightened.

"Lottie?"

"Massa Trumbeaux?"

Thank God.

"Whoa!" A man's voice bellowed from inside the barouche as it came to a stop. The young white man jumped out and ran toward Lottie, but before he could reach her Maurice had pulled her to his side. The man's steely eyes bored into Maurice. "What goes on here? Release my property immediately!"

Maurice placed himself in front of the girl. "Lottie, get in the carriage that's directly behind me. Hurry!" He pushed on her arm.

What was Maurice doing? Timothy bolted out of the carriage to help Lottie.

When the young man lunged at Maurice, his top hat tumbled to the wet brick below. Maurice raised his arm to block him. The man braced himself with widespread legs, and slipped his hand beneath the front opening of his frock overcoat.

Flick!

Maurice jumped back a step as the young man flashed a pocket blade menacingly close to his neck. The knife slashed the cape of Maurice's coat.

Click!

Maurice cocked the pistol he always carried in his outer pocket. Had he lost his mind? That wasn't part of the plan.

Timothy lifted Lottie into the carriage, his chest heaving. Then he climbed in next to her.

"Drop the knife or I'll fire!" Maurice looked angry enough to do it.

Not good. Timothy had never seen that side of Maurice.

The young man slowly lowered one hand, and the blade fell. As glinting metal pinged and bounced on the brick near his top hat, he raised his hand again. "Why are you stealing my property? Who are you?"

Maurice kept his pistol aimed. "She was stolen from me in Lexington. Her subsequent sale at Cheapside was fraudulent."

The young man's palms remained up. "How she got to auction is of no concern to me. I have the bill of sale stating she's legally mine. If you'll come with me, sir, I can show you—"

"All papers since her kidnapping are spurious documents! Her name is Lottie, and she was not for sale." Maurice had spoken much louder than he should have.

A man stood on the other side of the alley observing the altercation. Timothy feared a constable might show up any minute.

"I paid a sizable sum for her. Just who do you think you are?"

"My name is Maurice Trumbeaux, and I'm prepared to pay you for your loss."

"Trumbeaux? The textile magnate?"

"I am he."

The man put his hands down. "Well, my good sir … I, too, am from a family of reputable enterprise, and I do not wish to tarnish my father's excellent standing in the community. But with all due respect, Mr. Trumbeaux, I paid a—"

"How much do you want?"

"Three thousand."

Maurice disengaged the pistol, retrieved his pocket book and took out a roll of bills. Before handing the money to the young man, he removed a leather-bound portfolio from inside his overcoat as well as an inkhorn from his belt. "Three thousand, and I'll have you to sign this certificate." He handed the items over. "And we shall be done with it."

With a few strokes of the pen, the men completed the transaction.

Timothy's tense muscles relaxed. He smiled at Lottie. "You'll soon be home with your mama."

CHAPTER TWENTY-FOUR

Ruth's cottage

Timothy stood outside Ruth's little cottage with Maurice and Lottie, hiding in the shadows, while Cora rapped on the door. Cora brought a dessert for Ruth and Micah as an excuse for the visit. She stood there jiggling from head to toe, and Timothy almost laughed out loud.

Seeing Lottie shiver from the brisk, windy night air while they waited for someone to answer the door, Timothy removed his frock and draped it over her shoulders. He leaned over and cupped her ear. "Any moment now."

Micah pulled the door open. "Cora, what you doing here?"

"Brought you pumpkin cakes!"

Ruth walked up next to Micah. "Thank you, Cora. You so thoughtful." Silence followed for a few seconds as they stared at each other. "You like to come in, Cora?"

Cora went in by herself first and stood directly under the door frame.

Silence.

Timothy hugged Lottie close to him, noticing a glistening in her eyes. What was taking Cora so long to say something? If only she would hurry up and tell Ruth.

"What done got into you, Cora? You sure actin' strange.

Get in here and close the door." Ruth grabbed Cora's arm. "You lettin' all the cold air in."

"Massa here to see you, Ruth." Cora let out a huge squeal.

Finally.

"Massa Trumbeaux here? To see me?"

Cora stepped aside, and Maurice went in followed by Timothy and Lottie. Silence fell on everyone like a deafening roar. The wave of emotion in the room nearly brought Timothy to his knees. They had all waited and prayed for a long time for this moment, and God had been faithful to bring it to fruition.

Ruth parted her lips, but no words came out. Tears pooled in her eyes and spilled over.

"Mama."

"Lottie?" Ruth's tiny voice broke. "I can't believe it."

Lottie wrapped her arms around her dazed mother, their cheeks touching, their tears mingling.

"Oh, Mama, I missed you so."

"My baby, my precious girl. Thank the good Lord you safe." Ruth pushed away and planted her hands on Lottie's shoulders. "Nobody done hurt you, child?"

"No, Mama. Nobody hurt me."

Timothy knew that wasn't true. Lottie had confided to him that her young master had taken her as his mistress. But she'd made Timothy promise not to tell her mama. It would only crush Ruth's spirit even more. He agreed.

Lottie touched her mother's pregnant belly. "Massa Trumbeaux and Timothy tell me all about you and Micah and the baby."

"And you all right with this?"

"I'm very happy for you, Mama."

Timothy tossed a glance to Micah. What a relief that Lottie so readily accepted Micah and the baby.

Lottie faced Micah. "Mama couldn't have picked a better man to marry."

Micah smiled a proud papa smile. "That makes my heart happy, Lottie. Thank you."

Ruth stroked her daughter's face and hair then turned to face Maurice. "We can never thank you enough."

"It's Timothy you should thank." Maurice rested his hand on Timothy's shoulder. "If it weren't for this man, this happy reunion might never have happened."

"We be most grateful, my friend." Micah clamped Timothy's hand in a firm hold. "A miracle of God."

"You're right, Micah. It was a miracle." One of the many perks of Timothy's work. "Only God could have orchestrated something like this."

Micah switched his gaze from Timothy to Maurice and back to Timothy. "Don't you two have some place special you needin' to be right now? Your ladies been plannin' this night for months. Not polite to keep the ladies waiting."

"Come, Cora. Micah's right." Glancing at his pocket watch, Maurice signaled that it was time to leave. "It's past seven. Timothy and I are officially late to the Charity Ball." As Timothy held the door open, Maurice followed Cora out.

"Goodnight and God bless you, my friends." Timothy stepped out and closed the door.

As the three of them walked away, Maurice placed his hand on Cora's back. "Cora, would you mind arranging a second nosegay for Timothy to give his sweetheart while we dress for the ball? I especially like the dark red chrysanthemums."

Cora still had the jiggles. "Yessuh! I see to it right away."

"Thank you, Cora." Timothy winked, making Cora blush. "I'd probably be in trouble if I showed up without one, wouldn't I?" What would he do without Maurice to think of these things for him?

The Phoenix Hotel, downtown Lexington

The grand ballroom of the Phoenix Hotel glowed with candlelight from the dazzling crystal chandeliers while the fashion world of Lexington's finest made a fabulous statement at the Holiday Charity Ball. Haven had been dreaming for almost two months of being among the dancers with her handsome prince. But her prince failed to show up.

With a wistful sigh, she gazed upon the many lords and ladies enjoying each other's company. Of course, her sister had her beau with her. Everything always worked out perfectly for Harmony. She turned her head away so she wouldn't have to watch them dance. Would she ever be able to conquer that annoying jealousy? Something she needed to keep working on. She supposed she was lucky to have her brother's company. Harrison was such a good sport.

"Who's the pretty lady sitting over there—the one wearing the blue gown?" Harrison tossed his gaze in the direction of the Delaney family as he handed Haven a glass of punch. "I think she's been watching me."

Haven's brow arched. "That's Alifair Brooks—the lady you fetched me to help on the Fourth of July—the widow who had the baby."

"Really?" He took a drink of his punch and finished it off in one swallow. "Who's she with tonight?"

"Her brother and his wife. She doesn't have an escort, if that's what you're wondering." At least Haven wasn't the only lady at the ball with her brother.

Harrison set his empty glass on the table. "I think I may just have to strike up a conversation with the lovely widow."

"Would you like me to introduce you?" Haven wondered if she might end up a total wallflower after all.

"Yes … would you?" He crisscrossed the dance floor with Haven on his arm.

"Hello, Mr. and Mrs. Delaney … and Alifair." Haven smiled as if Alifair were her best friend. Anything to redirect the young widow's affections away from Timothy. After all, Harrison was a very handsome man. Maybe she should have arranged for the two of them to meet sooner. It might have saved her a lot of grief. But that was all water under the bridge now.

Avery Delaney rose from his chair. "Good evening, Miss Haywood. I was hoping Timothy would be here tonight."

"Me, too, Mr. Delaney. He was going to try, but we haven't seen him yet." She felt Harrison nudging her arm. "Oh … I'd like you all to meet my brother." She made eye contact with Alifair. "Alifair, this is Harrison Haywood."

In an instant, Harrison had his hand extended to Alifair. "I'm pleased to meet you, ma'am." The love-stricken look on Harrison's face—priceless.

Alifair's ivory complexion blushed to crimson. "My name is Alifair. Pleased to meet you, too."

Oh, how perfect!

"May I have the honor of this dance?" Harrison glanced at Haven and winked her a "thank you."

Haven sighed. "Enjoy your evening." Yes, she'd be a wallflower tonight, but this arrangement was worth it.

Shifting her gaze to the ballroom entrance, Haven gasped. "They made it!" She meandered her way through the maze of lords and ladies, meeting up with Jeannette Trumbeaux halfway. They hurried to meet their men.

The sight of Haven in her emerald green, velvet gown left Timothy breathless. "You look absolutely divine." He lifted her hand for a kiss.

"I'm so happy you're here!" Her eyes misted. "I was so worried about you. Did things go well in Louisville? Did Mr. Trumbeaux find the girl?"

"Yes! She's with her mother as we speak."

"Oh, Timothy, that's wonderful news!"

He held out the nosegay of dark red chrysanthemums. "For you, my lady."

"Oh, they're quite lovely, my lord. Thank you." She took the nosegay and stepped back. "How fine and dapper you look! Every fair maiden in the kingdom will surely try to steal you away from me."

"But my heart already belongs to the fairest maiden of them all, my lady." Timothy executed a princely bow, surprising himself with his ability to be charming.

Haven curtsied. "My prince doth make me blush."

"Mr. Delaney gave me this suit … early Christmas gift." He cupped her face and kissed her forehead. "You know, I've never been to a formal dance in my life."

"You'll be fine." She slipped her arm through his. "Let's see. The first thing we need to do is greet my family. Then we can be selfish and keep the rest of the evening to ourselves."

"That last part sounds wonderful." If he could take her away tonight, he'd do it. "Well, let's go find your family, shall we?"

"Ma's much better now. And this morning we received a telegram from Uncle Brady in Texas saying Howard showed up at his ranch. Howard wants to come home to make amends with Harley. It's been a very good day."

The musicians began to play another set, and the two love birds made all the obligatory greetings. But where was Harrison? Timothy spotted him first. "Will you look at that?"

"Oh, yes! I forgot to tell you. Harrison picked Alifair out of the crowd moments after we arrived. He thinks she's pretty." Haven sighed. "She is, isn't she?"

"What?" If he played dumb, would he get away with it?

"Pretty."

He cleared his throat. "I never noticed."

Grinning, Haven punched his arm. "Let's dance. I've been waiting a long time." She tugged on his arm as the next waltz began.

His feet stuck to the floor like glue.

"What's wrong?" She let go and backed away.

"Uh …" He faltered. "I don't know how to dance."

"Then you shall watch and observe the steps until you learn." She took his arm. "It's really very simple. I promise it will be magical, my handsome prince."

Haven left him with no choice. He picked up the movements the best he could, and Haven had him on the dance floor by the end of the second waltz.

"Forgive my clumsiness, my lady."

"You're doing quite well, my lord."

As the music died down, everyone turned to face the platform where a man's voice clamored for attention. Haven's pa? What was he doing?

"Ladies and gentlemen!" A hush fell over the spacious hall as Frank stood on the platform with his hand up in the air. "It is with great honor that I proudly announce the engagement of my daughter, Miss Harmony Haywood, to Mr. Larkin Smith." Frank gestured with a wave of his arm to the beaming couple standing next to him. As the orchestra burst into an upbeat piece, Frank kissed his daughter and shook hands with his future son-in-law.

"I don't know what to say." Haven looked stunned. "I had no idea. How did she manage to keep it a secret? It must have just happened tonight."

Timothy studied the situation. At least Frank Haywood approved of one daughter's suitor. Good for Larkin. He took Haven's hand in his. "Well then … shall we dance to celebrate?"

"I'd love to."

Having caught on to the dance steps quite well, he whirled Haven around the floor. Eventually, he maneuvered his lady into an adjoining hall. Perfect … no one in there.

His lips brushed her cheek as he pulled her against him in a solid embrace. His pulse quickened. "Haven, I want you to know …"

"Yes, Timothy?" Her face eased toward his lips as she drew rapid breaths.

"I love you, Haven." He gathered up the long, loose curls that spiraled down her back, weaving them through his fingers and kissed her temple. "So much."

Haven closed her eyes, pressing her fingers against the nape of his neck. She tipped her chin upward. "I love …" Their lips met.

His kiss claimed her as his own—and it was magical.

CHAPTER TWENTY-FIVE

The Delaney home

"Joyful, joyful, we adore Thee …" Timothy sang along with Melia as Alifair accompanied them on the harpsichord. "God of glory, Lord of love." Outside the parlor window, giant December snowflakes coated bare branches like powdered sugar frosting. Baby Sam gurgled and cooed on a quilt next to his mother, enjoying the cheerful music while Lazarus kept warm on a rug by the hearth.

Now that Harrison Haywood had swept Alifair off her feet, Timothy felt a lot more at ease around her. What a blessing when those two hit it off at the Holiday Charity Ball. Their courtship breathed new life into Alifair, and she seemed to be in an extra merry mood today.

Avery had taken the girls to the woods to gather evergreen and holly to decorate the house for Christmas, but he'd insisted they wait another week to cut a tree. Melia had large, festive red bows ready for the arrangements as well as hurricane lamps for the candles.

As they sang the last line of "God Rest Ye, Merry Gentlemen," the front door opened and in walked Avery and the girls, their arms piled high with pine branches and holly. "Sounds like Christmas is already here." Avery's voice rang out from the foyer. "Look what we brought home."

Timothy sprinted over to help Avery and the girls unload their sweet smelling harvest of evergreens. Timothy chuckled when Alifair broke into "Deck the Halls."

An hour later, the house had taken on a wonderful festive flavor. Timothy stayed long enough to help Avery hang decorations in those hard-to-reach places and after the women fashioned a wreath for the front door, he hung that up as well.

"Well, if that's all you need, I think I'll be on my way." As soon as he opened the front door, he practically ran into Harrison. "Come on in! I was just on my way out to the farm to see Haven."

"She's waiting for you." Harrison beamed as he stepped inside, ducking a sudden attack from Brillie and Sylvia. "Um, um, um … I love the smell of fresh pine."

"We got lots of pine!" Brillie hugged Harrison from one side while Sylvia embraced him from the other.

Alifair stood in the parlor entrance with Sam bundled in her arms. "Come join us for some Christmas music, Harrison."

"I will as soon as these girls release me." He looked helpless with the girls clinging to his arms. "I think I'm being held prisoner here."

Timothy knew that feeling, and he missed it. As he watched the girls lavish their attention on Harrison, jealousy trickled through him. Ha … they had a new man. Girls could be so fickle no matter what their age.

Haven Hill Farm

Timothy rode horseback to Haven Hill Farm, awed by the beauty of the virgin snow that blanketed the roadside. Only two inches, but still beautiful. A good six inches would have been perfect for a sleigh ride around the farm with Haven.

Maybe next time.

As soon as he reached the front lawn, a sudden bombardment of well-packed snowballs dropped from the sky, pelting him from head to foot. Hank's dog, Scratch, ran circles around him, barking nonstop, and wicked fits of boyish laughter echoed from high up in a tree.

He looked up. Big mistake. His nose became the perfect target for the next "snow bomb." Muttering and sputtering, he brushed the snow from his face while trying to calm his jittery horse.

"Hank! Andy!" The scolding voice came from Hank's mammy, Ella, who hurried toward the battle scene. But she tripped and fell, probably because of her oversized galoshes. Shaking her fist, she got right back up. "I declare—can't leave you rapscallions alone for ten minutes while I go to the outhouse!" She held her skirts out of the way and started running again. "I declare!"

Timothy dismounted, having gathered his wits about him enough to finally laugh. Using caution, he tipped his head back to see the enemy, cupped his mouth with both hands and hollered, "I surrender!"

"Hank, Andy, you get down from that tree right this minute! You hear me?" Ella stood below the branches, waggling her finger at the boys. "You 'pologize to Brother Tim, you little scamps, before I tie you both up to this here tree and throw snow at you until they ain't no more snow left on this hill."

"I think she means business, boys." He covered his mouth to hide his smirk.

The boys climbed down lickety-split, and Hank looked like he might be a smidgen remorseful. Maybe. "Sorry, Timothy. We meant to hit Ella, but then you came along."

Andy grinned. "It was too tempting."

"Why, you little varmints!" Ella swatted at them and missed.

"Oh, now, Ella." Timothy walked over to her and hugged her shoulder. "The boys are just having some winter fun. But

I came to see Haven, so I'd best get on up to the house."

Ella's eyes widened. "Miz Haven ain't there, Brother Tim."

"But she was expecting me. Where did she go?"

Andy piped in before Ella could speak. "My sissy, Sapphire, she having a baby. I ain't allowed to go home until Miz Haven come and say so."

He turned to Ella. "How long ago was this?"

"Less than half an hour. Ruby come up to the house to fetch Miz Haven."

"Thanks, Ella. I think I'll ride over to the cottage and keep Elias company." He mounted his horse and looked down at the boys. "Now you behave or I'll help Ella tie you up to this tree, and I'll throw snowballs at you." He chuckled and winked as he rode off. Glancing over his shoulder, he shouted at them. "And I'll show no mercy, you hear?"

Timothy found Elias outside his cottage, pacing in the yard and wearing a path through the snow. "Hello, Elias!" He hitched his horse to the post next to Haven's horse. "I thought I'd come and chat with you while I wait for Haven, if you don't mind."

Elias walked up to him. He looked both nervous and happy at the same time. "Oh no, suh, I don't mind. I welcome somebody to talk to."

"Tell me, Elias, does Harley know anything about this baby yet?"

Elias shrugged his shoulders. "I reckon you have to ask Miz Haven about that."

"I'm sorry, Elias. I can't imagine a worse thing happening to one's daughter." Timothy wondered how forgiving he would be if he were Elias. "It would be asking an awful lot of you to forgive Harley, but maybe someday the Lord will help you find it in your heart to do so."

"Oh, I forgive him. Haven say Massa Harley did ask forgiveness for having his way with Sapphire. But forgetting, well, that be impossible now with this baby to remind us every day. I just hope Sapphie able to love her child and care for it like a good mama." Elias glanced at his cottage. "But I forgive, yessuh, I do, 'cause Massa Jesus, he forgive me, and that what he want me to do."

Timothy put his hand to Elias's shoulder. "I couldn't have preached a better sermon."

A newborn baby's cries screeched from the little cottage, and ten-year-old Pearl came running out the door, leaving it wide open. "Pa! Pa! The baby here!"

Elias pivoted to face Pearl. "How's Sapphire?"

"Wait—I go find out." Pearl went back inside and returned within seconds. "Sapphie fine. And it a girl, Pa."

A voice yelled from within the house. "Close the door, Pearl! You lettin' all the cold air in."

Haven stayed next to Sapphire while Ruby watched her mama clean the baby by the warmth of the fire. Pearl sat like a good little girl at the table, waiting to see her new niece. When Anna finished bathing the baby, she let Ruby carry her over to Pearl. Haven wondered what emotions might be running through Anna now that the baby was here.

"What wrong with that baby's hair?" Pearl scrunched up her nose. "She different. It look kinda red, and her skin not as dark as us."

Anna's face froze, and Haven tensed. She kept her gaze fixed on Anna and waited for someone to say something.

Ruby broke the awkward silence. "She gots purty hair, Pearl."

"I know." Pearl smiled. "I like her." Thank goodness for Pearl's innocence.

Haven's tension relaxed a little when Anna took the baby from Ruby and carried her to Sapphire. "What you gonna name this baby?"

"Dunno, Ma." Sapphire stroked her baby's cheeks and hair. Haven studied Sapphire's expression. Were her motherly instincts kicking in?

Haven leaned over the baby, observing the new little

creature—her own family's flesh and blood. She was this little girl's aunt. The realization took her breath. Of all the babies she'd delivered, not a one had ever affected her like this child.

The reddish tint to the baby's hair caught her eye—clearly a hereditary trait of the Haywood family. *Just like Harley. Just like Pa.* She took the infant's tiny hand in hers. Tears rushed to her eyes as the baby wrapped its fingers around hers. "She's a jewel, Sapphire."

"A jewel." Sapphire kissed her baby's head. "That be her name then—Jewel."

"I love it!" Haven faced Sapphire's sisters. "What do you think of that, girls? Elias and Anna have a Sapphire, a Ruby and a Pearl, and now another 'jewel' is added to the family."

"Jewel be a fine name." Anna wore a softer look. "Pearl, tell your pa he can come in now. And don't hold that door open so long."

As Pearl trotted off to fetch her pa, Haven checked Sapphire one more time to make sure she was all right. "You did good, sweetie."

The door opened, and Elias followed Pearl into the house.

"Come see Jewel, Pa." Sapphire looked happy. She'd be a good mama after all.

Haven knew she didn't need to worry about Elias. His heart was as big as all outdoors, so full of love for everyone and everything. "They're both doing great, Elias."

"Thank you kindly for all you help, Miz Haven." Elias walked Haven to the door. "Timothy out there waitin' to see you. I invite him to come in, but he say no, he just wait outside."

"Thank you, Elias." Haven threw on her cloak, pulled on her galoshes and hurried out the door.

When Timothy saw Haven running toward him, he could tell from her harrowed face that she'd had a rough afternoon. If he could kiss all her troubles away, he would.

The snow crunched beneath her galoshes, and he spread his arms wide, pulling her into his embrace. As he held her, kissing the top of her head, she didn't say a word.

"It's all right. I'm here for you, Haven." He pressed her cheek against his chest, his head bent low over hers. "I'll hold you as long as you want."

For as strong a woman as Haven claimed to be, her frailty at that moment became crystal clear. He loved her all the more for it. "There now, let it all out."

A few minutes later, she lifted her head and met his gaze. "She's beautiful. Sapphire named her Jewel."

"I like that." He cupped her face, wiping her tears with his thumbs.

"She truly loves her child, Timothy."

"I thought she would." He pulled the hood of her cloak over her ears. "But what about Harley? Does he know yet?"

"I think so." Haven sniffled, and he handed her his hanky. She wiped her nose then stuffed the hanky into a pocket. "After Ruby came up to the house to get me, Pa said he would tell Harley about the baby and have a nice long talk with him. Harley's been sober over six weeks now."

"I'd like to meet Harley sometime, but I suppose today's not a good day. I'd better wait."

"You're probably right. Better wait." Haven slipped her arm through his as they walked toward the horses. "It makes me sad knowing Harley nor anyone else in my family will ever have anything to do with this baby. Except for Pa providing for her financially, no one will ever talk about her."

"At least we can be thankful your pa wants to provide for the child."

"She's my niece, Timothy. My flesh and blood." There came those tears again. She stopped walking and leaned into his chest. "I wish we could be together for Christmas. Do you really have to leave again?"

He hooked her chin with his finger and tipped her face up. "Sweetheart, you know I have to preach at my parents' church that morning."

"I'll miss you, but I understand."

He tapped the tip of her nose. "But hey … I'll be back

for New Year's Day. We'll spend an entire week together."

"Promise?"

"Promise." He intended to spend the rest of his life with her.

CHAPTER TWENTY-SIX

Sunday, January 1, 1860
Haven Hill Farm

Timothy relaxed into the plush comfort of the Haywood mansion's parlor sofa, crossed one leg over his knee and slipped his arm around Haven's shoulders. Nuzzling his nose against her cheek, he whispered, "Happy New Year."

Haven smiled, shifted her weight and wiggled closer. She met his gaze. "Happy New Year."

The Haywood family and guests had just finished a New Year's Day feast, and the three young courting couples had gathered together in the parlor. While the flames flickered and crackled in the fireplace, they enjoyed some rare time of talking and getting to know each other.

Larkin, who'd come from Louisville for the weekend, sat with Harmony on the settee. Alifair stayed close to the hearth keeping an eye on little Sam as he slept on a thick quilt by his mother's feet, and Harrison stretched out on the floor next to Sam.

"I've never seen your whole family so happy before." Timothy rubbed his belly. "And I'm stuffed. I think I ate too much."

Larkin wilted into the cushion, laughing. "I think we all

did."

Haven tapped Timothy's arm. "Would you be up to a chat with Harley—maybe get to know him a little better?"

"I'd love to. Didn't get a chance to talk to him at church this morning."

Timothy and Haven excused themselves and headed upstairs to Harley's room. They found Harley sitting on the edge of his bed, still in his church clothes. He had a Bible on his lap.

Timothy hesitated to go in when he saw Frank and Rebekah sitting in chairs facing Harley. The three of them appeared to be engaged in a serious conversation.

But Frank looked over his shoulder, smiled and waved them over. "Come on over, you two. Harley has some wonderful news to share."

"Oh, I love good news!" Haven took Timothy's hand, and they walked to the foot of Harley's bed. Her eyes sparkled as she palmed the cannonball finial on the mahogany bedpost. "Let's hear it, Harley."

"I made a decision this morning, sis." Harley's voice broke as he tapped his heart. "Right here."

Timothy grinned at Haven and took her hand, giving it a happy squeeze.

"I've decided that I'm ready to start living my life for Jesus. I'm through running from God." Harley held up his Bible. "I'm rededicating my life right here, right now."

Haven released his hand and rushed to embrace her brother. "This is the best news!"

"I can't think of a better way to begin the New Year." Timothy felt every ounce of Haven's joy as he shook Harley's hand. "I don't believe we've formally met."

"Happy to meet you, Timothy. During dinner, I was hoping we'd get a chance to talk, so I'm glad you came in to see me. Heard a lot about you." Harley chuckled. "All good, of course."

After Haven's parents left the room, Harley kept Timothy in stitches for the next hour with humorous childhood stories about Haven and Harmony. Did the twins really create all that mischief?

When Howard came in, they excused themselves, taking the opportunity to steal away. Haven slipped her arm through his as they went down the stairs. "Now that Harley has thoroughly embarrassed me, you'll have to tell me about some of your childhood shenanigans with your brothers."

"Maybe someday. I have something else in mind for today." He winked. "Do you remember when I told you I had a belated Christmas present to give you?"

"Yes! And I've been curious as a cat ever since."

"I'd like to take you out for a Sunday drive first. I have Avery's carriage, and your pa said it was all right with him—against his better judgment, I'm sure."

She punched his arm. "Why are you teasing me so?"

When they reached the bottom landing, he kissed her cheek. "I'll get the carriage ready then come back in to get you."

Along a country road

"Finally! I have you to myself." Timothy felt the pull of her gaze. The carriage rattled and the wheels creaked as the horses took them at a slow gait along the muddy road.

Haven snuggled close to his side and pulled a cozy red plaid, woolen blanket up to their necks. It worked perfectly to shield them from the cold January air. "Timothy, I think I'll die from curiosity if we don't exchange our Christmas gifts soon!" She looked up at him. Her eyes twinkled like a child's on Christmas morning. "How much longer?"

He slanted his gaze and gave her a sly grin. "Just be patient, my love. Not yet."

"What are we waiting for?" Even her voice sounded like a child's.

"You'll see. We're almost there."

"Oh, all right." She readjusted the blanket around their necks. No sun today. Only a hazy gray sky. "How's your friend Micah?"

"Micah and Ruth seem to be doing well adjusting to their new life with Lottie. I saw Micah yesterday. He said Lottie has accepted him as her stepfather. He's glad Ruth has Lottie with her since he can't go see her very often."

"You know, Timothy, I can see so clearly how wrong that is. It's just something I never thought about until I got to know you. What your friends have been through is so sad."

"Strange, isn't it? Once you're aware of how wrong something is, it becomes so glaring you can't help but see it." His mind flashed back over the past year. Haven had come so far in her convictions. "Did I tell you Maurice and Jeannette are leaving with their children in the morning to go to France? Micah said Maurice's father is very ill and may die soon."

Haven put her fingers to her lips. "Oh my … I'm so sorry. I do hope they get there in time to see his father."

"Keep them in your prayers." Timothy drove along the road a few more minutes before he pulled off to the side and parked the carriage.

"Are we going to open our presents now?" She really was a child at heart.

He laughed. "Yes, but you're not going to open it right here."

"Where then?"

"You're cute, you know it?" He started to climb down. "Come with me. You'll see."

She pulled on his arm. "Wait. I want you to open your gift here. It's too big to carry."

"All right." He sat back down. "If it's so big, why haven't I seen it? Where is it?"

"It's in the back under the seat." She climbed into the passenger section and opened the hatch over the luggage compartment. Her hand came to rest on a large box wrapped in brown paper and tied with a huge red ribbon. "See … this is for you."

"How in the world …?" Timothy chuckled as he watched her struggle to scoot the monstrosity out into the open. "Would you like some help?"

"I've got it. Here you go. Now, come back here with me." She panted to catch her breath. "Harrison loaded it in your carriage when you came back in the house to get me. Belated Merry Christmas, sweetheart."

"You're a sly one." He studied the package. "You weren't joking when you said it was big. Now what could this be?"

"Open it!"

"Yes, ma'am!" He started in, pulling the ribbon off first then attacking the brown paper in long, brutal tears. He shot her a curious look before making the final tear. His jaw dropped as he stared at the finely crafted pine toolbox.

"Well?" Haven ducked down and peered up into his face. "Do you like it?"

"Do I ever!" He widened his eyes. "I don't know what to say. I've never had a decent toolbox, much less one as fine as this." His hands stroked the exterior of the box, touching the side-mounted handles.

"Look inside." She could sure be bossy sometimes.

He lifted the hinged lid. Two large wooden trays rested inside.

"Now take out the trays." The cute kind of bossy.

He followed her instructions. Hidden beneath the trays she'd arranged a brand-new tool set. On each side of the box, he found small bins with lids and latches filled with nuts, bolts, screws, and nails.

She clasped her hands together. "I've never forgotten that day downtown when I crashed into you in front of the hardware store."

"Ha! I remember it well. I've never been happier about anyone crashing into me." He peeked into each bin. "Haven, you're amazing. There's a place for everything. Now I can stop swiping my mother's canning jars to put things in. Thank you, my love." He pushed the box aside and reined her in for a "thank you" kiss.

She muttered the words, "You're welcome," as his lips grazed hers.

"Now it's your turn." He stood and climbed down from the carriage. With his hands at her waist, he lifted her out. "Come with me."

Holding hands, they trudged into the woods, boots slushing through the thick wet earth. Their breath formed a fog in front of them, and the daylight waned under the towering woodland shadows. As the temperature dropped, they kept walking until they reached a small clearing.

Timothy turned her to face him. "Recognize this place?"

"Hmm … no." Haven shrugged. "Should I?"

"That's all right. It's been a while."

"Wait a minute." Her eyes lit. "I *do* recognize this clearing."

"I hoped you would! This is where you appeared like an angel to help me with Pete. Seriously … that was my first thought. There was a ray of sun breaking through the trees that morning at just the right angle to create an aura around you." Timothy treasured the image. "And you know what? You have been an angel to me. We're standing in the exact spot where you were that day."

"Yes, I remember it well. Funny thing about that—you saw an angel while I saw a man aiming a rifle at me. How could I forget?" Her laughter assured him she was teasing.

He quirked a brow. "I suppose you're never going to let me live that down, are you?"

"Only if you hurry up and give me my Christmas present. Where is it? Have you buried it in the woods or something?"

"Of course not, silly." He took her gloved hands in his. "Haven, I need to talk to you about something first."

"All right, Timothy." She worried her lip.

"First, I want you to know that I've never felt about anyone the way I feel about you. I love you, Haven."

"And I love you." Was she going to cry?

He caressed the back of her hand with his thumb. "Are

you willing to accept me and my beliefs about slavery knowing that I'll never compromise for anyone?"

"Yes, Timothy, I've thought it all out very carefully. I don't desire such a lifestyle either." Warmth radiated from her brown eyes. "And I admire you for being patient with Pa. I'm so thankful he's accepted you. Of course, you know Ma absolutely adores you."

"Ah, Haven." He pulled her close. "What about my work with the Underground Railroad?"

She squeezed his hands. "Your secrets are safe with me."

"Always? Even after we're … if we …?"

Haven looked at him askance. "Are you asking me to …?"

His heart raced like wildfire as he reached inside his coat pocket and pulled out a small box. "Will you marry me, Haven Haywood?" He held the box up for her to take. "Will you be my wife?"

Her trembling hand took the little box. "Yes, Timothy Locker, I will marry you!" She wrapped her arms around his neck and pressed her cheek to his.

He tipped her chin up to his face and smiled. "You can open your present now. You've been about to burst with curiosity all day, remember?"

Haven slowly lifted the lid from the little box and ran her gloved fingers over the delicate pearl ring secured in its soft satin bed. "Oh, Timothy, it's beautiful."

Timothy took the box, lifted out the ring then returned the box to his pocket. "Allow me." Taking her left hand in his, he removed her glove then slid the ring onto her finger. "There … this is our promise to each other."

"Timothy?"

"Shhh …" He pressed his finger against her lips. "I know what you're thinking. You're wondering what your pa will say, right?"

"You know me so well."

"I asked your parents after church if we could marry next month."

"And Pa gave us his blessing?"

"Hmm … that might be stretching it a bit." The thought of Frank giving his blessing … well, that would never happen. "But he did say yes!"

"That's good enough!" Hugging him, she pressed her cheek against his chest. "I love you, Timothy Locker. With all my heart."

"Happy New Year, my lady."

She lifted her face, and their breath mingled in a single fog. He kissed her long and slow, again and again, stopping only to catch a breath. He could have stayed there for hours in spite of the chilly air, but he reluctantly pulled away.

"I'd better get you home soon or your pa'll have a posse out looking for me."

One more kiss and he walked his betrothed back to the carriage.

CHAPTER TWENTY-SEVEN

Saturday, February 4, 1860
The Roberts farm

For the first time since riding the circuit for a month, Timothy had finally made it back to Lexington. But instead of heading out to Haven Hill like he'd planned, he found himself riding horseback with Leonard Thompson and Bear's boy, Moe, out to the Roberts farm. Moe had ridden into town to fetch them both at Micah's request.

The three rode up to the front of the house, and Moe dismounted first. "I take care of you horses. Micah say you have to hurry. Massa Roberts not have much time."

Timothy put a gentle hand to Moe's shoulder. "Try to stay calm, Moe."

The maidservant, Lucy, opened the front door. "Come in, Brother Leonard. You, too, Brother Tim. Massa in a terrible bad way, and Micah all upset."

Timothy removed his hat. "How is Mrs. Roberts?"

Lucy let out a pitiful groan. "Lawd o' mercy, Miz Cilla beside herself, snappin' at everyone. We all be afraid of her."

Timothy followed right behind Lucy up the stairs. "Does she know Micah asked us to come?"

Lucy shrugged. "Not sure, Brother Tim."

Leonard, following behind Timothy, cleared his throat. "I reckon we'll find out in a minute."

As they approached the entrance to John Roberts' room, Priscilla Roberts' voice shrilled into the hall. "If only you'd listen to me once in awhile, John." They could hear her pacing the floor as she fussed at her ailing husband.

Timothy and Leonard stood in the doorway until Micah noticed them and waved them over.

Mrs. Roberts gave them the evil eye, frowned and sat down in a chair on the opposite side of her husband's bed. "What are you two doing here?"

John raised his trembling hand. "I told … Micah to … ask them."

"Don't talk, John. You're straining yourself." She patted his arm and glanced at the door. "Where is that doctor? I sent Jack to get him almost an hour ago."

Micah looked at Timothy with teary eyes. "I been reading to Massa from the Good Book."

Timothy took John's hand. "Could I have prayer with you, John?"

Priscilla Roberts shot to her feet. "Not now. He's had enough of this nonsense."

"Pray for me … Brother Timothy." How wonderful to see John garner strength from the Lord in the face of opposition.

"Oh, for crying out loud." Mrs. Roberts marched out of the room.

"Father in heaven, we ask that you place your comforting hand on our brother in Christ. Ease his suffering and give him peace. Bless him, Lord, and all his household, especially his wife, during their time of need. In the blessed name of Jesus … amen."

"Thank … you, son."

Mrs. Roberts marched back in and plopped down in her chair. Frowning, she folded her arms.

Lucy poked her head inside the room. "Can I get Massa or Missus anything?"

"Don't disturb us, Lucy!" That woman … what could

possibly have caused her to become so miserable?

"Tea." John turned his head toward Lucy. "Thirsty … more tea."

"Well, don't just stand there, Lucy. Bring Master Roberts his cinnamon hawthorn tea."

"Yes, Miz Cilla."

A few minutes later, Lucy returned with a tray. "Here Massa's tea." She set it on the nightstand and left the room.

Mrs. Roberts propped her husband up with extra pillows and held the teacup while he sipped. When he finished, she shot Timothy and Leonard an icy stare.

John glanced at his wife. "Priscilla, please leave us … for a moment."

"John! What?"

"Let me talk with … these men … of God … alone."

"Why? Are you going to pray to your God again? Well, I ask you, John, where is your God now? I'm staying here." Her eyes darkened as she plopped into a chair.

Ignoring her, John turned his face to Micah. "Read to me again … the Good Book."

Micah sat next to John's bed, and Timothy handed him his Bible. Micah opened it to the Psalms.

As Micah read, Timothy sneaked a look at Mrs. Roberts, who seemed to bristle at the Word.

After a few minutes, Mrs. Roberts stood up. "That's enough for now. I'll not have you filling my husband's head with such infernal nonsense any longer." The brackishness of her voice took Timothy aback.

John suddenly cried out. "I'm going to see Jesus today!"

"Nonsense, John." She leaned over him. "The doctor will be here soon. You're not going anywhere!"

"Yes … it's time."

Mrs. Roberts glared at Timothy, Leonard and Micah.

John pressed his hands to his chest. "Tell me, Micah … about being with Jesus."

Micah flipped frantically through the pages of John's Bible until he came to Philippians, chapter one. "'… Christ shall be magnified in my body, whether it be by life or by death. For to me, to live is Christ and to die is gain.'"

"To die … is gain?"

Micah nodded. "Yes, Massa. Apostle Paul say so."

"To die … is gain." John smiled. "I like that."

"Stop it! You're not going to die, John."

"Yes, wife, I …" John's face twisted into a painful contortion, and his body lurched upward. He collapsed onto the bed, his arms limp at his sides.

Jack knocked on the doorjamb. "Doc Allen here now, Miz Cilla."

"John! The doctor's here now!" Mrs. Roberts made a sharp pivot. "Well, send him in, Jack!"

Dr. Allen stepped inside. "What seems to be—?"

"It's about time you got here!" Her snappish tone hissed across the room.

"I left home immediately, Mrs. Roberts." Dr. Allen kept a level voice as he checked John's wrist for a pulse, then listened to his heart. He looked up to meet her gaze. "I'm sorry, Mrs. Roberts. Your husband is dead."

Her head fell to John's chest. She held his hand and sobbed as Micah's lumbered walk to the door accompanied her lament.

Timothy and Leonard followed Micah down the stairs.

"You've had an exhausting day, Micah." Timothy draped his arm across Micah's shoulders. Nothing seemed adequate to console his friend.

"He gone." Dipping his head, Micah wiped his eyes. "Massa Roberts gone to be with Jesus."

The rest of the Roberts slaves had waited in the foyer for the news. Timothy looked around at all their faces. He wondered what lie ahead for them.

Leonard walked over to Lucy. "Keep an eye on Mrs. Roberts. Send for me if you need to. It's not easy, I know, but it's what God would have you do."

"Yessuh, Brother Thompson. I will."

Micah pulled Timothy aside. "I have to tell Ruth before

Miz Cilla notice I gone. What if she take away my passes to visit my family? The baby be due in a week or so, and I don't know if Miz Cilla gonna allow me to see my firstborn child." His tears spilled over.

"I'll ride out there with you, Micah." A stinging sensation mushroomed like flames in Timothy's cheeks. "Haven will understand why I'm late to see her." At least he hoped so.

Leonard faced Micah. "I'll be back tomorrow to see if Mrs. Roberts needs help with the burial. Stay strong, my friend."

Haven Hill Farm

The gray February sky painted a bleak view through the window in the parlor where Haven and her sister sat with Ma and Alifair, sewing and knitting. But wedding talk and Baby Sam kept things lively and bright.

Sam played on the carpet, occasionally pushing himself up on his hands and knees. Haven hadn't realized how much she loved being around babies that age until Alifair started bringing Sam with her to visit. She giggled when he grunted and scooted one whole inch. That little fella could take off crawling any moment.

Haven focused on her knitting as she waited for Timothy to arrive. Why was he so late? She never knew it was possible to miss anyone as much as she missed him.

With their wedding being only two weeks away, her mind darted in a thousand different directions. Nonstop. Was she doing the right thing? Did her gown need to be taken in a little more? Was Timothy in danger? Oh, the secrets that filled her heart with fear. *Lord, help me.*

And whatsoever ye do, do it heartily, as to the Lord, and not unto men.

"What's the matter, sweetheart? You seem distracted today." Ma rested her work on her lap. "Is it Timothy?"

Harmony and Alifair both stopped their needlework, and Haven knitted faster. Why was everyone staring at her? How much did Alifair know? Had Avery and Melia sworn Alifair to silence, too?

Haven forced a laugh. "You know I'm always thinking about Timothy, Ma."

Ma smiled. "For a moment there, I thought you might be getting cold feet about the wedding."

"Oh, Ma. Of course not." Haven frowned. "Don't say that!"

Harmony pulled her knitting needle from the second slipper she'd just finished for Larkin. "We still haven't set a date. Larkin wants to get married right away, but I've always dreamed of a June wedding, perhaps down by the lake." She held up both slippers, comparing one to the other.

"A June wedding by the lake would be lovely, dear." Ma sewed another embroidery stitch on her pillowcase. "But since you already have your gown, you could always change your mind, you know. As a matter of fact, I was just thinking how special it would be for my two lovely daughters to have a double wedding."

"Oh, I don't know, Ma. What do you think, Haven?"

Did Harmony actually want to know what she thought?

Haven beamed. "Sounds like a grand idea to me." She drew a deep breath and exhaled. Surely Timothy wouldn't have any objections. "It certainly would be easier on Ma and Pa."

Ma had the silliest dreamy look on her face. "I can picture it now … both my girls in their beautiful gowns, Pa escorting you down the aisle, a daughter on each arm." She wilted into the sofa with a sigh.

"All right, Ma, you talked me into it." Harmony actually looked excited. "I know Larkin will be thrilled. If it were up to him, we'd get married tomorrow!"

Haven got up to hug her sister in a rare show of affection. Then she hugged Ma, whose dreamy look morphed into sheer joy.

Alifair, who'd remained silent during the wedding talk, set her knitting aside and clasped her hands together. "Perfect!"

The afternoon slipped away, and Timothy never showed up. Haven knew there would be times like this, and she was just going to have to get used to it. She had to trust him. And she did.

Just as the household call to supper came, Haven heard the clippety-clop of a single horse approaching the house. Peering out her bedroom window, she gasped at the sight of her knight in shining armor riding up on his steed … well, Danny Boy, anyway. She waved to them then flew down the stairs to meet Timothy at the door.

"Are you all right?" She pulled him inside and closed the door. "I've been worried about you all day."

As Noah took his hat and frock, Timothy reined Haven in for a hug, the I-haven't-seen-you-for-a-month kind. "I'm sorry I wasn't able to let you know I'd be late, but the day took some unexpected turns. Long story short, Micah's master died today. Micah sent for me and Leonard to be with him."

Haven pulled away and peered into his tired eyes. "Oh, Timothy, I'm so sorry to hear that. I knew it must be something serious."

"I went with Micah to the Trumbeaux Estate so he could tell Ruth what happened."

"I'm glad you could be there for him." She took his hand. "Come with me. You're just in time to dine with the family." Scanning the foyer to see if they were alone, she turned to face him. Without hesitation, she threw her arms around his neck and planted a big kiss on his lips. "You don't know how much I've missed you."

"I've missed you more." He tapped her nose.

"I don't see how, my lord."

"We can debate that later, my lady." He lowered his lips to hers and kissed her again.

Rapid clicking of boot heels striking the marble floor echoed off the walls and ceiling, startling Haven and

Timothy.

"Timothy! You're back!" Haven's little brother slammed into his side. "You going to eat with us?"

"Hey there, Hank! Good to see you. I just got into town this morning." Timothy roughed up the boy's hair. "And yes, I'll stay for supper."

Hank straightened his hair, frowning. "Why does everyone do that?"

With both her hands on Hank's shoulders, Haven turned him toward the dining parlor. "Go sit down. We'll be there in a minute." She pushed his back.

"All right." Hank tromped away.

Haven peered into Timothy's eyes. "Now where were we?"

Saying nothing, he kissed her again then pulled away. "I think we'd better get in there before your pa comes out."

His kiss lingering on her lips, she slipped her arm through his and walked with him to join the family. Why couldn't they just skip supper?

CHAPTER TWENTY-EIGHT

Monday, February 13, 1860
The Delaney home

"Melia!" Timothy zipped across the foyer to the staircase as the grandfather clock tolled a quarter past nine in the morning. Market day.

"Merciful heavens!" Melia nearly collided with him at the bottom landing. "What is it, Timothy?"

"Where's Avery? We have an emergency."

"He took Sylvia back to school. They left an hour ago. Said he'd be leaving straight from the school for Louisville to speak at a bankers' leadership meeting." Melia pressed her hand against her belly. "What kind of emergency?"

"Melia." Timothy buried his face in his hands. "It's horrible … just horrible. Please, Lord, have mercy." He doubled over from the pain in his gut. Searching for the right words, he slumped down to sit on the step.

Tears drenched Melia's cheeks. "Did something happen to Haven?"

"No … it's …" He met her gaze. "They've got Micah."

Brillie walked over to them, looking distressed. "What you mean, Bro'er Tim?"

"Who has Micah?" Melia sat down beside him, sliding

Brillie onto her lap.

Timothy wiped his watery eyes. "Cheapside has him. Priscilla Roberts sold him to Baxter and Drake first thing this morning. No warning, no nothing."

Brillie's hands flew to her cheeks. "No, Bro'er Tim!"

Melia looped her arms around Brillie. "How did you find out?"

"I stopped by the blacksmith shop a little while ago to chat with Micah. I wanted to catch him before he began his work. His boss told me about it, and he was as shocked as I am."

"How much time do we have?" Melia glanced at the clock.

"Maybe a little over two hours. Hardly enough time to collect sufficient funds. It would take a miracle."

"Mercy, Timothy. You have to try." Melia eased Brillie off her lap and stood up. "Wait here. I'll be right back." She hurried up the steps and returned a few minutes later with a small reticule. "How much do you think he'd sell for?"

"I have no idea, Melia. His education could work for him or against him."

Melia took his hand and placed the reticule in it. "It's not much, but take it. Alifair pitched in, too. It's all the money we could find in this house. I wish Avery was still here."

"Thanks, Melia. Every little bit helps." Timothy emptied the contents of his own wallet into Melia's reticule. "I have to let Leonard know. Maybe we can get this collection snowballing."

He flew out the door as quickly as he'd entered.

❧

Leonard Thompson's church study

"Come in, Timothy." Smiling, Leonard pushed away from his desk and rose to his feet.

Timothy closed the door behind him. "I have bad news, Leonard. Priscilla Roberts sold Micah this morning."

Leonard's smile vanished. He set his pen down on a stack of sermon notes. "No!"

"He's going to auction in a couple of hours."

Leonard slumped down in his chair. "My God, no."

"I've got a start of over a hundred dollars." Timothy held up Melia's reticule. "If you can get the word spreading quickly to the other ministers, say like Watson, McKinney, Good and whoever else … maybe, by the grace of God, we can scrape up the money in time. I'm on my way to the Trumbeaux Estate to tell Ruth. She needs to know. I'm hoping Maurice will put up the money for Ruth's sake."

"But Maurice and his family are still in Paris, son."

"Oh, you're right! In all this frenzy, I completely forgot. This is a nightmare." Timothy dropped his head and leaned over Leonard's desk, bracing himself with both hands. Another sucker punch and so little time. "God, help us."

"I'll get with the ministers." Leonard grabbed his hat and coat. "Why don't you try Frank Haywood? Now that you're about to be his son-in-law, maybe he'll listen to your plea."

Timothy opened the study door. "The man doesn't like me, but I'll give it a try. Meet me at Cheapside in two hours."

Dr. Wright's office

"Good morning, Timothy." Nurse Sarah Goolsby stepped from behind the counter as Timothy burst into the waiting room of Dr. Wright's office. "Is there something I can do for—"

"I need to see Haven immediately." Timothy started to walk back to the patient room.

Sarah stepped in front of him. "Excuse me, but you can't go back there."

Timothy's eyes did a quick sweep of the patients in the waiting room as they all turned their heads toward him. He lowered his voice. "Where is Haven? Is she here?"

"She is, but she's helping Dr. Schneider with a patient."

"I need to see her right now. It's important, Sarah." Timothy frowned. "And who's Dr. Schneider?"

"Dr. Schneider's filling in for Dr. Wright. If you'll have a seat, Haven will be right out."

"Please, you don't understand. This is an emergency."

"Timothy?" Haven walked into the waiting room. "What are you doing here?"

He took a few steps toward her. "Haven, I need your help. It's urgent."

"What happened?"

Looking around at all the inquisitive faces, he gulped a huge lump of despair. "Can we talk in private for a moment?"

Haven tossed a look to Sarah.

"Just for a moment, Haven." If Sarah hadn't been Haven's best friend, she'd probably be reprimanding her by now. All because of him.

He held the door for Haven as they stepped outside. The sun peeked through the clouds on this unseasonably mild day, belying the atmosphere of pain and chaos festering a few blocks away at Cheapside.

"What's this all about, Timothy?" Haven's natural rosy color had paled.

He clamped his hands on her shoulders. "Listen carefully, Haven. My friend, Micah, was sold to Baxter and Drake this morning, and he's now in the pen awaiting auction—today!"

"Oh, Timothy, no! Not that sweet man."

"We need to raise money fast, and you can help us if we hurry."

"I have a little cash, but it's at home. What do you want me to do?"

Timothy held her gaze. "I need you to ask your pa to contribute cash so we can purchase Micah at the auction. Will you do that, Haven?"

"Oh, Timothy, Pa will never go for—"

"Haven!"

Covering her ears, she backed away from him, her eyes

wide. She looked as though she'd come face to face with a monster.

"I'm sorry, sweetheart. I'm so sorry. Please, will you at least give it a try?" His heart pounded like a call to battle from a hundred drums.

Doubt etched away at Haven's confidence in Timothy. She suddenly didn't know the man standing before her at all. What would she be getting herself into if she shared a life with someone like that? Did she really want to go through with the wedding? Words stuck to her tongue.

His head facing down, Timothy spoke in a deep, deliberate voice as if to the boardwalk. "There's an innocent man a few blocks away from here, sitting in a pen like an animal, chained by his hands and feet to countless other men, about to be sold to only God knows whom, and for no other reason than the fact that his skin is black." When he lifted his face, she saw so much pain in his eyes. "Micah has a family, for heaven's sake, and his wife's expecting a baby any day. At least give it a try."

As he released his grip, her shoulders slumped. She turned away for a couple of seconds. Remembering her scripture, she faced him again. "You're right, Timothy. I must do this as if I'm doing it for God and trust the outcome to Him."

"Thank you, sweetheart." He blew out a lengthy breath of air. "Let's go! Time's running out!"

She dashed into the doctor's office, and Timothy followed her. All those waiting patients staring at them—no time to worry about that now.

As Sarah emerged from the patient room, Haven ran over to her. "Sarah, I need to leave. It can't be helped, and I'll explain later. Tell Dr. Schneider for me."

"All right, Haven. I'll cover for—"

"Nurse Haywood!" Dr. Schneider stepped into the room. "I'm afraid I can't allow you to leave. If you do, I'll have to report your action to Dr. Wright, in which case you may find your position here terminated."

Haven glanced at Sarah and Timothy then marched right over to the coat rack on the wall. She plucked her mantle from the hook and turned back to face Dr. Schneider. "I'm sorry, Dr. Schneider, but I must go."

Timothy grabbed her hand, pulling her to the door. "We have to hurry!"

They raced two blocks to the livery and rented two horses. From there they rode horseback to Haven Hill, galloping at a furious speed.

Haven Hill Farm

"Haven,. what are you doing here? I thought you went to work this morning." Pa shot a quick glance to Timothy and nodded. He appeared to be in somewhat of a hurry as he and Noah worked on the harness for two quarter horses. "I was just getting my wagon ready for a trip to Cheapside."

"I did go to work this morning, but I need your help with something, Pa." She dismounted and walked toward him.

Pa stopped what he was doing and faced her. "Sure, honey, what's the matter?"

"Pa, you know the slave named Micah—the one who does farrier work for you?"

"Yes, I know the one."

"Mrs. Roberts sold him to a firm, and he's going to auction today." Haven kept her eyes locked on her pa. "We can't let that happen, Pa."

"Why are you telling me this, Haven?" He turned away, grabbed the reins and ran them through the harness guides.

"I need to ask you a favor, Pa." Had she lost him before she even made her request? "Would you please contribute some cash to help us purchase him today?"

Pa ignored the question as he made the final adjustments to the harness, speaking to Noah instead. "You can leave now, Noah. I'll finish up."

"Pa?" She closed the distance between them.

"I can't do that, honey. I already have plans for other purchases I need to make." He tugged on one of the straps. "Now, if you two will excuse me, I have to get going."

"Excuse me, Frank." Timothy squared his shoulders. "Don't you know that Micah is a preacher of God's Word?" He took a step forward as Pa hopped into the seat of his wagon. "And he has a family with a baby on the way."

"I'm sorry, but I said I can't help you." Pa picked up the reins and looked at Haven. "I've got my share of burden without worrying about someone else's." He clicked to his horses. "I'm sorry, Haven. Good-bye."

Haven quivered from head to toe as her pa drove away. How could Pa be so callous? She cast a misty-eyed glance to Timothy. "We tried. God knows we tried."

"I know. Thank you, sweetheart." He stroked her back. "C'mon … let's stop by the house so you can collect your cash, then we'll ride over to the Trumbeaux Estate. Ruth needs to know."

Still unsettled from the sting of Pa's refusal, Haven wiped the tears from her eyes.

The Trumbeaux Estate

The Trumbeaux family's butler answered the door. "Massa Trumbeaux not here, sir."

Timothy removed his hat. "We've come to see Ruth, but she wasn't at her cottage. Is she here by any chance?"

"Yessuh, she here." The butler stepped aside as Cora bumped him out of her way.

Cora stood over the threshold. "Brother Tim, fancy seeing you here today." She glanced at Haven and flashed her usual buoyant smile.

Timothy placed his hand on Haven's shoulder. "Cora, this is Haven Haywood."

"Oh, sure! Nurse Haywood—I hear about you plenty. Come on in." Cora pulled Haven inside by the arm. "Well, if that don't beat all. A nurse show up just when we need her. Ain't the Good Lord wonderful? Sure enough, he send a nurse to help Ruth with the baby."

"I'm sorry, Cora, but we can't stay." Timothy quirked a brow. "Am I to understand that Ruth is in labor as we speak?"

"Yessuh, she start about an hour ago." Cora's brows dipped to her nose, and she eyed him like an eagle focused on its prey. "What you mean you can't stay?"

Why did Ruth have to go into labor today? How was he going to tell them about Micah? A seering pain shot through his gut.

Timothy looked at Haven then back to Cora. "We need to get back to town right away, Cora."

Cora shifted her weight to one foot and planted her hand on her hip. "Well, then, will you please go tell Micah his wife having the baby?"

Timothy swallowed hard, his eyes stinging. "Cora, I'm afraid we have some very bad news."

"What bad news, Brother Tim? Can't be no bad news today. This a happy day."

Timothy slipped his hand under Cora's elbow, just in case, and braced himself to tell her. "I'm sorry, Cora, but Mrs. Roberts sold Micah. He's at Cheapside awaiting auction."

"No-o-o!" Cora dropped to her knees, and her wails echoed off the foyer walls. "Can't be true. Say it ain't so."

Lottie bounded into the foyer and gasped. She ran over to Cora and helped Timothy and Jim get the flustered woman back on her feet.

Ruth's voice rang out from the servants' quarters off the kitchen. "Lottie? What wrong with Cora?"

Timothy told Lottie about Micah, and Cora convinced Haven to stay with Ruth. Then Cora offered to gather a collection from the Trumbeaux employees while Timothy waited. When she returned a few minutes later, she handed him a modest sum.

"How can I ever thank you, Cora?" He gave her a quick hug and flew out the door.

She followed him onto the portico and hollered. "I take care of Ruth. You just bring Micah back!"

CHAPTER TWENTY-NINE

Cheapside auction

Adrenaline kicked in a second time for Timothy as his rented horse galloped back into town at full tilt. So little time left. After returning the horse to the livery, he forged through the horde of buyers and traders on the Cheapside lawn. Eyes darting here and there, he searched for Leonard but couldn't find him.

With about ten minutes to spare, he elbowed his way back through the growing mob to locate the keeper of the slave pen. The thick, repugnant odor of cigars hung in a haze of smoke everywhere he turned. Still no sign of Leonard.

As the squalid building came into view, he noticed a coffle of men chained together being led from the building to a long bench situated on the far side of a fenced area. That's where they'd stay until it was time for their final inspection. He walked up to the fence and surveyed the long line, spotting Micah near the end.

Fighting to keep the acids in his stomach down, he stared and flailed his arms in the air until he got Micah's attention. Timothy pointed upward to heaven, but Micah, his hands bound, could only nod. He glanced at the clock tower—five minutes until the auction.

Seeing the keeper of the pen, a burly-looking man with his whip in one hand and a notebook in the other, Timothy hollered until the man looked at him. The keeper tramped toward Timothy, somewhat annoyed, but Timothy didn't care.

"Excuse me, sir." Timothy pointed to the notebook. "Could you tell me what chattel number you have for Micah Hall?"

The man scowled and skimmed over the page with his index finger. "Thirty-one." Slapping the notebook shut, he trudged back to watch over his "goods."

Where could Leonard be? Timothy stood at the back of the lawn and waited as the auctioneer took his place at the stand. Timothy prayed, but was he asking God for too much?

Noon. It was time. The traders grew quiet and put out their cigars. While the auction guard led Chattel No. 1 to the stand, the traders got their catalogues, pencils and purses ready. The auctioneer began his chant, and the greedy men called out their bids like a pack of ravenous dogs.

One human chattel after another as well as oxen, mules and miscellaneous farm equipment, became the property of a new owner with each slam of the auctioneer's hammer.

Timothy paced back and forth, keeping an eye out in all directions for Leonard. A crop of curly red hair in the middle of the crowd caught his attention. Was that Frank Haywood? Several top hats soon blocked his view.

The image of Leonard shouting to the redheaded man on a horse flashed through his mind: *"Just once why can't you work with us instead of against us?"* Timothy's nostrils flared. God forbid that he'd ever take his anger toward Frank out on Haven.

Number 28 stood on the block. Amidst the clamor, Timothy heard his name. Turning, he saw Leonard approaching with three other pastors—Watson, McKinney and Good. At least now they stood a chance of rescuing Micah.

"Any luck with Frank?" Despite the chilly air, Leonard

wiped beads of sweat from his brow.

"None … but we did try. He's got his own agenda." Timothy showed him the reticule from Melia. "I've got a hundred and fifty dollars here from other sources."

"We came up with seven hundred from our four churches combined." Leonard's words put Timothy somewhat at ease. "That's eight fifty. That should do it, don't you think?"

"I'm not so sure." Pastor McKinney skewed one side of his face. "I've seen some surprisingly high bids before."

The hammer went down on the sale of Number 30. Leonard, being the designated bidder, shut his eyes and quietly mouthed a prayer as Micah stepped onto the block. Leonard looked faint and began to sway. Timothy and Pastor Watson grabbed his arms until he had sure footing again.

"You have to do this, Leonard. For Micah and Ruth and their children." Timothy never imagined this would be so hard.

The auctioneer's chanting began and Timothy's heartbeat raced against the bidding. He prayed for Leonard to draw on the strength of the Lord.

Leonard stood tall and, as always, he marked his opportunities with expert precision.

"Six hundred. Who'll give me six hundred?"

"Six fifty!"

"Six fifty. Do I hear seven hundred?"

Leonard cupped his mouth and shouted, "Seven hundred!"

Timothy fought hard to keep his stomach from coming up.

"Eight hundred!" Which bidder was that?

"Eight hundred." The auctioneer pointed to someone at the front. "Do I hear eight fifty? Who'll give me eight fifty?"

Leonard held his hand up high. "Eight fifty!"

But the bidding went higher still.

Both Timothy and Leonard fell to their knees—defeated—as the numbers faded into oblivion. How could God let this happen?

Timothy jolted to attention when the auctioneer declared the price of Micah's life. "One thousand dollars once! One thousand twice …"

They watched the auctioneer raise the hammer into the air. Time seemed to fall into suspended animation as the hammer began its descent. All four ministers jumped with a start as a loud voice bellowed from the middle of the crowd.

"Eleven hundred!" Whose bid was that?

The hammer came down. "Sold!" The auctioneer pointed to a man in the crowd. "Sold to the red-haired gentleman over there for eleven hundred dollars."

"That's Frank Haywood." Emory Good slapped Leonard on the back. "I don't believe it."

"I don't believe it either!" Timothy grabbed Leonard's arm. "Praise God!"

Frank approached them. "He's all yours, fellows." He spoke directly to Leonard, looking as serious as if it were any run-of-the-mill business deal. "I'll have his manumission papers drawn up tomorrow. We can settle up with the money after the auction."

Leonard shook Frank's hand. "You're full of surprises, sir. I can't thank you enough."

Thank you, Lord, for working miracles in people. For a split second, Timothy wanted to hug his future father-in-law. He quickly dismissed the idea and shook his hand instead. "You'll never know how much this means to me, Frank. Thank you."

"You're welcome. Be a pity to lose a good farrier." Frank gave him a softer look than he'd seen before. Maybe they'd be friends after all.

As Leonard crossed the street to find his wife, Timothy spotted a woman preparing to get into a carriage. Priscilla Roberts. Had she been there the whole time? He caught her gaze for a couple of seconds before she snapped her head away and climbed inside.

God have mercy on her soul.

⸙

The Trumbeaux Estate

Timothy walked with Micah to the house servants' door of the Trumbeaux mansion. As they stood there, the muffled voices of the women inside permeated the walls. He had already told Micah that Ruth was in labor, but Micah appeared to be in a daze.

"Are you going to knock or are you just going to stand there staring at the door all day?" Laughing, he put a hand of encouragement to Micah's back.

"What so funny?"

"You are." He nudged Micah's arm. "Now go on and knock!"

Micah lifted his knuckles to the door and hesitated. "What if . . ."

A woman let out a loud, throaty wail. Micah gasped. His knuckles hit the door, hammering away faster than a woodpecker.

"Now who that be?" Cora's voice. Timothy would recognize it anywhere. Her grumbling carried through the closed door as her footsteps approached. "I'm a comin'. Just hold you horses!" Her ramblings faded into low, unintelligible mumbling before the door swung open.

"Cora, where's Ruth?" Micah craned his neck, looking past Cora's wide frame. "She all right?"

"Micah! Oh, praise the Lord God Almighty—He done save Micah! Thank you, Jesus!" Cora practically jumped onto the back porch, closing the door behind her. With a jubilant squeal, she threw her arms around Micah and squeezed him as he gasped for air.

Another groan came from inside. Micah lunged for the door, but Cora raised both hands and blocked him. "Huh-uh," she declared. "You wife be fine, Micah. You ain't got no business in there right now. That be for the womenfolk. You hear me? You menfolk just have to wait until this here baby get born."

"You sure Ruth be fine?"

"I declare! If Cora say Ruth be fine, then she be fine." She stomped her foot. "And I say Ruth be fine! Now you two go around to the front door and tell Jim that Cora say you have to wait in the parlor. Then when it the right time, I come and tell you." She spun on her heel, her skirts swirling after her as she went back into the house and closed the door in their faces.

Timothy waited with Micah in the parlor as Cora had ordered. Neither one said a word. Occasionally, they exchanged glances, but otherwise they just stared at the fire, watching the flames flicker and dance while they sipped the coffee that Jim brought them.

The long-awaited sound finally pierced the silence. The vigorous squeals sent Micah to his feet and out of the parlor in a flash.

Smirking, Timothy watched Micah pace the foyer. How much longer would they have to wait? These baby deliveries sure did take a long time.

"You can come in now, Papa." Cora's beaming face was a sight for sore eyes. "You, too, Brother Tim. Come see the baby."

Ruth lay in the bed, cradling a tiny new creature in her arms, and Lottie smiled at them from the edge of her mother's bed.

Timothy went straight to Haven's side and whispered in her ear. "Your pa came through for us."

Haven's eyes brimmed. She smiled and turned her gaze on Micah. "Another answered prayer."

"Come see you son, Papa." Ruth looked beautiful with her long, tight curls tied in a ribbon at the back of her neck, and a few stray tendrils framing her face. She parted the blanket to expose the infant's body.

Micah bent low and kissed Ruth's forehead then caressed his son's tender head and tiny feet. "Thank you, Jesus."

Timothy stepped a little closer to Ruth for a better look at the baby. "What will you call him?"

Ruth looked up at Micah. "What his name be, Papa?"

Micah lifted the child from Ruth's arms. "His name is Ransom."

A loving smile graced Ruth's lips. "That a good name, Papa."

"Just as the Lord Jesus sacrifice his life as a ransom to set me free from the shackles of my sin, so on this day, my brothers and sisters in Christ pay a ransom to set me free from the shackles of slavery." Micah's words prompted a myriad of emotions in Timothy's already exhausted spirit. "I name my son Ransom as a reminder of this day."

Amazed at the picture of redemption made manifest in Micah and his family, Timothy silently gave thanks to God. Cheapside had lost its power over them.

He pulled Haven close to his side. She looked exhausted, too. When she leaned her head against his shoulder and rested her hand on his chest, his mind raced ahead to their wedding—less than one week away.

His love for her still frightened him beyond anything he could ever explain.

CHAPTER THIRTY

Haven Hill Farm
February 19, 1860

"Molleeee!" Harmony's voice blared from her room and echoed into the powder room where Haven sat at the vanity. Could that sound be any more irritating?

Haven puffed her cheeks. Surprisingly, Harmony had been rather quiet at church that morning. Why couldn't she have stayed that way? Things had to calm down before the wedding guests started to arrive. They just had to.

"I right here, Miz Hominy." Poor Molly … all out of breath from being at Harmony's beck and call. "What you need me to do?"

"Everything, Molly! I need everything. My attendant isn't here yet, and it's getting late!" Harmony's constant griping grated on Haven's last nerve. My goodness, how did she ever keep it up?

"Yes, Miz Hominy."

Haven rested her elbow on the vanity and palmed her chin, staring at her reflection in the mirror. Maybe a double wedding with her sister wasn't such a good idea after all. She drummed her fingers on the glass-covered surface. Too late now.

Sarah would be there any minute. Sarah … her best friend would stand with her during the ceremony. If she decided to return to work for Dr. Wright after the wedding, things would sure be different between her and Sarah. What would Sarah tease her about?

A smile tugged her lips as she thought about how Harmony and Larkin would be making their home in Louisville. The distance between them would be a blessing.

She and Timothy agreed to temporary residence in Avery Delaney's apartment. Their future was still up in the air. Timothy had been considering the possibility of preaching at his home church in Ohio should their aging preacher decide to step down. She rather liked that idea. At least he wouldn't be riding the circuit, and she'd see him a lot more often.

Oh, that Timothy's parents could have come to Kentucky for the wedding. She had hoped to meet his mother, but it was much too far away for them. Timothy said his ailing granny lived with his parents, and they couldn't leave her. Haven wondered what Mama Locker would think of her. Someday soon.

A tap on the powder room's open door followed by a soothing female voice broke into her pensive moment. "It's me … Sarah."

"Sarah!" Haven jumped up and threw her arms around her friend. "Am I ever glad to see you!"

"Look at you! You're not even in your gown yet, and you look radiant!" Sarah flung her bridesmaid dress over a chair in the corner.

"Oh, Sarah, I'm so hap—"

"Molly! Where is my other silk pump?"

Haven and Sarah jumped together before bursting into full-blown laughter.

"That's what I've had to listen to all day, Sarah. I don't know how she does it."

"Poor Molly." Sarah wiped "laughing" tears off her cheek.

"I know. Bless her heart. I thought the same thing." Haven slipped her arm into Sarah's. "Can you believe I'll soon be Mrs. Timothy Locker? I feel so happy."

"I teased you right into making it happen." Sarah winked. "I knew you'd get married before me."

"Now I'll have to tease you instead." Haven pointed to Sarah's gown on the chair. "Bring your dress to my room. We'll help each other get ready."

While the Haywood men idled away the pre-wedding time in the library, Timothy lingered in the foyer to chat with Micah.

"Thanks for coming, my friend." He scanned Micah from head to toe and whistled. "Don't you look like a dandy?"

Micah held both arms out straight to model his new tailcoat and stuck one foot forward to show off a shiny new pair of shoes. "So you like my style?"

Timothy applauded. "I do indeed!"

"Leonard helped me with these clothes. Ruth say she not recognize me." Micah did a full-circle turn, showing off.

Timothy laughed. "Leonard has good taste."

Frank hadn't formally invited Micah to the wedding, but he'd told Timothy that Micah could come. How big of Frank to be so thoughtful. Micah kept a low profile and stayed in the foyer away from the white guests—an unfortunate side effect of Cheapside's power that would not go away even though the chains had been broken.

When Leonard arrived with his family, Timothy took the opportunity to excuse himself while his two friends kept each other engaged in conversation. He hated to leave Micah's company, but he had to spend some time mingling with his future in-laws.

As a string quartet in a corner of the large foyer entertained everyone with fine, classical music, Timothy meandered his way through wave after wave of colorful hoop skirts and dozens of people he'd never met. Haven's uncle, Brady Haywood, happened to be one of those people. He'd come all the way from Texas and brought his family with him. The two of them hit it off well.

"Haven's had nothing but good things to say about ya,

son." Brady slapped a solid hand to Timothy's back. "Hope you know what a treasure you're about to marry."

"Yes, sir, I do." Timothy found it hard to believe that Frank and Brady could actually be brothers.

"Uncle Brady!" Hank plowed into Brady's leg. "This is the bestest day ever! You're here, and I'm getting two new brothers!"

"Can't beat that with a stick, can ya, little colt?" Brady looped his arms around Hank. "And two fine brothers, they are!"

Just as Hank started to run off, Mrs. Haywood made an appearance at the open door of the library. She nabbed the boy as he ran by. "Hank, dear, tell your pa it's time for him to come upstairs to get your sisters."

"Sure thing, Ma."

The double doors to the large parlor had been left open, giving the spectators a view of the bridal procession as they descended the staircase. Timothy followed Harrison, who'd been given the honor of officiating, and took his place next to Larkin, pausing to catch a glimpse of the brides through the entrance. A collective "ahh" rippled across the room as Frank Haywood made his way down the stairs with a daughter on each arm.

Both brides wore silk gowns, one in dusty rose and the other in powder blue. Their lace veils graced their upswept hair, leaving their glowing faces uncovered.

Timothy gaped. Had his eyes ever beheld a vision more heavenly than this? And those nosegays of pink blush hothouse roses—surely created for angels to carry.

While Larkin maintained a statuesque form next to him, Timothy worried his buckling knees might take him down in front of everyone. And why did men have to wear such a ridiculous accessory as a throat-choking cravat? He tried in vain to adjust the torture device, chuckling to himself as he remembered Micah fought the same battle on his wedding day.

He had to focus … had to keep his eyes on his bride—the charm of her smile, the flow of her dress—but … oh no! Which bride was Haven? He gulped. No doubt everyone in the room heard it.

As the brides drew nearer, he flashed Harrison the most pitiful, lost puppy look he could make.

Harrison leaned close to his ear. "Haven's wearing rose."

Timothy exhaled, his heart throbbing as Frank placed Haven's hand into his, and Harrison masterfully guided the two couples through their vows. Timothy's shoulders heaved. He'd made it through the hard part.

Then the kiss.

His neck and cheeks warmed, and Haven's face rivaled her pink nosegay. Why did people always erupt into applause during a wedding kiss? He tuned it all out as he and Mrs. Timothy Locker followed Mr. and Mrs. Larkin Smith out of the parlor.

Classical music filled the grand foyer as the guests enjoyed a lavish buffet. Mrs. Haywood stood like the lovely matriarch that she was next to Frank, and the newlyweds took the center of the floor for the first dance.

"You remember your dancing lessons quite well, my lord." Haven's smile lit the room.

"Oh, my lady, in my heart I've never stopped dancing with you since the night of the ball." Memories of a whirlwind year gone by flooded Timothy's mind.

Though marred by shadows of Cheapside, it all seemed like a dream.

ABOUT THE AUTHOR

Judy Gerlach is a Lexington, Kentucky, author whose publishing credits include Lillenas Drama Publishing as well as several nonfiction stories published in separate anthology books by Adams Media. Her short story, *CSI: Christmas*, was selected to appear in *The Daily Advocate* newspaper, Greenville, Ohio, December 15, 2014, as part of a series about the Christmas Spirit.

A native of Ohio, Judy moved to Kentucky with her family in 1982 and has lived in Lexington ever since. She works as a personal assistant for her husband Greg's video production company, Gerlach Productions. Judy and Greg call Southland Christian their church home. They have four grown children (three daughters and a son) and four grandchildren.

A bit of trivia about Judy: Born a Real McCoy, she is a bona fide descendant of Kentucky's Pike County McCoy family known for their role in the famous 19th century Hatfields and McCoys feud. Her great-grandfather, Asa McCoy, was a young boy during that time and witnessed a little of the feud firsthand.

www.judygerlach.com

Made in the USA
Columbia, SC
24 November 2018